THE BARGAIN

THE BARGAIN

DUANE A. EIDE

iUniverse, Inc.
Bloomington

The Bargain

This is a work of fiction. All of the characters, names, incidents, organizations, and dialogue in this novel are either the products of the author's imagination or are used fictitiously.

iUniverse books may be ordered through booksellers or by contacting:

iUniverse
1663 Liberty Drive
Bloomington, IN 47403
www.iuniverse.com
1-800-Authors (1-800-288-4677)

ISBN: 978-1-4620-4312-5 (sc)
ISBN: 978-1-4620-4313-2 (ebk)

Printed in the United States of America

iUniverse rev. date: 08/02/2011

CHAPTER 1

Justin placed his briefcase on the hood of his car. The others had left, and he stood alone in the teachers' dark, parking lot. The night shined, fresh and clear. A gentle breeze whispered through the pines that surrounded the school, the moon just rising above the tree tops. Placing his hands in his pockets, Justin rested against the front fender of his car, looking up at the thousands of stars that twinkled above him.

Had he done the right thing? Was the teachers' proposal really that crucial? Should his committee have taken the salary offer? It represented more money than any previous negotiating committee had been offered. Justin shrugged his shoulders in resignation to the vote for rejection that his committee had taken. He reached for his briefcase. As he did, the screeching of tires penetrated the still night air.

Suddenly, a car turned into the far end of the parking lot, accelerated and headed directly for Justin. He stood immobilized as he watched the car speeding toward him. Should he run or should he stand by the car? He had little time to decide. Before he could move, the car swerved, missing the rear fender of his car by inches and continued toward the far end of the parking lot where, with smoke billowing from tires gnawing at the blacktop, it did a screaming three hundred sixty degree turn.

For an instant, the car remained still, the odor of burned rubber drifting across the parking lot. Then it came again.

The headlights jumped and smoke poured from the rear tires. Justin rushed to the other side of the car, peering over the top to watch two headlights rapidly approach.

With but a few feet to spare, the car braked, the back swinging wildly, then coming to an abrupt stop, almost parallel with Justin's car. Two young men jumped out and walked menacingly toward where Justin stood astonished by the events of the last few minutes.

"Kind of late for you to be out, isn't it, Mr. Starling?" The voice was sneering and vaguely familiar. "We came to see that you get home safely. Wouldn't want nothing to happen to the great Mr. Starling."

"What do you want?" Justin's voice trembled.

"Just told you. You don't listen very well, Mr. Starling."

The two young men moved around the car to face Justin. Justin recognized one as Randy Wilcox but had never seen the other before.

Fear gripped Justin. Trying to sound natural, he stated, "Look, it's late. I'm tired, and I want to go home. If you don't mind, excuse me."

"Not being very friendly to one of your former students, Mr. Starling," Randy growled. "You always had a few words for me when I was in your class." He stepped closer, his breath blowing directly into Justin's face.

"I'm sorry things haven't worked out for you," Justin voiced, sensing the danger he was in. "But this is not the place to discuss it."

"Why not! You fucking teachers are all alike. In school you're big shit. But we ain't in school now. How's it feel, Mr. Starling?" Hatred clung to every word Randy spoke.

Justin moved back a step and bumped into Randy's companion whom Justin had almost forgotten about. In an instant, his arms were pinned behind his back while Randy plunged forward with a fist in his stomach. Justin doubled over with a groan; a knee came up sharply, cracking him in the mouth. Blood filled his mouth and pain exploded throughout his face. As Justin stood trapped by the other person, Randy continued to ravage him with punches to the face and body. Soon, Justin could feel nothing; he only knew that someone was pounding him, again and again. Then there was nothing. The person holding Justin let him go. He crumbled to the hard blacktop, blood flowing form his mouth and nose. Giving the lifeless form one last kick, Randy turned and walked to his car. Justin, again, was alone.

CHAPTER 2

Connie Shetland abhorred defeat. In her life, she experienced very little of it. The teachers' rejection of the board's salary offer was to her a personal defeat. She spent hours justifying the offer to other board members. Board chairman Harold Baylor provided the most resistance. Connie despised him, repulsed at the thought of sitting across from him for hours, watching him slowly fall victim to the alcohol he couldn't handle. He became increasingly disgusting as he slobbered his drinks and slurred his words. In the end, she succeeded in securing his agreement to a new salary offer for the teachers.

As Connie rushed from the negotiating meeting, she fought to control her anger and resentment. She was not accustomed to losing her self-control in public and certainly did not want to display any signs of weakness in front of the teachers. She had felt confident that the teachers would give in, lured by the smell of more money. She acquired the support of the board, but now surely they would question her judgement.

The board's support she urgently needed. In another month, the board held its annual meeting. New officers were elected and new members officially began their terms of service. Connie wanted that chairmanship desperately. It would give her even more visibility in the community which is exactly what she needed and desired to realize her political ambitions.

Now, sitting in her car, Connie could only think of what the teachers' rejection of the money offer might mean: possible mediation; hours of tedious meetings with no guarantee of any satisfactory results; a potential strike which could anger and fragment the community; criticism of the board for inefficiency in failing to resolve the conflicts with its employees. For all of this, she blamed Justin Starling. Grasping the steering wheel fiercely, she cursed, "Damn! Damn! Starling, you bastard!" She then started the car and raced out of the parking lot.

Tossing her sweater and purse on the entry floor, Connie stormed upstairs. She rushed into her bedroom, slammed the door behind her, throwing herself onto her bed. Rarely, in her life had she been incapable of handling any situation or crisis she faced. She vowed she would handle this one. She needed time, and she might need help. Justin Starling had to learn a lesson. He was the one responsible for holding up settlement of the contract. He refused to respond to reason, clinging to his ridiculous, idealistic notions about issues, such as class size and teacher assignments. If reason didn't work, Connie determined some time ago that other means would have to be used.

Sitting up, Connie ran her fingers through her hair and gently rubbed her temples. She breathed deeply and rose, standing at the side of her bed. Since she left the meeting immediately, she assumed Justin Starling might still be in or near the school someplace. It was yet early. If Randy would catch him in the parking lot, perhaps some physical intimidation would offer more persuasion than mere words.

She walked around her bed toward the windows that made up much of one wall of the bedroom. With arms folded tightly across her chest, she stood rigid before the windows, studying the darkness outside. Dropping her arms to her side, she turned to stare at the phone beside her bed. She would have to decide quickly or surely Justin would leave the school. Randy would need little encouragement to get revenge on Starling. But to seek Randy's cooperation was repugnant to Connie. Choices were few; risks were obvious. Resolved, Connie walked deliberately to her bed, reached for the phone and dialed.

"Hello, Mother? Sorry to bother you."

"Is anything wrong?" Since Connie seldom called her, a note of surprise was in her mother's voice.

"No, just need to talk to Randy. Is he there?"

"I think so. But what on earth for?"

"A personal matter, Mother. Could I talk to him?" Connie answered with impatience.

"Is he in trouble again?"

"No, Mother. Just let me talk to him will you, please."

"Just a minute."

Connie tapped her finger nervously on the bed as she waited.

A deep, youthful voice said, "Hello."

"Randy, this is Connie. How've you been?"

"What the hell do you care?"

Connie cringed at the contempt in Randy's voice and with reluctance but determination asked, "How about a favor?"

"A favor! You're kidding," Randy laughed.

"No, I'm serious."

"What is it?"

Connie paused, anxious that her request would not sound too blatant or pleading. "Look, Randy," she spoke slowly and distinctly, "you know Mr. Starling from the high school?"

"Damn right I do," Randy answered bitterly.

"I think if you hurry, you can catch him in the parking lot at the high school. He may need . . ." and Connie stopped then started again. "He may need some help. I believe he's alone."

Randy said nothing for a moment then began, "Help doing what?"

"Why not go find out," Connie urged.

"What's in it for me?"

"Satisfaction."

"Bull shit!" Randy bellowed in the phone.

"All right, you'll be paid."

"How much?" Randy insisted.

"Fifty bucks," Connie answered tentatively.

"Must be pretty important to you. Where'd you say he was?"

"School parking lot if you hurry."

"What you got going with this guy?" Randy asked caustically.

"Do you want to go or not?"

"Fifty bucks is fifty bucks."

"I don't have to remind you to keep this conversation to yourself," Connie advised, "and there might be more money in the future. Open your mouth and I'll deny everything you say. And you know who they'll believe. Got it?"

"Got it," Randy acknowledged as he hung up.

CHAPTER 3

Connie replaced the receiver. She sat transfixed for several minutes, her mind reliving the agony and the embarrassment Randy caused the past five or six years. Randy Wilcox was a well adjusted young boy, an only child, an only grandchild and Connie's only nephew. Connie possessed no special affection for kids but tolerated Randy. His mother, Connie's older sister, married right out of high school and moved with her husband to a small community about one hundred miles north of Twin Pines. Connie rarely saw her sister and her family. Only occasionally on holidays did they get together at their parents' home in Twin Pines. Not proud of her sister, Connie took very little interest in her life.

Quiet and withdrawn, Randy made few friends. He would spend hours playing by himself, content to be alone. He adapted well to school, however, getting along well with his teachers and experiencing no problems with other students.

Just after Randy's eleventh birthday, Connie's sister and her husband decided to take a short vacation alone. In his parents' absence, Randy was sent to Twin Pines to stay with his grandparents for a few days. Randy's parents were gone for only two days when Connie received a call from her mother, who in near panic explained that there had been an accident. Critically injured, Randy's parents were not expected to live. The next few hours still remained a blur for Connie: a frantic trip to the small remote hospital; the discovery that her sister died from her injuries shortly before Connie's arrival and the death a day later of Randy's father.

Randy displayed little emotion through the funeral and the days that followed. He talked little, preferring to be alone. He continued to stay with his grandparents, but regardless of what they tried, Randy withdrew more and more into himself.

Connie and her parents had to make decisions about Randy's future. She did not want him in her house. Her involvement in outside activities prevented it. Besides, she simply did not want the extra burden. Her parents were in their sixties but willing to assume the responsibility for Randy. Consequently, at eleven years old Randy Wilcox began an entirely new life with his grandparents in Twin Pines.

Randy attended school but associated with no one. He rarely talked to anyone. He found enjoyment in none of the activities he formerly spent hours doing. His attitude toward school deteriorated, and he frequently faced reprimand for his indifference and lack of cooperation. His grandparents sought help from the school psychologist who agreed to talk with Randy. He resisted the psychologists's efforts to address his problems, absolutely refusing to discuss his parents' accident and death. Connie remained uninvolved, choosing not to be identified in anyway with Randy Wilcox. Her parents requested her assistance, but she discreetly declined to help.

As Randy entered middle school, he brought with him more belligerence and hostility. Confrontations with teachers occurred with increased frequency. He flaunted authority and created trouble in nearly every class he attended. Connie's parents attended conferences to discuss Randy's behavior, but no one seemed to know what to do about him. The grandparents suffered extreme frustration with both Randy and the school's inability to find some answers to his problems.

Even though Connie was not directly involved, she, too, developed a resentment for the school's inept handling of Randy's situation. She considered these numerous problems an imposition on her life. She struggled with the fear that she would be associated too often with her nephew. As a result, she seldom talked about him or his difficulties.

When Randy was in the ninth grade, Connie successfully ran for the Twin Pines School Board. Now, more than ever she was determined to dissociate herself from him. She reasoned that having a nephew who was the nemesis of the entire school would reflect poorly on a school board member. Even though few people, including teachers, knew that Randy was her nephew, she resented the fact that the school personnel had done little to reduce the embarrassment and maybe the guilt that Randy's intransigence caused. How much this resentment influenced her decision to seek a school board position, even Connie did not know. She hoped that soon the turmoil Randy created would end. It didn't.

Randy stumbled through middle school, antagonizing nearly everyone in school with whom he came in contact. His reputation preceded him to the high school where all teachers were apprehensive about having to put up with Randy Wilcox in their classes. Though approaching maturity reduced the number of minor encounters Randy had in school, those he did have were more serious.

He was suspended from school for threatening his sophomore social studies teacher. He was given several hours of detention (none of which he served) for fighting with other students. He was involved in several instances of vandalism in the school and was strongly suspected of drug use. Still, he managed to accumulate nearly enough credits to graduate, to the relief of Connie's parents. Only a junior English credit stood in his way. To make up this credit, he enrolled in Justin Starling's junior composition class, the only class that would fit into Randy's schedule.

Justin experienced few discipline problems with Randy. Randy, simply, refused to accept the responsibility required for success in a writing class. He completed few of the assignments, while doing very poorly on the ones he did hand in. By half way through the second semester, Randy's grade in

Justin's class was such that he couldn't conceivably pass. That precluded Randy's graduation.

In an after school conference to discuss Randy's alternatives, Randy's grandparents implored Randy's teachers and the principal to devise some means that would allow him to graduate. The school personnel remained firm in their recommendation that Randy return the next year to take another semester of English.

Realizing that all hope was lost, Randy flew into a rage, condemning the school, threatening the teachers, particularly Justin, and storming out of the conference room. His grandparents sat dismayed and ashamed of what had finally become of their grandson. The next day Randy Wilcox dropped out of school for good.

CHAPTER 4

Justin Starling's world was hard and cold. There was excruciating pain. Then there was none. There was nothing. In those brief moments of awareness he felt ribs aching as if squeezed in a gigantic vise. The moments of intense pain grew longer. The taste of blood filled his mouth. Blood gurgled as air passed through his nose. He choked, then coughed; more blood filled his mouth. He spat it out.

Conscious now, Justin attempted reconstructing what had happened: the speeding car, Randy Wilcox, the fight. He tried to move, but pain shot relentlessly through his head. He managed to get up on his hands and knees. His head swam with pain. Crawling toward his car, he pressed his hands painfully against small stones loosened from the blacktop. Once he reached the car, he collapsed face down.

Justin rolled over onto his back. The moon glowed brightly directly above him. He had no idea of the time. How long had he lain there? He must try to get into the car. The keys? Where were the keys? Gently getting on his hands and knees, he forced himself to a standing position next to the car. His head was spinning, but he remained standing. He reached into his pockets. His fingers touched the keys.

Justin fumbled for his handkerchief; pain penetrated his left side. He tried to wipe his face. His nose and mouth were much too sore. Pain surged through his head again. He carefully touched his mouth, his hand gliding over swollen lips. His teeth seemed all there though his nose continued to throb. Justin knew he had to get home. Using the car for support, he maneuvered himself slowly around to the driver's side, opened the door and struggled in. He sat for a moment, letting his head clear. With trembling fingers he inserted the key, started the engine, and slipped the car into gear. In ten minutes he would be home.

"My God!" Justin exclaimed as he surveyed his face in the bathroom mirror. Dried blood and bits of gravel stuck to his face and clung to his thick blond hair, his upper lip swollen to twice its normal size. Already traces of bluish purple colored the skin under his eyes. His nose curved awkwardly to the left.

One hell of a way to get out of a day of school, Justin thought, raising his arms in a helpless gesture. He would have to call early in the morning so that a sub could take over for him. He didn't like the thought of missing school. Preparations for the sub and picking up where the sub left off sometimes made missing school more of a headache than it was worth. Now, he had no choice. He needed to see a doctor. Besides, he looked like hell. What would he say had happened? The truth would just cause more trouble, and Justin had enough of that already. Maybe he would take more than one day off. He'd decide after seeing the doctor and after getting some sleep.

Justin did't bother to fold back the covers on his bed. He lay on top. On his back he found some comfort, but breathing was difficult. Relaxing as much as he could, he tried to sleep. His mind rebelled. Instead, what happened tonight, what had happened the past few months tumbled over in his head. That bastard Randy Wilcox. While still in school, he caused nothing but trouble, Justin recalled. The audacity of that worthless . . . Justin slapped his bed in anger.

In his mind, too, Justin dwelled on the six months he had battled the school board of the Twin Pines School District. As chairman of the teachers' negotiating team, he devoted countless hours, weekdays, weekends, to the matters which now prevented a contract settlement. All his effort accomplished nothing.

Only with reluctance had Justin accepted the job of chairman. Unionism didn't, initially in his career at least, impress him. He taught English at Twin Pines High School where membership in the Twin Pines Federation of Teachers was one hundred percent. As a result, ten years ago when he accepted the job in Twin Pines, he also joined the federation of teachers. During the intervening ten years, Justin served the organization in various capacities as building steward, secretary, and now negotiating chairman.

Why he subjected himself to these added responsibilities he, with greater frequency, asked himself? A definitive answer eluded him. Maybe the answer lay hidden in some feeling of commitment, some desire for recognition and involvement, or maybe sheer stupidity. As he now suffered in pain on his bed, he leaned toward stupidity.

Somewhere, though, he acquired a desire to excel, to be the best in what he did. Certainly, this quality, if he, indeed, even possessed it then, lay dormant while Justin attended high school. However, during his four years of college, the desire emerged and grew stronger, resulting in his decision to major in English leading to a career in teaching.

Justin coughed, spitting more blood into the tissues he gripped in his hand. He carefully turned onto his side. Pain around his left rib cage forced him to change positions again. He tried his right side. That was tolerable. Breathing came easier, but his nose continued the persistent throbbing. Though exhausted, he still couldn't fall asleep. The pain and soreness were one thing. The vivid image of Randy Wilcox's sneering, contemptuous face was another. Ironically, Justin was reminded of the expected role of public schools to provide the best for all students. Just how much professional time and money had the district wasted on Randy Wilcox? What good had it done?

Carefully, Justin rolled onto his back. Again, gazing into the darkness of his bedroom, he concluded that circumstances demanded he escape to somewhere for a few days. Perhaps, by Monday evidence of his beating would be less visible. A friend of Justin's had always left an open invitation to a cabin in a remote wooded area east of Twin Pines. Two or three days, Justin thought, would give him the temporary escape he needed. He would call his friend tomorrow. First, to arrange for a sub, he would have to call the school before six thirty in the morning.

At six fifteen the sound of the clock radio awakened Justin from a night of pain and restlessness. Drifting in and out of sleep, he wrestled with the incident in the parking lot, his body aching each time he moved. He could scarcely open his eyes. Swelling invaded nearly his entire face. His mouth and teeth were sore. Thankfully, the taste of blood all but disappeared, replaced by a stale dryness which made swallowing difficult.

Justin eased himself up to a sitting position on the edge of his bed. Dizziness forced him to lie back down. He tried again. This time the spinning in his head gradually diminished.

Though talking was difficult, his voice distorted by soreness and swelling, Justin arranged for the school to hire a sub, explaining simply that he wasn't feeling well. Six thirty in the morning was too early to call for a doctor's appointment so Justin lay back on the bed. He touched the tender areas around his nose and mouth. He began making plans for his recovery. He'd have to call Bob Turner, who owned the small cabin. He wasn't sure of the cabin's exact location but knew it wasn't more than an hour's drive from Twin Pines.

Turner was an old name in Twin Pines. Born in Twin Pines, Bob, about the same age as Justin, never left. He now operated a small grocery store not far from Justin's house. Over the past three or four years, Bob became a close friend. He often spoke of his cabin and the perfect opportunity it offered to get away for a few days. Not much of an outdoorsman, Justin didn't enjoy "roughing it." He, therefore, never accepted Bob's invitations to use the cabin. Now, he would.

Justin raised himself from his bed and walked to the bathroom. A shower would probably help wash away some of the soreness. He regretted being unable to brush his teeth; his bruised lips and sore teeth prevented it. He would have to devise some other means of eliminating the horrible taste that lingered in his mouth. About the shower, he was right; never before in his life had he so enjoyed one.

CHAPTER 5

Vincent Shetland was in no condition to go to work this Friday morning. Men's night at the Twin Pines Country Club inevitably lasted too long, and he always drank too much. Friday at the Twin Pines State Bank was the longest day of the week, not until after eight o'clock would he lock the doors and escape the misery of Thursday night's over indulgence. Even though vice president of the bank, Vince shouldered the responsibility, most of the time, for opening and closing.

Slowly sipping a cup of coffee that had little effect on the dull gnawing pain he felt in his head, Vince grimaced at the thought of the nearly three hundred dollars he lost in last night's poker game. Vince, an inveterate gambler, should have been more accustomed to losing. Nonetheless, it always devastated him. If Connie discovered exactly how much he lost, she would be furious. This morning he certainly was in no condition to deal with her censure.

Recently, he absorbed more than his share of abuse from Connie. Their ten years of marriage failed to develop into the understanding, tolerant relationship the community assumed existed between Connie and Vince Shetland. Maybe at one time this was true, not now. After a three year romance and an impressive wedding, the Shetlands settled down to begin life as husband and wife.

Early in their marriage, Connie resisted having children and the constraints that came with them. When the Shetlands learned of Vince's sterility, she was temporarily distraught. Resourceful and aggressive, however, Connie soon turned her attention to community affairs. She became chairperson of the Twin Pines' annual Sugar Beet Festival, headed the local campaign for the improvement of city parks and finally successfully ran for the school board of the Twin Pines School District. Currently, into her second term as a school board director, she served as a veteran member of the board's negotiating team.

"Vince, remember the dinner at the club tonight," she now yelled from the upstairs bathroom. "And would you please deposit some money in my checking account. I need it for a dress I saw yesterday. Will you be home for lunch today?"

"Don't think so," Vince mumbled.

"See you tonight," Connie again yelled from above. "We should be out there by nine so get home as soon as you can. I have a lot to do today and must get going. I'm going to take a shower so put your dishes in the washer."

Another dinner at the club did not appeal to Vince, especially tonight. What could he do? More money for a God damned dress. My God, would there be no end? With his frequent gambling debts and Connie's insatiable thirst for anything expensive, Vince's salary from the bank simply did not reach. He made a good income, but the demands on that income stretched beyond what it could possibly cover. This plus the hangover he now suffered made the day already unbearably depressing. Nonetheless, if he was to be at the bank at eight thirty, he had to leave and attempt to deal somehow with the problems which pressed ever more heavily upon his throbbing head.

Connie relaxed completely standing beneath her shower with rivers of soap suds and hot steamy water rushing over her trim body. At thirty-two, she was unusually attractive, perhaps even more so than as an active, vivacious high school student. Maturity produced a refinement and a polish in Connie that magnified her physical appeal.

Years of attention only made Connie more aware of her own body. She took pride in what she saw as she stood before the full-length mirror attached to the door of her bathroom. Long, rich black hair hung wet and dripping about her shoulders, already tanned by the late spring sun. Her breasts, never large, were, nonetheless, gracefully firm with a slight hint of the sag that occurs only too quickly. Her stomach was flat and her buttocks full, curving sharply down toward shapely legs, also a golden tan.

At five feet six inches, one hundred eighteen pounds, Connie stood before the mirror with confidence in herself, in her appearance, in her accomplishments, in her ability to attract the attention of almost any man, and in her ability to control any situation in which she found herself. Undoubtedly, she mused, Justin Starling lacked knowledge of her influence. Soon he would know the truth.

CHAPTER 6

Vince's eyes studied the clock. Only five minutes elapsed since the last time he looked. One fifteen, in five long hours he could lock the door. Then he would have to spend another evening at the club.

The day dragged interminably. His head still ached with a dull throb which four aspirins had done little to allay. Fridays, invariably busy days at the bank, imposed constant demands on Vince's time while contributing to his suffering. Vince now looked forward to maybe a few minutes' rest and a chance to let his small lunch settle.

Leaning back lazily in his chair, he placed his feet comfortably upon the corner of the desk. In his own mind he several times threatened to give up the bank business. He just was not cut out for the limitations imposed on him by a rigid bank routine. His position as vice president required his presence at the bank more than he liked.

Vince's father, Charles Shetland, managed the Twin Pines State Bank for almost thirty-five years. During that time he distinguished himself as a capable executive, not domineering and exacting but able to extract devotion from his employees. Charles Shetland had not pushed his son into banking. He said little about what profession Vince should pursue. He frequently reminded Vince, "Son, your life is yours. Just remember: know what you want then make the most of it."

Vince, as an inhibited, creative teenager, found great satisfaction in painting and ceramics. Time he spent alone in his makeshift studio provided his greatest source of enjoyment. Inherently, quiet, almost shy, Vince, nonetheless, enjoyed acceptance by nearly all his high school classmates. He resisted the thought of going away to college but possessed sufficient intelligence to realize the value of a college degree for his future.

Charles Shetland refrained from guiding his son toward any particular college. However, he did encourage him to attend one. Money was not a major factor in the deciding which college. Vince ultimately selected the University of Minnesota in Minneapolis with the intention of majoring in art with a minor in business.

The first two college years gave him a sense of accomplishment and direction. During the summer before his junior year, he met Connie Winters, who just graduated from high school. Her aggressiveness and assertiveness contrasted sharply with Vince's unassuming withdrawal. Nonetheless, Vince fell desperately in love with Connie. A year later his interest in art waned. Business became his major at the university.

He discussed a possible position at the bank with his father, expressing concern that the art world was too financially insecure. Vince's father, of course, expressed delight in his son's following him as eventual bank president. He did, though, caution his son about making a hasty decision. Connie deserved more than he could provide for her as an artist, Vince affirmed. Besides, banking did well for his father, and as far as Vince was concerned, one could do a lot worse in life than his father did in his.

Connie did not feel as intense about Vince as he did about her. However, she found his warmth, sincerity, and devotion appealing. They dated often that first summer and after Vince returned to college, saw each other during breaks and vacations. Connie worked as a secretary after high school, having no desire to attend college. Academically capable of succeeding in college, she exhibited more of an interest in owning a car and in buying new clothes. Those could only be acquired with a job. Her extraordinary good looks and attractive figure served her well in the search for a job which she acquired after only two interviews.

Vince's decision to change his major to business delayed his graduation by two full quarters. Determined to obtain his degree, he willingly devoted his time to the extra quarters and finally gradated with a bachelor's degree in business. Following his graduation, he assumed the position of teller at the Twin Pines State Bank. His diligence in performing his duties along with the influence of his father advanced him rapidly to his present position as vice president. Nearly everybody accepted as inevitable that he would eventually assume the presidency of the bank. Not quite a year following his entrance into the banking business, Vince and Connie married, establishing them as respected members of the Twin Pines community.

That was ten years ago, and now as Vince sat suffering from last night's over indulgence, he thought of abandoning the banking business which failed to provide him with the challenges, the satisfaction or the financial security he anticipated. Connie's demands on his money had become excessive. His failure to provide for her at a level she required was a source of growing frustration for Vince. In addition, his gambling did not help matters any. In recent months he lost much more money than he cared to contemplate but still was unable to resist the lure of the Thursday night poker table at the country club. Something would have to change soon. His ability to deal with his present situation was rapidly eroding.

CHAPTER 7

Vince dropped his feet from the top of his desk. He massaged his eyes and forehead. With his hands on the arm rests, he slowly raised himself out of his chair and walked to the coffee pot. Before he reached it, the phone rang.

"Mr. Shetland, Paul Bennett is here to see you," announced his secretary.

Wearily, Vince replied, "Send him in."

A large man, well built with broad shoulders and thinning reddish hair, entered Vince's office, smiling and amiably extending his hand toward Vince.

"How's the head today, old buddy?" Paul asked in a playful tone.

"Not too good but I guess I'll make it. Have a seat," Vince directed while seating himself at his desk.

Vince knew why Paul Bennett was there. Vince owed him almost two thousand dollars in gambling debts. Paul was a friend of Vince's, not an intimate friend but still a friend. A successful real estate agent in Twin Pines, Paul Bennett over the years established himself as a reliable, hardworking realtor who did the most for his clients. At the same time he enjoyed an impressive income.

He loved to play cards as did Vince. The only difference was he enjoyed much more success at it than did Vince. In the past months Vince turned to Paul several times to cover him when his money did not stretch the evening on a given

Thursday night. Vince simply was reluctant to write so many checks to pay off his gambling losses. Besides, even Connie started to ask more questions about his poker playing.

"Vince," Paul began more seriously, "I don't want to take up much of your time, but I do want to remind you that two thousand dollars is a lot of money. Not to pressure you, but I could use some of it."

"I know. I know," Vince quickly replied. "I should have paid you long ago. No reason for your having to come here to ask for it." Vince exhaled loudly, resting his elbows on the top of his desk. "Look, Paul, I can't quite make the full amount right now. How about five hundred now and I'll try to get the whole thing taken care of in the next couple weeks."

"Fine, Vince. As I said, I don't want to be a jerk about this, but I think it should be cleaned up before too much longer."

"I agree," Vince smiled. "Here, I'll write you a check which can be sort of my first installment."

Vince's feeble attempt at humor produced a small grin on Paul Bennett's face. Vince reached into the top desk drawer for his checkbook, wrote out the check, got up, and handed it to Paul.

"I'll make sure you won't have to come in for the rest of the money." Vince promised. "I'll send you the rest in a couple weeks. Maybe not all at once but you will get it."

"Great," Paul exclaimed with a much bigger smile on his face. "By the way, are you and Connie going to the dinner at the club tonight?"

"Yes, I guess so," Vince answered glumly. "Not too excited about it but the situation is out of my hands. Connie decided that we are going, so we are going."

"I know how that is," Paul agreed, "Not much different at our house. Well, won't keep you any longer," Paul said as he rose from his chair. "Got a few good prospects this afternoon so better get with it. Thanks for the money. See you tonight."

"Sorry if I have caused any inconvenience," Vince apologized as Paul opened the door and left.

Vince's head pounded more violently than it had all day. He took two more aspirin, aware that they probably would have little effect. He leaned back in his chair, covering his face with his hands, wondering what had gone wrong with his job, his marriage, his life?

CHAPTER 8

In his mind Vince retraced the gradual deterioration of his relationship with Connie. His sterility, no doubt, was a big factor, but other factors had their impact: Connie's involvement in community and school affairs and her almost insatiable desire for things, all of which cost money, were two important ones. Connie's frequent absence from home also became depressing to Vince. At first, his lingering interest in art filled the idle moments, but over time this ceased. The cocktail after work assumed more importance, and soon three or four cocktails were not uncommon. Men's night at the club emerged as the highlight of the week as well as a diversion from the otherwise lonely evening at home.

In the beginning Vince gambled only because everyone else did. The excitement of his early winning inspired and intrigued him. Furthermore, his earnings provided some small help with the numerous bills that he or Connie incurred each month.

Vince's income at the bank exceeded that of most other professionals in Twin Pines. It still didn't go far enough. This, right now, more than anything else, was the source of his misery. Again, the phone interrupted Vince's thoughts.

"Yes," Vince answered.

This time a man's voice said, "Vince, are you busy?"

"No," Vince said quietly.

"Could you come to my office for a minute? I have something I'd like to discuss with you." It was Vince's father.

"Okay. Be right there but I have a few things to take care of first."

"Fine," replied his father.

Vince refilled his coffee cup, took a swallow and walked to the small mirror across his office from his disk. He briefly studied himself in the mirror, straightening his tie while observing the pale, drawn look of his face.

Vince knocked gently on the door to his father's office, located across the bank lobby from his own and up a short flight of stairs. Not waiting for any invitation to enter, he opened the door and walked in. Behind a simple but impressive oak desk sat Charles Shetland, a grey haired man of sixty who shared with his son the same unassuming, reserved appearance.

"Afternoon, Vince. Please sit down. Your day going any better?"

"I guess so. Still a bit tired but nothing that some sleep wouldn't take care of," Vince replied.

His father settled back in his chair, observing Vince closely. "You don't look good today. Are you sure it's just a lack of sleep?"

"I'm fine, really I am," Vince assured his father. "Men's night at the club runs little late some times. Last night was one of those times."

"I see." His father glanced down at his suit jacket brushing away a piece of lint. He again made eye contact with his son. "It isn't only today. Lately you have not been yourself, more withdrawn or something. You simply don't look good. Is there something on your mind, something I can help you with?"

"No, Dad," Vince expressed impatiently, waving his hand in rejection of his father's offer. "Really, I'm fine."

"Okay, son. You should know how you feel, but remember, I'm not only your boss but still your father. If something is bothering you, please feel free to discuss it with me."

"Thank you," Vince said. "I appreciate that. He started to rise out of his chair. "Is there anything else?"

"Yes, there is." His father sat straighter in his chair, assuming a more business like countenance. "Three times in the past four months either yours or Connie's account has been overdrawn. I know that happens occasionally, but it's happening a little too often in your case. After all, you are a banker and should display a little more care in managing your own money."

Vince settled back into his chair. "I know. I know," he sighed moving his head slowly from side to side. "Things have been a bit tight lately, too many needs and not enough revenue to cover them."

"Are you sure you are discussing only needs?" His father interrupted.

"For some maybe not, but for us, yes, I am talking about needs. Connie enjoys expensive things, and I feel responsible to provide them for her. At times, this places a great burden on our accounts, but I'll see to it that it won't happen again."

"It's none of my business what you spend you money on, Vince. I don't want to meddle in your private affairs. The bank is my business, and when it becomes involved, I feel it is my obligation to inquire into the circumstances."

"I understand completely," Vince agreed. "I'm at fault and assume full responsibility. I'm sorry that this happened." Vince stared at the floor for a moment then looked up at his father. "Dad, I'll take care of it immediately."

Vince rose slowly from his chair, turned, and walked toward the door. With a quick glance toward his father, Vince said, "Talk to you later." He closed the door behind him.

Crossing the bank lobby toward his own office, Vince felt a strange sense of remorse. His father was never threatening, but Vince for the first time in years felt guilty, as if he had disappointed his father. The pain in his head was now unimportant. More important was somehow to straighten out their accounts. He suddenly remembered that Connie had instructed him to put more money into hers.

"Shit!" Vince uttered, audibly. "That's all I need."

CHAPTER 9

Vince walked slowly in the direction of his office and, before entering, requested his secretary to bring his account records. Once in his office he sat behind his desk rubbing his eyes gently with the tips of his fingers.

A gentle knock sounded on the door. "Come in," Vince said quietly.

"Your records, Mr. Shetland." His secretary handed him a large folder containing copies of all deposits, withdrawals, loans, interest payments, and receipts.

"Thank you," Vince said without looking up. "Could you hold my calls for a while?"

"Certainly. Anything else you need?"

"No, not right now. Thank you."

As the secretary closed the door, Vince opened the file and began studying the data that it contained: checking account balance, five hundred dollars with several checks, he assumed, still outstanding including, for sure, the one he just wrote to Paul Bennett; savings account balance, three thousand dollars, a large share of which would have to go for taxes on their home; Connie's checking account, overdrawn.

Vince looked up at the clock, three forty-five. Money had to come from someplace. He could not absorb another loan and the resulting monthly payment. The money in his two accounts was committed already. Making out a deposit slip for Connie's checking account followed by a failure to withdraw money from his savings account would disrupt balances. In the banking business, a two to three hundred dollar discrepancy aroused considerable alarm. If somehow he could temporarily conceal the false transaction, he would make up for it in a few weeks. Nobody would know the difference.

Unaccustomed to dishonesty, Vince's mind rebelled at even his contemplating a means by which he could accomplish what he did not want but which he needed. Trying to overcome the restraints of his conscience, Vince pushed himself to devise a plan that would place money into his account without a legitimate deposit.

Vince inadvertently picked up a pencil and started doodling on his desk pad. He stared vacantly at the meaningless shapes that appeared on the pad. All transactions at the Twin Pines State Bank ultimately ended up in a computer. Once there ended any further manipulation. Vince concluded to himself.

He knew little about computer programming. He did know the rigid control imposed on access to computer data. Even if access were gained, little could be done without detection to alter what was stored there. However, Vince imagined, if somehow the data were examined before transfer to the computer, conceivably some changes could be made.

Records of all transactions for the day were placed in the vault at closing time. He was generally responsible for closing; thus the opportunity was available for him to tamper with the transaction data. Perhaps it was worth a try. For now, though, he would simply deposit three hundred dollars into Connie's account without a withdrawal from his savings. In the meantime he would have to think carefully about what to do in the future.

Vince found what he contemplated difficult to believe. He wiped the perspiration from his upper lip. How could he think of embezzlement, embezzlement from his father's bank? Some justification soothed his conscience when he assured himself that it would only be for a while, just long enough for him to reorganize his finances and attempt to control his wife's spending and his own gambling.

"It was really just a loan," Vince whispered to himself. "A loan handled differently, that's all." Besides he desperately needed the money, and no other answer occurred to him at the moment.

Vince jumped when the phone rang. Though he had instructed his secretary to hold his calls, he answered anyway.

"Sorry to disturb you, Mr. Shetland," apologized his secretary. "But Mrs. Shetland is on the line."

"Put her on," Vince answered tersely.

"Vince?" Connie's voice came alive on the line.

"Yes?"

"Did you deposit some money in my account?"

"Yes, I did."

"Good. Remember the dinner tonight. We should be out there by nine o'clock."

"Yes, I remember," Vince responded unenthusiastically. "I'll do my best. Should be out of here by eight, depending on how well closing goes. Are you going to be at home, or should I meet you at the club?"

"If you're not home by eight thirty, I'll meet you there. If you are, we'll drive out together." Connie replied.

"Okay, see you later," Vince said as he hung up the phone.

He eased himself out of his chair and walked slowly out of his office into the lobby of the bank, filled now by customers completing their banking before the weekend. He stepped back into his office, filled out a deposit slip for three hundred dollars, and placed it in his file lying open on his desk.

With nervous hands, he placed his pen on his desk. Beads of perspiration formed around his nose and across his forehead. A chill raced through his body. Slowly, he pushed his chair away from his desk, rose, and wiped his face with a tissue he grabbed from the box on the corner of his desk. Slumping into his chair again, he ran his fingers through his hair and rubbed his eyes, his mind drifting to the ecstasy of the previous night. In his memory he could still sense the seductive smell of Connie's body. When he entered the bedroom, she sat by the phone in deep meditation.

CHAPTER 10

"What are you doing?"

Startled by Vince's quiet entrance to the bedroom, Connie bluntly replied, "Nothing."

Vince walked slowly around the bed and sat down next to Connie. He had hardly seen her the last few days. They had spoken little. He felt alone, alienated from the one person he loved most in the world. Connie knew nothing of his increasing frustration with the bank and with his constant worry over money which she spent so freely. Despite the issue of money, he regretted most their gradual drifting apart: Connie into the world of community politics and he into the world of loneliness and doubt. He suffered this anguish alone.

Now he wanted to talk with Connie, not about anything in particular, just talk. He loved Connie and needed her. No longer sure if she still loved him, he craved reassurance. She appeared upset, but an urgent need to reaffirm his relationship with his wife, the few drinks at the club and his dismay over another loss at the poker table gave him the strength to insist they talk.

'How was your meeting tonight?" Vince asked quietly.

Connie shrugged her shoulders and with obvious reluctance to discuss the subject said, "We didn't settle. That should tell you how it was."

"I'm sorry to hear that."

"Don't be. We're not done yet."

They both sat on the bed, staring into the dim light of the bedroom. Vince moved uncomfortably, started to say something, then stopped.

Connie stood up. "I'm going to bed."

Vince grasped her hand in his. "Sit down. Please?" He pleaded. Still holding her hand, Vince said softly, "Connie, I love you. I think you know that, but I feel we are drifting farther and farther apart."

"What makes you think that?" Connie looked directly at Vince for only an instant then looked away.

"Connie, look at me." Vince held her hands firmly. "Are all these meetings and commitments you have really necessary? I don't think I've seen you more than a couple times all week."

Connie sensed a greater urgency in Vince's voice than at previous times when they discussed her involvement in school and community affairs. "We've discussed all this so many times already. Of course, they are important to me. Otherwise I wouldn't do them. I've told you that before." Connie's voice sounded intense, strained. "This is only a beginning. There's a big world out there, and I'm going to take advantage of as much of it as I possibly can. People need direction. They need to be controlled. I think I can give that direction and assume that control."

"But at what cost? I don't mean necessarily just money. We really don't have a marriage. We just live in the same house." Both his eyes and voice pleaded with his wife.

"What do you want?" Connie raised her arms for emphasis. "Should I sit here at home all day waiting for you to come home so you can take me in your arms and kiss me?"

Vince reached for her hands again. "No, that's not what I mean, and you know it," he replied in clear frustration. "We don't really share anything. We scarcely know where each other is most of the time. We just go our separate ways and meet occasionally in the bedroom.

Connie did need Vince, too. Not in the same way he needed her. She needed him if she was to realize any of her goals.

He had a good job, a respectable income, and was looked up to in the community. At least for now, her ambitions were unattainable without Vince. To maintain some semblance of a happy marriage was imperative. Connie knew this. She realized she must be careful or Vince could become another problem she'd have to deal with.

Connie extracted her hands from Vince's grasp. She cradled his face between her hands. "I'm sorry," she said tenderly. Leaning forward, she kissed him softly on the lips.

He put his arms around her and held her tightly. Releasing her, he leaned to kiss her lips, parted and waiting. As they kissed, desire which Vince had not felt for weeks surged through his body. His hand reached for Connie's firm, rounded breast. She made no attempt to stop him. She began to breathe heavily as their kisses became more impassioned. All thoughts of meetings and commitments, Justin Starling and Randy Wilcox, faded as Connie submitted to her husband's advances.

Vince hastily unbuttoned Connie's blouse. She reached behind her back, unlatching her bra. Her white breasts, contrasting vividly with the tan of her shoulders, dropped gracefully from the loosened bra, her nipples enlarged and erect. Vince cupped his hands over each breast, slowly moving them in a circular motion.

Urging Connie back on the bed, Vince buried his face in her breasts, nibbling feverishly on her dark firm nipples. Connie stroked his head, pressing it to her bosom, moaning quietly in sensual pleasure.

She took Vince's hand and placed it between her legs, holding it there tightly as she arched her back. Vince pulled her skirt up around her waist and reached inside her delicate underwear. Connie pushed rhythmically as Vince move his hand back and forth through the dense black, pubic hair. She moaned her satisfaction while pushing his hand harder against her crotch.

Vince struggled to take his pants down while Connie's hand waited anxiously to grasp his erection. He rolled over on top of her. Her hips moved more rapidly, with an almost circular motion. Consumed in desire, Vince's motion matched hers perfectly. As he pushed, seeking the greatest penetration, Connie did likewise. A flood of sensation stormed through their bodies exploding in pure delight. Then both lay still, breathing heavily, exhausted.

"I love you," Vince whispered.

"I know. Let's go to sleep. I'm tired," Connie answered.

Vince too was tired last night, and sleep came quickly for the first time in several nights. Despite the good night's sleep, he still felt drained and lifeless as he now quickly straightened his desk, secured his tie, and tugged at his trousers. Tonight, he still faced another dinner at the club.

CHAPTER 11

The doctor's examination revealed a broken nose, three loose teeth, a small cut on Justin's upper lip and bruised ribs. After resetting Justin's nose, the doctor advised a couple days' rest. The teeth would tighten themselves, but the doctor advised taking time to adjust to the trauma of the beating and to give his body a chance to heal. Despite his inquiries, Justin insisted that the doctor refrain from reporting the incident. Instead, he would handle it his own way. Exactly what that way would be, he was not at all sure. The doctor agreed, giving Justin a prescription for mild pain killers.

Bob Turner expressed delight when Justin called about the cabin. No one was scheduled to use it for at least the next two weeks. Justin could have it for as many days as he wished. Early that evening Bob would stop by Justin's house to discuss details on how to get to the cabin and provisions Justin needed once he got there. How Justin would explain his condition to Bob remained undetermined.

Justin, lying on the sofa in his living room, had just dozed off when the ring of the phone brought him back to consciousness. Groggy, Justin made his way to the kitchen phone. He still hadn't fallen victim to the ubiquitous cell phone.

"Hello," Justin answered with some effort.

"Justin?"

"Speaking."

"This is Norma. What's the matter with you? I hardly recognized your voice."

"I ran into sort of a problem last night after the meeting."

"What kind of problem?" There was an urgency in Norma's voice.

Justin ran his hand over his sore lips and stared at the clock over the sink. "I'd rather not go into it now. Could you stop by the house on your way home from school?" Justin knew his voice sounded distorted.

"Sure. Are you all right?"

"Yes, I'm fine. Let's see. It's now three o'clock. When are you leaving school?"

"I can leave right now."

"Okay, stop by then. We need to discuss some things."

"Be there in a few minutes."

"Good, see you then. Bye." Justin replaced the receiver.

Norm Metcalf, a respected member of the Twin Pines High School staff, had taught home economics for twenty-three years. During that time she established a sound program, attractive to both boys and girls. Norma, a fighter for the rights of teachers, had been a union member ever since she started teaching, and she started her career in Twin Pines. Had her philosophical inclinations been different, she would have made an excellent advocate for women's rights regardless of the profession.

Besides her teaching career, Norma was a dedicated housewife and mother of two grown sons. Perceptive and articulate, Norma quickly detected superficiality and tokenism in education and quickly denounced it. No dreamer, Norma's twenty-three years of experience had refined her into an outstanding teacher who knew what students needed and what to expect of them. Not uncommonly, students were turned away from her classes because of space restrictions in the home economics facility.

Standing in the kitchen, Justin realized he hadn't eaten anything all day. What could he eat? Merely opening his mouth caused pain. He settled for a glass of milk, cringing as the cold liquid passed over his sensitive teeth.

The doorbell rang before Justin could get back to the living room and the sofa. He peeked out the front window. There stood Norma.

Her mouth open and eyes wide, Norma stood on the front steps speechless.

"Come on in," Justin mumbled.

"My God! What happened to you?" she gasped.

"I said I had a little problem last night."

"A little problem! What on earth happened?"

"I got the shit kicked out of me. That's what happened."

"Where?" Norma was obviously mystified by Justin's appearance.

"In the school parking lot."

"After the meeting?"

"Yes." Justin moved aside. "Here, sit down. We don't need to stand in the middle of the floor." Justin directed Norma to a large stuffed chair. He took the sofa. "There wasn't much else to say after last night's meeting and everyone just . . . well disappeared."

"Yes, I know," Norma concurred.

"I was standing by my car," Justin continued. "Everyone else apparently had left. This car came speeding into the parking lot."

Norma sat spellbound, her face contorting as Justin described the savage assault.

"Have you reported this to the police?" she asked as Justin completed his story.

"No."

"You certainly are, aren't you?" she replied firmly.

"I don't know. What good would it do? It would only make a bigger deal out of it than it really was. Besides, reporting it would only give Randy more satisfaction than he already has."

"But are you going to let that . . . that animal get away with it?" Norma pleaded.

"I really don't know what I'm going to do, Norma. My gut reaction is to do to him what he did to me. What would that solve? I would only be lowering myself to his level. I don't particularly want the whole school or the whole town to feast on it. Reporting it would be like announcing it on the radio."

"Don't you suppose people are going to find out anyway?" Norma asked.

"Yes, eventually, I suppose. But Randy doesn't have much contact with the school anymore so I doubt if many kids will even know about it. In a few days the swelling and black around my eyes will disappear, and no one will know." Justin paused for a moment to touch his tender nose. He resumed. "As a teacher or as a negotiator or for whatever the reason, I just don't want this mess publicized any more than it has to be."

"I guess I understand. It just seems so damned unjust for some wild kid to assault someone viciously and get away with it."

"What would the police do anyway, Norma? Randy is a minor. So they slap his hands and put him in the custody of his parents which is probably the source of the trouble anyway."

"He doesn't have any parents," Norma reminded Justin.

"He doesn't?" Justin answered with mild surprise.

"You knew that, certainly. The people you met with in that fateful conference were his grandparents. His parents were killed a few years ago in a car accident."

"That's right. I guess I do remember that. Just the same, I don't think the police would do much about it anyway." Justin leaned back in the sofa, rubbing his eyes gently.

"I just wonder how Randy knew you'd be in the parking lot at ten o'clock at night?" Norma asked absently.

"Probably just coincidence."

"I don't know if this makes any difference, Justin, but you know, don't you, that Rand Wilcox is Connie Shetland's nephew?"

Justin shot up from his reclining position, clutching his head in his hands to ease the pain that again exploded there. "What did you say?" he uttered in an anguished whisper.

"Randy Wilcox is Connie Shetland's nephew," Norma calmly repeated.

Justin said nothing. He just stared at Norma.

"You must have known that, considering your involvement with Randy,"

"My God! I just never had any reason to make that connection. I can't believe it!" Justin got up painfully to walk to the other side of the room, still rubbing carefully the sides of his head. "Considering what the school had to go through with that kid, how could I possibly have not known?"

"I don't think Connie wanted anyone to know. At least the fewer the better," Norma explained.

"Nonetheless, the school officials certainly must have known." Justin spoke almost accusingly.

"I'm sure they did," Norma confirmed. "No doubt they assumed the teachers did too. In view of Connie's position in the community, I suspect they were discreet in discussing it."

Justin walked back to the sofa and sat down. "This is too ridiculous to even contemplate, but, Norma, last Friday I met with Connie Shetland, at her request, at the Pine Inn."

"You met with her?" Norma spoke with alarm.

"Yes, about a week ago. She called the school."

CHAPTER 12

The sound of the lounge intercom phone startled Justin from his thoughts. "I'll get it," Justin volunteered as he eased himself out of his chair to walk to the small, black wall phone by the door.

"Lounge," Justin said as he picked up the receiver.

A firm voice asked, "Is Mr. Starling there?"

"Speaking," Justin replied.

"Mr, Starling, you have a phone call in the office."

"Who is it?"

"It's Mrs. Shetland. Shall I have her call back or do you wish to talk to her now?"

Justin scratched his head. What could she want, he asked himself? "Yes, I guess I can take the call now. Be right there."

During the six or seven negotiating meetings, Mrs. Shetland said very little. Her presence could hardly be missed, but board chairman Baylor generally dominated the meetings, seldom permitting the other members of the board's negotiating team to say anything.

Justin, on occasion, speculated why such a stunningly attractive woman would want to spend her time entangled with teacher contract negotiations or with school matters of any type. Women like her, he thought, should be reserved for the country club or the fashionable Caribbean beaches.

As Justin made his way to the office, only a short distance down the hall from the lounge, he continued to wander what she could want. No doubt, it had something to do with negotiations, but why call him during school hours and why Mrs. Shetland?

Once in the office, Justin closed the door after him and was motioned to the phone sitting on one of the three desks behind the main counter. With some apprehension in his voice, Justin said, "Hello, Justin Starling speaking."

"Good morning, Mr. Starling. This is Connie Shetland. I hope I haven't taken you away from your work." The voice was calm, refined and friendly.

"No, of course not."

"Mr. Starling, I would like the opportunity to talk to you in private. I was wondering if you would be so kind as to meet me later today so we could talk?"

Justin hesitated, his finger reaching to scratch a nonexistent itch on his cheek. "Could I ask exactly what you wish to talk to me about?"

"Naturally, it has to do with negotiations," Connie continued in a more commanding tone. "But I would rather not pursue it by phone. Could you meet me say at about four thirty this afternoon at the Pine Inn just south of town?"

With reluctance but also with deep curiosity, Justin agreed.

"Fine, I'll expect to see you then at about four thirty this afternoon. Thank you, Mr. Starling. Good bye."

As Justin put down the receiver, several thoughts tumbled over in his mind: What about negotiations? Why in such a remote location? Wasn't she aware of the ethics of negotiations which, except at official meetings, generally precluded contract discussions between members of the two committees? Had the other board committee members sent her to disarm him or to lure him into some concessions?

Bewildered but still a little annoyed at the thought of having to meet with someone at four thirty on a Friday, Justin headed upstairs for his fourth hour class and more compositions. Fortunately, he would not have to lecture today nor would he have to engage in any class discussions. The afternoon meeting would make difficult any concentration on academic matters.

CHAPTER 13

Driving south out of Twin Pines at four fifteen, Justin still struggled with several questions bothering him all day. His reluctance to go through with this meeting increased as the day progressed and at one time, Justin almost decided that he would call Mrs. Shetland and cancel their appointment. However, curiosity and maybe a little inexperience were factors in his rejection of that plan. Besides, he simply could think of no diplomatic escape from his commitment.

In ten years, Justin seldom visited the Pine Inn. It was not the type of restaurant or lounge that many of the faculty members chose for their dining pleasure. It was gorgeously situated in a large grove of pine trees, overlooking a small ravine in which nestled a small stream whose name Justin forgot. Many of the community leaders, the mayor, the president of the local chamber of commerce, the members of the Lions Club and Rotary Club, used the Pine Inn as their refuge from daily routines, a refuge they sought nearly every day.

Justin turned off the road and entered the spacious parking lot adjacent to the Inn. His work with negotiations and other union affairs had given him a degree of confidence in dealing with school board members. Not often did they intimidate him even though at one time early in his career board members made him very uneasy. Now, some of the old uneasiness surfaced as he pushed open the large oak door and walked into the Pine Inn.

Lighting was tastefully done. Its contrast with the bright sunlight outside made Justin squint. A hostess quickly acknowledged his presence and inquired, "May I help you, sir?"

"Yes, I'm to meet Mrs. Shetland at four thirty. Has she arrived yet?"

"Are you Mr. Starling?"

"Yes, I am."

"Right this way, Mr. Starling."

The hostess led Justin into a dimly lighted lounge with several tables spaced at comfortable distances. Large, richly cushioned chairs encircled each table. Justin noticed Connie Shetland seated alone at a table off to one end of the bar.

As he and the hostess approached, Connie smiled radiantly and greeted him with a pleasant, "So glad you could come. Please sit down. What could I offer you to drink?"

Connie Shetland was even more captivating than Just realized. Her tan, accentuated by the dim light of the lounge, complimented her rich black hair spilling gently over her shoulders. She wore a tightly fitting tube top that provided a tantalizing glimpse of the tops of her breasts. Thrown over her shoulders, a white sweater contrasted beautifully with her brown skin.

The hostess stood by patiently as Justin deliberated briefly. "Oh, I'll have just a bourbon and water, thank you."

"Put it on my tab please," Connie instructed the hostess who dutifully walked to the bar.

Connie sat for several seconds studying Justin, her large brown eyes locked on his face. "Well, Mr. Starling, I assume you had a productive day at school."

"Fridays are not always the most productive, but I must confess they have a certain appeal to them," Justin responded a little too abruptly. He felt uncomfortable and on guard, a feeling he had not experienced for quite some time.

"What are your plans for the summer?" Connie asked as she appeared to sense Justin's uneasiness and tried to engage in some friendly conversation.

Before Justin would answer, a waitress brought his drink. Taking a small swallow, Justin replied, "Not much in particular. I may take a short trip up into Canada if I ever complete several small jobs around my house which must be attended to, but nothing is really very definite."

"The opportunity for time off certainly must be a strong incentive for pursuing a teaching career, isn't it?"

Justin took another swallow of his drink. It was potent. Already the alcohol produced an effect. Justin could feel some of the tension leaving is body. "It may appear that way," he agreed, "but the summer months can create a problem for some people."

"A problem?" Connie repeated.

"I suppose not really a problem," Justin conceded. "But sitting idly around for three months can drive one crazy and having to search for a job simply to occupy one's time is less than desirable. Nonetheless, I do look forward to some of the breaks which most of us desperately need."

"Yes, how you people survive the rigors of the classroom as skillfully as you do is miraculous. I know I couldn't do it."

Justin smiled. He couldn't remember the number of times he heard that from people who had essentially no idea of what emotional and intellectual pressures a classroom of thirty students five times a day five days a week for nine months exacted. Not looking for any sympathy, Justin studied his glass and replied, "All professions impose their own unique demands on people."

Connie paused as if planning her approach. Her eyes followed her delicately manicured finger as it traced the rim of her glass. She looked up to Justin. "Mr. Starling, it is precisely to discuss these demands that I have asked you to join me here today."

Shifting her body in her chair, Connie assumed a more formal position. "We have negotiated now for several months, and very little has been accomplished. I think you will agree with me on that. Oh, yes some minor items have been wrapped up, but some important issues remain unresolved. One of them is class size; another is teacher instructional assignments in a day."

As she spoke, Justin sipped his drink slowly, giving the impression that he was carefully absorbing each word. He was hearing her, but his mind was not focusing on what she was saying. Instead, Justin still thought of why she asked to meet him in the first place. What was her motive?

At one time, Justin was aware, negotiating committees settled contracts in dark corners of bars even in Twin Pines. Public employee bargaining laws changed all that, however. All bargaining was now done, by law, in public meetings, and Justin deliberately avoided private contract discussions with any members of the board's negotiating team. He had scarcely spoken to Connie Shetland before about anything let alone contract matters.

As Justin pretended to listen, Connie continued. "These issues are important matters, but haven't you magnified them a bit out of proportion? Do you fully realize the extensive cost of implementing what you ask? Are you really willing to forestall settlement on issues you are sure to lose on?"

"Mrs. Shetland," Justin interrupted, "exactly whom do you represent?"

"Do I have to represent anybody?" Connie sharply replied, her dark eyes flashing.

"Has the board asked you to talk to me privately or have you decided to do so on your own?"

"Does it really matter?" Connie sat up straighter in her chair, assuming a more commanding position. "I'm only interested in getting these negotiations completed so the district can get on with its other business. If somehow I can facilitate this whole process, I think that can be to everyone's benefit."

"What affect does what we discuss here have on what happens at the negotiating table?" Justin asked, beginning to feel impatient with the whole situation.

Connie continued in a tone more harsh and authoritative. "I have not said much at our meetings. That does not mean that I have been happy with the way they have been handled. Harold Baylor is not always the most tactful man nor does he necessarily possess the sharpest insight into the problems that we have dealt with these past months."

"And I suppose you do," Justin replied sarcastically.

"No, I don't mean to suggest that at all," Connie asserted. "It's just that at times the issues get clouded by a lot of discussion while very little if any movement is made toward some compromise. As it stands now, we have the impression that unless something is done about the class size and instructional assignment matters, no settlement can possibly be reached." Connie showed increasing tension in both her tone of voice and in her body language. "I personally don't think people are so locked on one or two issues they can't be persuaded or encouraged to reexamine their positions. I'm not sure to what extent the rest of the staff supports you in your campaign for these issues, but I do know that money is very important to most people."

The implications of these remarks forced Justin into a defensive position. He moved his drink aside, folding his hands on the table in front of him. Anger surged in his chest and tingled at the base of his neck. He suppressed the temptation to release his anger and to insist that Connie say exactly what she meant. However, since he was still reluctant to continue this conversation, he said nothing. He sat rigidly, puzzled and a little intimidated by this attractive woman who sat across from him.

Connie sensed Justin's growing irritation and pursued the topic cautiously. "Let's be realistic, Mr. Starling. Not this board or any other board anyplace is going to relinquish its authority to determine the size of the classes in its schools or how many classes its teachers teach. Regardless of the merits of your arguments and they do have merit, we simply can't risk the possible economic consequences. If thirty students made an impossible teaching-learning environment, I am not sure. I am sure that this district can't afford to commit itself to the demands you're making."

Leaning closer to the table with arms spread, Connie lowered her voice for emphasis. "What I'm proposing is that you temper your stand on these issues, and I think I can persuade the other board members to reevaluate what at the last meeting was termed our final offer."

In disgust, Justin turned his head, surveying the room behind him, looking for nothing, only gathering his composure. Focusing his attention again directly into the dark intriguing eyes across the table, Justin, with feigned alarm, said, "Why, Mrs. Shetland, that sounds like a bribe."

"Call it what you want!" Connie shot back, unmoved by Justin's accusation. "I said I was realistic about this whole thing. Money is a powerful motivator. If the salary schedule provides big enough raises, you people will forget about class size and teaching assignments, and you know it."

"If you believe teachers teach only for the money, I wonder what the hell you're doing on the board." Justin no longer bothered to restrain his anger.

"Oh, come on, Mr. Starling, you know as well as I do that dedication is wonderful. It just doesn't pay the bills."

"No, it doesn't. But it goes a long way in getting the damned job done." Justin's eyes burned with contempt. "You're wrong, Mrs. Shetland, oh, so wrong!" Justin, now assumed a more confrontational position with elbows planted securely on the table. "You first demean the motives of teachers, then you seem to think I have the influence to change their thinking on two critical issues that drastically affect their working conditions. Even if I did agree with you, that would guarantee nothing."

"Don't sell yourself short," Connie went on. "You do an impressive job as chairman, at least from what I have observed. You are a man of conviction. That attracts others to your support. What you recommend, I am sure, would carry considerable influence."

Justin ignored her compliment. He slumped in his chair, smiled, and placed his hands, palms down, on the padded armrests of his chair. "The question of my influence is really irrelevant. What you are suggesting I do, if not illegal, is surely unethical. Though I'm no purist, I do have, I hope, enough integrity and conviction simply to forget that this meeting ever took place."

Connie refused to be distracted from her purpose. "Let me repeat, Mr. Starling. You don't stand a chance of changing the current policy on class size or teacher assignments. Don't you see that I'm giving you an out, more money for your giving in on these issues. You remain unwilling to compromise, and you'll lose the money too. I know Harold Baylor. He can be very vindictive."

"He can be anyway he wants," Justin retorted. "He's not dealing with a group of kids looking for handouts. If he doesn't like our proposals, that's his business. We feel justified in what we are asking. That's important to us."

"You really, then, don't have the best interests of the district in mind," Connie said, obviously beginning to feel frustration in her inability to gain control over Justin.

Justin sat ever straighter in his chair, his face turning red and the muscles in his neck taut. "Mrs. Shetland, if you really believe that, you have no damn business dealing with school issues at all. The interests of the district are precisely what we have in mind. We are concerned about the conditions under which we teach and under which the kids learn. If there's any more important district interest, I'd like to know what it is."

"That sounds good," Connie answered with glaring irritation. "Let's be practical. The district can afford only so much. We do not have limitless resources. Sure, we want quality education as much as you do, but this has to be defined by what the district can afford."

"This district has never levied to its full capacity in the ten years I have been here," Justin countered vehemently. "If money were such a problem and quality education were such a high priority, then why hasn't the district taken advantage of this discretionary levy that the law allows?"

"People are suffering now because of high taxes. To burden them with more is unthinkable, at least as far as this board is concerned."

"Then don't talk platitudes!" Justin raised his voice a bit more than he intended. "If the best education is what this district wants to offer, then damn it, offer it and don't sit around complaining about the tremendous tax burden."

Silence fell across the table. Justin twisted slowly his now empty glass and glanced at his watch. "I must be leaving," he announced. "As I told you before, I'll try to forget this meeting every took place. Thanks for the drink."

Connie set her jaw and warned, "I don't give up easily. There are other ways to deal with the unreasonable."

Justin pushed his chair back and without another word got up, turned, and headed for the door. It was five thirty when he got into his car and started back to Twin Pines. He tried to ignore most of what Connie had said, but her final comments proved increasingly difficult to dismiss. What, he thought, did she mean by, "There are other ways?"

CHAPTER 14

Perplexed, Norma stared at Justin, attempting to see some connections between his meeting with Connie and last night's attack in the parking lot. "Do you mean that you think that she had something to do with what Randy did to you last night?"

"If you hadn't told me of her relationship to Randy, the thought would never have occurred to me. But now . . . I don't know. God, this is incredible."

Justin was now more troubled than ever. Connie Shetland appeared to be an ambitious woman, capable, Justin was sure, of manipulation and deceit to achieve what she wanted. She proved that at the Pine Inn. That she would resort to beatings was something else. Her final words from that meeting flashed though Justin's mind, "There are other ways to deal with the unreasonable."

"I can't believe it either," Norma admitted.

Justin and Norma sat silently, thinking of what they both admitted they couldn't believe.

Norma broke the silence. "What's next?"

"I don't know. All I do know is I'm leaving town for a couple days. I have to heal a little before anything else."

"May I ask where you're going?" Norma said cautiously.

"Cabin about an hour from here. By the way would you kind of keep in touch with my sub? I'll write out instructions for you and call the school. Maybe if my sub has questions, you can try to answer them. It's just review anyway. I'll be back to school Monday, I think."

"Be glad to," Norma replied.

Justin prepared the instructions for his sub and gave them to Norma. They discussed briefly what next must be done about negotiations. Then Norma left, advising Justin to take care of himself.

Hunger urged Justin back to the kitchen where he boiled two eggs. With careful effort he ate both, at least for now appeasing his hunger. Before he could clear the dishes, the doorbell rang. It was Bob Turner.

CHAPTER 15

Vince touched Connie on the arm. "Let's go home. It's almost twelve thirty, and I've had a long day."

"In a little while," Connie said moving her arm away from Vince's hand. "We both have cars here. If you want to go home so badly, go. I'll come later," Connie whispered irritably.

Connie left for the club before Vince arrived home from the bank. Though the arrangement established she wait until eight thirty, at eight o'clock when Vince arrived home, she had already left. Her not waiting disturbed him, but Connie usually did what she wanted.

Having taken his time getting showered and dressed, Vince did not arrived at the club until after nine thirty. His late arrival was conspicuous since all the other people were seated and awaiting their dinners when Vince entered the club dining room.

He located Connie seated with the McGuires, with whom, for years, they shared a friendship, and took his place across table from his wife.

"Get locked in the vault?" Ted McGuire asked humorously.

"No, just a few last minute problems, nothing serious. Good to see you, Ted. How's it going?" Vince inquired.

"If somebody around here would buy a car, I would be happier but otherwise, I guess, I'll survive," Ted laughed.

"Good evening, dear," Connie said with evident coolness.

Vince looked at her, hurt by the rudeness of her greeting. "Have you already ordered?" He asked.

"Just a round of drinks. What'll you have? I'm buying," volunteered Ted.

"Oh, I suppose a Manhattan on the rocks will do. Thank you."

Vince drank two Manhattans before dinner. They didn't really help his exhausted, depressed condition. He managed to make occasional contributions to the light conversation that was maintained at his table. Ultimately, the drinks and the meal made Vince only more tired. By twelve fifteen he was ready to go home. Connie was not. He did not insist.

"If you want to stay, you better stay. I have to go home and get some sleep," Vince told Connie quietly.

"Fine. Don't wait up," Connie answered as she got up and moved toward a group of people gathered near the bar.

In the darkness of the garage, Vince fumbled for the house key. Opening the door, he stepped into the small entry that led to the kitchen. Switching on the outside lights for Connie, he went directly up the stairs to the master bedroom, turned on the light, and quickly undressed. Opening the bedroom window to allow the spring night air to filter in, Vince then turned off the light and with an audible sigh of relief lay down heavily in the large king size bed.

Never could Vince remember being so totally exhausted, yet he lay staring at the ceiling of the bedroom, the events of the day tumbling over in his mind. The throbbing pain above and behind his eyes returned. He couldn't go to sleep. Instead, his mind began exploring what to do next. He had to discuss with Connie the embezzlement, his feelings of alienation and frustration, the whole matter, especially the embezzlement. Though it involved only three hundred dollars, that he succumbed to the temptation overwhelmed him with guilt.

Already, his preoccupation with being discovered made him detached and edgy. He needed Connie's cooperation.

Surely, he thought, she would understand if he explained their financial crisis frankly and rationally. He would simply have to pay off Paul Bennett and attempt to persuade Connie to live within the limits of his income. To go on like this was ridiculous. He could no longer tolerate it.

He thought he heard Connie's car in the driveway. He tensed. It must have been something else because no one entered the house. As tired and distraught as Vince was, he still couldn't sleep. He go up, drank a glass of water, and again lay back in bed, gazing at the shapes that danced across the bedroom walls as the light of the moon filtered through the gently swaying trees outside the bedroom window.

The rumble of the closing garage door startled Vince. He hadn't fallen asleep but had reached that threshold when sleep almost takes over. Tension returned as Vince rolled over on his back to await Connie's appearance in the bedroom.

He heard her keys drop on the kitchen counter; the hall closet open and close as she put her coat away. Perspiration formed on Vince's forehead as he contemplated the approach he would use with his wife. He waited but could hear no other sounds. The door opened, and he could see Connie's shape outlined by the dim hall light behind her. She did not turn on the bedroom light but carefully found her way in the semidarkness of the bedroom to her dresser.

As she began to undress, Vince, in a submissive tone asked, "Did you have a good time?"

"You were there," Connie snapped.

"Yes, I know."

Silence filled the bedroom.

"Connie, I think we need to talk."

"Didn't we do that last night? Go to sleep."

"I can't."

"You were so tired you said." Irritation grew in Connie's voice.

"I know I said that, and I am tired," Vince continued, "but there are some urgent matters we need to discuss. I want to discuss them now."

"Look, I've had a long day. Can't we talk in the morning?"

"We're going to talk now," Vince said with authority. "Connie, we simply cannot continue living the way we have been. I mean, I can't afford to maintain the pace of these past few months."

"What the hell is that supposed to mean?" Connie growled as she tossed her necklace on the dresser.

"It means that we spend too damn much money for my income to cover, and unless some adjustments are made soon, we are going to dig a hole we'll never get out of."

"That's you problem, not mine." Connie's voice remained calm but precise. "I have other things to worry about. You're the banker. You're supposed to know how to handle money. If you haven't done you job, don't place the blame on me."

Vince sat up in the bed, his arms draped over his knees. "I'm not placing the blame on anyone. We both spend money, foolishly at times. We both need to try to be more careful. That's all I'm asking. I know you have obligations because of your position in this town. We just have to be realistic."

"Yes, I'll be realistic!" Connie exploded in the darkness of the bedroom. She stepped closer to the bed, staring at her husband. "I do have obligations in this town, and before long I'm going to have a lot more. I have only begun. This community needs someone with ambition, with the vision to see the need for improvements and courage to see them through. The school board is a start, Vince, only a start. There is going to be more after that and don't you come around whining about changing my style of living. I married you to provide for me. I expect you to do just that. That is what is realistic. Don't you forget it."

Connie breathed hard as she climbed out of her dress and tossed it across a chair. Before she disappeared into the bathroom, she turned and said, "If you want me to take over managing the money, I will, but then what would I need you for? You have spent more money foolishly, as you put it, than I ever will. Thursday nights at the club, I understand, are getting more expensive each week. Now excuse me, but I need to get ready for bed." She slammed the bathroom door behind her.

Vince lay down with his hands behind his head. The discussion did not go as he had anticipated. Only more antagonism and tension. He couldn't possibly broach the subject of embezzlement. He felt inadequate and more depressed. Once a fulfilling relationship with his wife he now viewed as a near nightmare. Connie seemed unwilling to acknowledge his position or to understand the gravity of their situation.

Staring into the space of the moonlighted room, Vince saw nothing. He desperately groped for some means of resolving the dilemma he faced. To continue as in the past would require more borrowing, honestly or dishonestly. To change their habits seemed, right now, out of the question as far as Connie was concerned. Vince thought of separation, but he still loved her. He never lost that fascination he first felt for Connie. To give her up was more than he dared to do.

What Connie felt for him he was not sure. That hadn't mattered that much at first. Now Vince needed someone to share the burden of the problems that confronted him. Somewhere along the way during their ten years of marriage, Connie changed. She no longer displayed the affection and tenderness evident early in their relationship and in their marriage. She became obsessed with her role in the community and recently spoke of bigger ambitions: city council, mayor, state representative. There was no limit to what she might achieve, she reminded Vince a few days before.

Connie returned from the bathroom. Without a word she climbed into bed. She remained absolutely silent. Within minutes all Vince could hear was her quiet, rhythmic breathing. If only he could fall asleep as quickly, but what about tomorrow?

What will it bring? The problems wouldn't vanish during the night.

Overcome by all that had happened in so short a time, Vince closed his eyes, fighting back the tears, shutting out the dreadful emptiness of his bedroom.

CHAPTER 16

Justin went to bed shortly after completing the cabin arrangement with Bob Turner. He awakened just before dawn and decided to leave while the rest of the city slept.

Traces of the sun peeked over the tops of the distant pine trees as Justin drove east out of Twin Pines. He felt more refreshed than he had felt in days. The swelling in his lips had decreased. His nose and ribs were still sore, but the pills the doctor prescribed reduced the pain.

The sun rose to a gorgeous morning, calm, clear and serene. Not another car in sight. Justin savored the freshness of the morning and the delicate smells of late spring. The wild flowers and grass lining the road glistened with morning dew. The tress that bordered the road on both sides stood tall and unmoving.

Though the cabin was only about forty miles from Twin Pines, the drive was slow. The highway, in good repair, featured several curves and small hills requiring a careful speed. Justin didn't mind. He enjoyed every minute of his solitary drive.

For the moment, anyway, he tried to forget Norma's disturbing revelation about Connie Shetland and Randy Wilcox. His mind wondered, drifting back to the recent meeting just before his beating.

"You teachers simply must realize that this community is dedicated to quality education, and as an elected representative of this community, I absolutely refuse to see this school district operate in the red. What you have asked for is unrealistic and irresponsible. What you teachers need to do is display some of the dedication to your profession that his community expected of you when it hired you to serve its young people."

"Bull shit!" Justin spit out in the silence of his car.

Those were the closing remarks of school board chairman and negotiator Harold Baylor, a fitting conclusion to a meeting both tense and unproductive, the meeting after which Randy Wilcox seized the opportunity, apparently, to get even with his former teacher, Justin Starling.

Justin gently ran his hand over his nose, the most vivid reminder of the parking lot incident. Despite his efforts to enjoy the peacefulness and beauty of the morning, Justin's mind seemed trapped by the affairs that for the last few weeks commanded his complete attention.

Again his thoughts dragged him back to the last negotiating meeting. Besides the unmitigated arrogance of chairman Baylor, Justin's own committee bickered over contract language just before the meeting with the board. To his dismay, his own committee stood divided on what was more important, placing money in fringe benefits, such as insurance, or concentrating on the salary schedule.

Of his committee members, only Ruth Wirth, an experienced teacher with some twenty-seven years spent teaching third and fourth graders, and Robert Medford, a soft spoken but highly competent middle school math teacher, joined with Justin in his insistence on consistency and committee unanimity. The others on the committee, Rita Mathews, a young, third year teacher whose teaching salary supplemented her husband's income from a lucrative insurance business; Shawn Kelly, a forty year old middle school social studies teacher who was dedicated to two things: money and Shawn Kelly; and Norma Metcalf wavered in their commitment to a unified effort by the committee. Personal interests were difficult to ignore. Justin recently concluded that within his own committee personal interests interfered with a settlement.

The sun now shown fully in Justin's eyes. A magnificent morning. As he continued his slow journey to Bob Turner's remote cabin, the arrogant tones of Harold Baylor's monotonous voice echoed in Justin's mind.

"Mr. Starling, this, I believe, is our seventh meeting. We feel we have been more than patient in our attention to your concerns about class size, teacher assignments, declining enrollments, curriculum reductions, and potential staff cuts. We have listened to your pleas to preserve programs as they exist and to ensure quality education by limiting class size. At the same time we have endured your lengthy justification for a sizable increase in salary.

"Let me remind you, Mr. Starling, that we on this negotiating board and the entire school board of Twin Pines want more than anything else quality education in our community. Also, let me remind you, Mr. Starling and your committee, that we cannot have quality education and begin to afford the type of salaries you have asked for in your latest proposal.

"We have offered you what, in our opinion, is a reasonable salary schedule. However, in the true sense of negotiations, we are prepared to offer you an adjusted salary schedule above which I previously refused to go. That you deserve more, there is no doubt. The district just cannot pay any more. This, I must advise you, will be our final offer. If you find this salary schedule unacceptable, your only recourse, I guess, would be to seek mediation, a costly, time consuming alternative."

Baylor's oration still rolled in Justin's head. He heard all that bull shit before. How could that bastard talk about quality education but refuse to pay for it? Justin shook his head with renewed anger.

He caught himself slipping over the center line of the highway. Quickly bringing his car back onto his side of the road, he managed a smile. A hint of pain trickled from the cut on his lip.

Making speeches was not one of Justin's strengths. He now recalled, though, with some pride his spontaneous yet vehement response to the pompous board chairman.

"Quality education is an impressive phrase. People use it kind of like they use 'good morning.' I don't know what quality eduction means to you, Mr. Baylor, but damn it, you will not get it for nothing! Programs cost money. Materials and books cost money. Classes of manageable sizes cost money and yes, Mr. Baylor, good dedicated, well trained teachers cost money. If you think what happens in a class of thirty fourth graders is of the same educational quality as in a class of twenty fourth graders, then you know virtually nothing about the nature of education and the interaction between teachers and students.

"If this community is really serious when it commits itself to quality education, then I must confess I can't believe it is unwilling to provide the economic resources the schools need to ensure this quality. Finally, Mr. Baylor, if you are really serious about your so call final offer, then so be it. With one thing I agree. Mediation is time consuming. But, Mr. Baylor, I submit if it means some small victory for us as teachers, it will mean a much bigger victory for the kids of this school district. Then every damned minute will have been worth the wait."

CHAPTER 17

Justin suddenly took note of where he was. Bob Turner warned him that though the cabin was only a few hundred yards from the highway, it was almost impossible to see until one was virtually right next to it. Bob instructed Justin to watch his mileage carefully. After driving about forty-three miles, he would approach a steep hill which descended to a small creek, named Beaver Creek, at the bottom. Near the bottom of the hill just before the bridge over the creek, he would find a small gravel road off to the right. This small road wound upward to the cabin.

Justin hadn't watched the odometer carefully. Had he gone too far? He thought he traveled about forty miles. He began to watch more carefully the road and the signs which would warn of the approaching hill.

Bob's directions were precise. In minutes Justin saw the sign advising truckers of the steep grade ahead. He hadn't gone too far. Slowing the car, Justin watched carefully on the right for a break in the heavy forest which would mark the entrance road to the cabin. The bridge stood clearly visible far below. Drawing nearer that bridge, Justin spotted the small gravel road.

The small gravel road was indeed just that; scarcely two tracks melted upward into the heavy forest. Justin stopped his car, surveyed the area briefly, shrugged his shoulders, and shifted the car into gear. Snaking sharply right then left, the road led Justin up one steep incline after another. His small car strained for power, bits of gravel shooting from under the rear tires. Visions of a breakdown or of getting stuck formed in Justin's mind as the car lurched, climbing the primitive road.

Almost as if someone had suddenly flashed a picture on a screen, the cabin appeared. Justin stopped immediately in front of the cabin. There the road ended. He sat for a moment simply absorbing the view of the cabin and relaxing after the climb from the highway. He shut off his car and opened the door. The quiet overwhelmed him, the absolute privacy. Only the occasional sound of a bird broke the pervasive silence. The trees, all pine and birch, concealed the cabin on three sides. The fourth side, the front, provided an unobstructed view of the trees concealing the entrance road and the steep incline, descending to the highway below.

Bod had said little about the cabin itself. Justin expected some simple frame structure sufficient for protection from the elements but nothing more. He was so wrong. Not large, the cabin, an attractive A-frame with large front windows, overlooked the highway, bridge, and creek below.

Inside, Justin discovered to his amazement the cabin offered modern plumbing, electricity, and nearly all the amenities of home. He walked to the large windows he saw from the outside, pulled back the curtains, and was treated to a panoramic view that extended for what seemed miles. Because of its position, shrouded on three sides by trees and built upon a bluff, the cabin sat barely visible from the highway. The highway and small creek bridge, however, were clearly visible from the cabin.

Justin drank in the absolute solitude that filled the cabin. He stretched out on the comfortable sofa to one side of the window and could feel the tension flowing from his body. He was in a world all alone. He loved it.

CHAPTER 18

Justin slept on the sofa until nearly noon. The quiet, the remoteness and the feeling of escape over came the tension and pain he felt the past two days. He relaxed completely. The afternoon he devoted to exploring the area around the cabin. Justin looked in awe at the beauty of the site and the density of the trees and undergrowth. The cabin was constructed on a natural platform about half way up a large bluff. The design of the cabin and the contour of the land were perfectly compatible.

Beaver Creek ran just a few yards from the cabin. Justin followed its winding course toward the highway below. In places the creek trickled quietly. In others it raced turbulently as it dropped a few more feet toward the floor of the small valley which the cabin overlooked. Justin was impressed with the beauty and serenity of this place, finding almost incomprehensible the thought that a mere forty miles away lay an entirely different world.

Though he tried to, Justin couldn't dismiss the events of the past few days. Most troublesome right now was his discovery of the relationship between Connie Shetland and Randy Wilcox. As he walked aimlessly along the banks of the creek, Justin tried to erase the thought that lingered in his mind, the thought that Connie had anything to do with what Randy did to him. Connie might be ambitious and perhaps even unscrupulous, but from what Justin know of her she was not ruthless. At least he didn't think so.

Justin decided definitely to reject reporting to the police his encounter with Randy. Convinced it would accomplish very little, he concluded that the sooner the incident was forgotten the better. Besides, he did have mediation to look forward to. Getting the contract settled had top priority.

During the afternoon, Justin worked on the compositions he promised to return to his students. Though it required countless hours of preparation and correcting time, Justin took seriously his responsibility as writing instructor for the juniors in Twin Pines High School who enrolled in Composition II.

Writing was a national disgrace said much of the popular media. Justin dismissed most of what he read about education in the news media and questioned the validity of the rest of it. Too many people with very specious credentials established themselves as authorities on all matters related to public education.

Still, that many of the two hundred or so juniors at Twin Pines High School suffered serious deficiencies in written expression was no secret. The English Department in the past two years had made an effort to address these deficiencies, not only among juniors but among sophomores and seniors as well.

Writing teachers, in particular, but all English teachers at Twin Pines High School had two years ago embarked on a "significant curriculum revision" which featured renewed attention to writing. Combined with this renewed attention to writing, the English Department submitted a request to the building administration and ultimately to the superintendent and the school board for special consideration for reduced class sizes for English teachers.

The high school principal claimed his hands were tied by budgetary restrictions making impossible any commitment to such special considerations. "I am given a building staff allocation which does not permit such latitude," he lamented.

"If you can persuade other departments to take on larger classes, maybe there is some chance for your request. As it stands, I am powerless to make any promises on reduced class sizes."

The school board reviewed the request with only superficial concern. The board looked with disfavor on the additional costs involved in class size reductions. The English Department subsequently received commendation for its efforts to "overcome the impoverished condition of students' writing skills," as one board member had put it, and were encouraged, in essence, to carry on the good fight but to carry it on alone.

Justin's resentment of the casual treatment the English Department received in what he considered a critical matter, at least partially, motivated him to accept the chairmanship of the negotiating committee. If by no other means, perhaps, he thought, some concessions on class size particularly for English teachers could be obtained at the bargaining table.

With his pencil, Justin gently traced the contours of his delicately sore nose as he grasped the stack of papers on the table before him. He thought about his third hour class which then sat before a substitute teacher. Justin wondered if his absence really made a difference to his students. He hoped it did. He shook his head mildly, reprimanding himself for frivolous thoughts.

Justin shuffled the papers, tapping them on the table. He set the pile in front of him, placing the top paper off to the side. With red pencil in hand he glanced at whose paper would be evaluated first. In meticulously precise hand writing, the name "Kitty Wilder" appeared in the upper right had corner. He sat back in his chair, looking into the quiet space of the cabin.

The special relationship he shared with her puzzled him. In his ten years of teaching, she was one of the more charming and delightful students to sit in one of his classes. As a member of his junior Composition II class, she had distinguished herself not only as a student but also as a very mature and enjoyable friend. Justin truly liked most of his students. Rarely, though, had he experienced anyone quite like Kitty Wilder. She certainly was not the most beautiful girl in the school, nor was she the most popular, nor despite her impressive academic performance was she the smartest. What, Justin supposed, made her a special person was some intangible quality derived from a combination of intelligence, personality, and maturity. Whatever the explanation, Justin chuckled to himself, a part of the answer lay in her marvelously disarming smile.

Justin valued the relationship with Kitty as he did with most of his students. He knew, at the same time, what rumors of anything special between him and one of his students could mean to his career. He also knew the sinister satisfaction someone might glean from corrupting the congenial, professional relationship he enjoyed with Kitty as well as with most of his one hundred thirty-five students.

With a shrug of his shoulders, Justin nudged his chair closer to the table where he sat correcting papers. Right now Kitty's paper simply was the first of twenty-nine others he had to correct.

CHAPTER 19

How many times he drove east out of Twin Pines, Shawn Kelly had no idea. Every curve and hill remained etched in his memory. Yet, he couldn't remember ever taking this highway in daylight. Always at night, near midnight, he made his drops and pickups. Now as he followed the beam of his headlights reaching into the darkness he pondered how much longer this game he played would continue.

Within the past week even the local press featured an article about the increase in drug abuse among students in the Twin Pines schools. That Shawn heard nothing more about the article failed to allay his apprehension. Not a sensitive man, Shawn, until three years ago, always lived inside the law, frequently at the fringes of legality but still inside. Drug activities these past three years proved lucrative for Shawn, peace of mind elusive.

Compunction about the young lives he might be destroying never deterred him. In his opinion most teenagers ran around doing whatever they damned pleased. They drank, engaged in sex and violated nearly every law of common decency Shawn ever heard of. Associate these kids with drugs and the public responded with shock. The community then mobilized to protect its innocent young people from the evils of drugs. Shawn believed that as long as kids insisted on making their own decisions, and they decided to use drugs, that was their problem. They should accept the consequences.

His twenty years of teaching convinced him, that teenagers were the most contemptible creatures on earth. Their inconsistent behavior, their mood swings, their arrogant disrespect for adults despite their dependence on them, and their indifference rendered them repugnant to Shawn. Yet he remained in teaching. Even he, at times, couldn't explain why, but the explanation probably depended, more than anything else, on the vacations and on how little Shawn really did as a teacher.

He was never an ambitious teacher, and twenty years in the profession convinced him that he could get by doing virtually nothing outside the classroom. In the classroom he got along on lesson plans, tests, and daily activities he prepared years ago. Shawn concluded that if the money was adequate and if he could tolerate the students, teaching would offer him the freedom to do many of the things he enjoyed. To ensure the money remained adequate, he volunteered to serve on the teachers' negotiating committee.

Shawn liked his life in Twin Pines. That is, his life outside the school. He golfed, skied, traveled, drove impressive cars, and bought expensive clothes. He had very few domestic obligations, no family, no wife, just a small apartment. He was married, but that lasted only three years. Marriage proved too confining and just before coming to Twin Pines, he got a divorce. Since then, for him, women were objects of entertainment only.

At a young age, Shawn adopted a hedonistic philosophy of life. Growing up in Chicago, he saw his father and mother deprived of nearly all pleasures of life. Work was all they knew. Before finishing high school, Shawn joined the Army where he received his high school diploma and where he discovered the importance of an education in his pursuit of pleasure.

While stationed in Germany, he fell victim to the charm of a young American nurse working in an Army hospital. They were married after a short romance but soon realized that neither could tolerate the demands marriage imposed. When

Shawn took the teaching job at Twin Pines, she refused to go with him.

In Germany Shawn also first experienced drugs. The military was an absolute bore for Shawn. His job as a typist required very little of him. By three thirty each day he was off duty with very little to do. Drugs of a variety of types were readily available, even in the enlisted men's club. The drugs, especially marijuana, produced a mild euphoria which for a while Shawn found exciting. He, too, enjoyed the relaxation the drugs gave him without the hangover characteristic of alcohol. Gradually, however, he tired of using drugs of any kind.

Potential addition concerned him from the beginning, but Shawn believed he possessed the strength to avert that. He simply didn't enjoy the results anymore. Taking drugs made him vulnerable, he felt, to anyone around him. He despised being vulnerable to anyone.

Rather than in bars and clubs, Shawn started to pass his leisure time investigating a means to a college education. Ultimately, he enrolled in a military sponsored program which enabled him to take selected, transferable college courses at a small college near his base. Upon his discharge from the Army, he returned to the United States, finishing his teaching degree two years later.

Teaching jobs were plentiful then. Shawn could have acquired a job almost anywhere. The lure of Twin Pines was its remoteness, its proximity to several ski areas and its contrast to any other place Shawn had previously lived. In September, not quite three months after his graduation, Shawn Kelly, twenty-four and on the verge of divorce, was introduced on the first day of the fall, Twin Pines teacher workshop as a new middle school, social studies teacher, a position he had retained for twenty years.

CHAPTER 20

Drug activities had given Shawn the best of two worlds; he enjoyed the ease with which he could maintain his teaching career, yet benefit from the money generated by the drug world. Nonetheless, getting caught bothered him. It bothered him with increased frequency. He abhorred the thought of prison. Complete freedom was much too precious. His growing reluctance likely was evident Thursday night when his phone contact called.

"Hello, Shawn. How's it going?" asked a deep voice that Shawn recognized immediately.

Shawn's hand tightened on the receiver. "Fine," was his feeble response.

"Are you keeping the stuff moving?"

Shawn dismissed this as a superfluous question. The caller knew damned well the stuff was moving. "Sure, but the local hypocrites have taken a sudden interest in the welfare of their kids."

"You don't say. What's up?"

Shawn turned and sat on the sofa next to the telephone table. He breathed more easily. "Some young reporter for the local paper has been sneaking around the schools asking questions about drug use."

The voice on the line mumbled, "No shit."

"She wrote in an article last week that half the damn students in town are hooked."

"Where'd she get her information?" the voice growled.

"I don't know, but I suppose she asked a bunch of kids."

"Well, do you see any serious problems?"

"No, not if we lay low for a while," Shawn advised.

"Lay low! Christ we can't sit around while some young asshole tries to make a name for herself. We got to keep this stuff moving. In fact, I have a delivery planned for you this weekend."

Shawn felt a warm surge in his throat. "Maybe we'd better hold off this time. I don't know how distribution will be affected by this article, but I don't want responsibility for too much if it doesn't move."

"Shit, you don't have to worry. All you do is pick it up and drop it off at another place. No sweat off your balls."

Shawn weakly replied, "There might be more snooping around because of the article."

"Bull shit! Look, you have a pickup this weekend, and you'll make it. Your job is to see to it that the stuff moves, not to worry about some God damned article. If you don't do your job, my ass gets chewed. When my ass gets chewed, I get upset. Understand?"

As he now drove the familiar road, Shawn asked himself if it was all worth it? The money was good, but the risk was considerable. Twice removed from direct involvement in the local drug scene, Shawn still felt much more accessible than he preferred. He never knew or even saw the street men. His immediate contact he knew vaguely and met only occasionally. He understood very clearly that this business was not based on trust and integrity. It was based on muscle, money, and intimidation.

Shawn performed the function of a middleman who both picked up and dropped off the product. The area around Twin Pines was well suited to such activities because of its remoteness, its heavy forested areas, and its, so far, freedom from suspicion.

CHAPTER 21

For the past three years Shawn's involvement in drug dealing was both simple and profitable. The money he earned was strictly cash. It helped to pay for his expensive tastes and to satisfy his need for the good time. The money he earned as a teacher would just not go far enough. For the first few years the inadequacy of his teacher income compelled him to take out loans to cover the expenses of his summer trips. A new car when he wanted one was impossible, and for two successive Christmas vacations he had been forced to cancel ski trips to Colorado. Then he met one of his Army acquaintances in Mexico. It was spring break for Shawn, and he longed for some sun, sand, and excitement. Mexico provided the answer since he had but one week off.

Quite by accident, Shawn ran into Fred Wyman in Puerto Vallarta, Mexico. Shawn barely recognized him and certainly couldn't remember his name even though they served together in Germany.

Over a couple of drinks they reminisced about Germany, about the Army and about the present. Fred alluded to his business but never really revealed what type of business. Not particularly interested, Shawn didn't pursue the topic. Before the evening concluded, Shawn expressed his disillusionment with the financial side of teaching.

When they finally did leave the bar, they exchanged addresses. Shawn had no reason to believe that he would ever hear from or see Fred Wyman again.

He was wrong. Ten months later Fred called.

"Hello, Shawn?"

"Yes?"

"Fred Wyman here."

"What the hell are you doing in this part of the country?" Shawn asked in disbelief.

"I'm not exactly in your part of the country. I'm calling from Minneapolis."

"What the hell you doing in Minneapolis?"

"Just setting up new territory. Be up your way in a few days. How about getting together for dinner?"

"Great, any time," Shawn acknowledged.

"I'll be in next Tuesday. I'll give you a call."

"Fine. I'm usually around any time after four."

"Good. See you then."

Shawn thought little of the meeting and assumed that Fred engaged in some type of sales work. Nonetheless, the meeting aroused his curiosity. When Tuesday arrived, Shawn made sure that he was home immediately after school. Fred did call as he promised. They planned to meet at eight o'clock that evening.

Following the exchange of usual pleasantries, small talk and delicious prime rib dinner, Fred began to reveal the purpose for his visit. "How would you like to make some extra money, Shawn?"

"Who wouldn't?" Shawn relaxed in his chair.

"I thought you'd feel that way. I think I told you I'm setting up a new territory in this part of the state. I simply need someone to help me manage it."

"You realize I still teach," Shawn reminded Fred.

"Of course. This wouldn't take much of your time. Your teaching, come to think about it, might be a real asset for the business."

Leaning forward and resting his arms on the table, Shawn asked bluntly, "Just what is you business?"

"I was waiting for you to ask. I think I know the kind of man you are. If I didn't, I wouldn't be here. So I won't beat around the bush." Fred also leaned forward, assuming an air of confidentiality. "Now this must always remain just between the two of us. Can I have your word on that?"

"Sure," Shawn agreed.

"Without mutual trust in this, it will never work. Understand?"

"Sure, I understand." Shawn's curiosity was stretched to its limit.

"I deal in drugs, those that make life just a bit more enjoyable," Fred asserted quietly, assuredly, with not a hint of misgiving.

In disbelief, Shawn slumped back in his chair. He stared at Fred, unable to comprehend the casual manner in which Fred revealed his occupation. Shawn sat speechless.

Fred smiled furtively. "Well, what do you say?"

"I didn't know what you did for a living. My God, I never dreamed of this."

"You just never know, do you?" Fred said calmly. "Oh, I was reluctant at first, too. I guess the proposition wasn't laid on me quire so bluntly. I didn't intend to shock you, but I believe in coming to the point." Fred raised his hand and for emphasis pointed his finger in the direction of Shawn. "Look, we need good people, people who can keep their mouth shut and simply do their job. I think you're that kind of person."

"I don't know," haltingly, Shawn search for some response. "I need the money, but I don't want to risk sending the rest of my life in jail to get it."

"There's a risk all right. I can't deny that. Then isn't there some risk in anything that pays off well? It's just a matter of how big a chance you're willing to take," Fred explained then sat watching Shawn's reaction. "I'm not suggesting you walk the streets. I need someone to make the pick ups and occasional drops. You'll work with one person and not very directly. The less we see one another the better we'll be."

"But why here in Twin Pines?" Shawn asked, still bewildered by the discussion.

"Relatively virgin territory. We feel there's a lot of potential here. Getting in early will be to your advantage."

"I don't know. Kids give me a pain in the ass so that part of it doesn't bother me. It's just I've never done anything like this before."

Fred sensed he'd scored. He didn't want to push it. "You don't have to decide right now. Think about it for a few days. I'll get back to you."

Shawn slept very little that night. He just could not conceive of himself as a pusher. Though that would not directly be his role, that's what he would be doing. Also, what repercussions would follow Shawn's refusal to accept the proposal? Fred had admitted his role in dealing with drugs. Would he feel secure knowing that Shawn knew of this involvement but refused his offer?

The risk all around was substantial. Fred admitted that. His admission, however, did not include Shawn's potential refusal.

Shawn figured that discretion and some brains, could reduce the dangers. The organization was already set up. Shawn would do no recruiting, just serve as a middleman. His immediate boss would contact him only by phone to confirm shipments. They would not meet.

For several days Shawn debated the proposition. Ultimately, the lure of money, maybe large chunks of money, influenced his decision. When Fred called back, Shawn accepted the offer.

CHAPTER 22

Three years had elapsed since then. Now Shawn drove mechanically, questioning the validity of the decision three years ago. Maybe this minor complication would pass. Until that time Shawn would have to take extra precautions. Obviously, his phone contact wasn't much concerned. The shipment was coming as usual. Shawn just didn't like the threat that this situation posed.

The green Beaver Creek sign reflected in Shawn's headlights. He slowed and pulled onto the small road on the right, just before the bridge. Where the road led he didn't know. He only found parking there convenient. In the past three years, not once had he seen another person use that road.

Shawn's routine was simple: retrieve the package from a small compartment hidden under the Beaver Creek Bridge, deliver it a couple miles down the road, and place it in a container beneath a large birch tree standing only a few feet from a historic marker, historic for reasons Shawn did not know or care. Who placed the drugs or the money Shawn picked up was also a mystery to him. Why drops and pickups couldn't be made in the same spot, Shawn didn't know. He did what he was told.

Rapidly, Shawn crossed the highway, descending the bank and walking to the familiar spot under the bridge. Standing beneath the container, he unlocked it and reached for the package inside. As he did, a twig snapped in the distance.

Shawn jumped, plunging into the shadows provided by the bridge supports. He listened, motionless. He fought to control his breathing, to overcome the feeling of panic. He listened but heard nothing.

Shawn breathed deeply. He'd have to look around before attempting to take the package again. The sound apparently came from the other side of the bridge or beyond. Shawn carefully inched his way up the embankment onto the shoulder of the road. He peered into the darkness across the road but could see nothing. The moon shone brightly. Towering trees cast long shadows all around him.

Shawn dashed across the open road and down the bank on the other side. He slipped into the dense undergrowth and waited. Another crack, then a splash. Someone was there! Shawn's heart raced. He stood still, listening, eyes trying to penetrate the darkness of the forest. Then he moved cautiously toward the sounds. The creek came into view. A shadow moved. It was more than just a shadow.

Directly in front of him stood a person, near the bridge. Shawn froze, examining the shape more carefully. It appeared to be a man. Fear surged in Shawn's throat. He wanted to vomit. He swallowed hard, catching his breath. Had he been followed? Surely, if the man was after him, he would not have been so careless. What was he doing here? Shawn's mind raced. His heart pounded. What should he do?

With some new found resolve, he kneeled and searched the ground beneath him. He needed a heavy twig, solid enough to give a substantial blow without breaking. He felt something just big enough to grasp securely in his hand. He picked it up slowly. It would work.

The man still stood by the creek, just looking into the sky. Shawn crept forward a few more feet. His heart hammered against his ribs. He lunged forward, the small branch poised above his head. He swung as hard as the could. The branch struck. The man never knew what hit him. He fell instantly to the ground, unmoving.

For seconds Shawn stood transfixed, wanting to run but gripped by some magnetism of the figure slumped on the ground before him. Shawn looked at the small branch in his hand as if it were some foreign object then tossed it aside. He walked closer to the body on the ground. The force of the blow had thrown the man forward so that his face was concealed. Shawn's hand shook as he reached down to roll the man over. He gasped. The man was Justin Starling.

Fear and confusion consumed him. He stood up, ran, stumbled, got up, and ran again toward the compartment under the bridge support. He grabbed the package, clambered up the embankment, then ran to his car. Gravel flew as his car squealed onto the highway.

CHAPTER 23

The pain had virtually disappeared from Justin's mouth and nose. Only soreness remained. His teeth were yet sensitive to hot and cold, but with care he could eat most anything.

Late Friday afternoon Justin ate a light meal then decided to take a short nap. Sleep came immediately. When he awoke, darkness surrounded him. He sat up quickly, momentarily disoriented. Feeling his way to the other end of the sofa, Justin switched on a table lamp.

It was after eleven o'clock. He slept for five hours. Wide awake now, Justin poured himself a glass of milk and walked to the large windows which overlooked the valley below. Intermittent clouds appeared as strange dark shapes in an otherwise bright, night sky. The moon, peeking in and out from behind the clouds, created eerie but fascinating shadows among the trees. The bridge and highway were clearly visible below. Not a car was in sight.

Justin finished his milk. Impressed with the idea of a midnight walk, he retraced his earlier route, enjoying the freshness of the night air. The sounds of the night echoed all around him, an occasional rustle of leaves, a hoot of an owl, and the incessant chorus of frogs. Like earlier in the day, the presence of so much life in nature failed to alter the sensation of his being completely alone.

He felt better than he had for days. Pausing by the creek, he sat on the base of a fallen tree. Despite the serenity of this place, Justin sat powerless to resist the images of the previous few days from drifting through his mind.

Connie Shetland, Harold Baylor, Randy Wilcox, the negotiating committee, the strike possibility. These names, these ideas tumbled over in his head. While they did, he stared into the virtually cloudless, night sky. The negotiating committee. "What a horse shit job," Justin muttered aloud to himself. Seven, eight meetings or whatever and essentially nothing of significance accomplished.

Justin generally admired the members of his committee and respected their dedication, especially that of Norma Metcalf. She served as an excellent release for Justin. Sound judgement and clear perception of the issues dividing the board and the teachers enabled Norma to respond intelligently to Justin's opinions and refections on the whole negotiating process. Since they shared third hour preparation, they found time to discuss the problems created by the negotiations stalemate.

The other committee members, Ruth Wirth, Rita Williams, Shawn Kelly and Bob Medford, Justin admired for their willingness to serve. He had reservations, though, about their motives. Not knowing Ruth, Rita, and Bob as well as he knew Norma, he felt unsure about exactly how they viewed the unresolved issues which divided the school board and the teachers' committee.

On the other hand, Justin harbored little doubt about the motives and values of Shawn Kelly. Justin acknowledged that Shawn was a handsome man. Reddish, blonde hair accentuated his ruddy complexion. Despite his forty-three years, he retained a youthful appearance with the build of a professional football player. At six feet three, two hundred pounds, he presented an imposing figure in any classroom.

Added to his appearance, Shawn was kind of a smooth operator, Justin concluded after only casual contact and simple observation. To Justin, Shawn was not the kind who generally selected teaching for a career, maybe some kind of sales work but not teaching. Shawn enjoyed the big cars, the expensive clothes, the vacations in tropical paradises that are usually associated with the more affluent. His only concern in negotiations was money. As long as the raise was adequate, whatever else was included or excluded from the contract made little difference to him.

In contrast, Bob Medford attempted to consider all sides of an issue. Small and soft spoken, Bob listened, reluctant to engage in arguments with anyone. His math skill made him a valuable asset in preparing salary schedules and calculating costs.

Rita Williams, Justin had always considered attractive, not beautiful but attractive. Of course, attractiveness failed to guarantee an effective negotiator. However, Justin recognized Rita's willingness to serve her profession even though her income was a mere supplement to that of her successful husband, who earned an apparent comfortable living in the insurance business.

Generally, Justin received support from all his committee members. Nonetheless, he understood that each one came to the committee with a range of motivations, objectives, and priorities. He realized that his job was to coordinate this range, to provide leadership that would embrace diverse opinions, finally bringing the committee to a unified position on the major issues. Not an easy job, but one made possible by Justin's willingness to seek the opinions of others and to listen to what they had to say.

Justin gingerly pressed the contours of this nose between his fingers. Closing his eyes, he massaged his nose tenderly. Paradoxically, despite the calm, peacefulness of the night, Justin was struck by the continued and near infinite variety of sounds that pervaded the night. The frogs carried on an unending chorus, while the distinct hoot of owls punctuated the night air. Twigs snapped, leaves rustled, and pine needles whispered as a gentle breeze stirred the night air.

Rising from his seat on the fallen tree, Justin walked closer to the creek and crouched lower to see the water. The class size and teacher assignment issues were becoming, even to him, an agony. Norma had told him the other day in the lounge that she was apprehensive about achieving any concessions from the board on these matters. Administrative prerogatives, enrollment declines, learning environment, class size, economic capabilities of the community, strike, quality of education. Justin threw up his hands, "Bull shit! It's all bull shit!"

To Justin it was a matter of priorities, and the only ones that mattered were those that offered the best for the students in Twin Pines. All the other stuff just clouded the priorities while satisfying personal goals of some people with inflated egos.

Continuing his progress toward the bridge, his path lighted by the now clear, brilliant moon, Justin, for some reason, thought of the article he recently read on drug abuse in the Twin Pines schools. In all that had happened the last two or three days, he hadn't given that article much thought.

What were the reported statistics? Justin probed his memory. Fifty or sixty percent of the students at the middle and high school levels had either tried some drug or were regular users? "Incredible!" Justin declared to himself. He promised he would have to investigate more fully the allegations contained in that newspaper article. So many things to do. Even in this remote, secluded place, he found no escape. Instead, the solitude tended to provoke reflections.

CHAPTER 24

Justin delighted in being alone. It gave him time to think, to sort out the problems that faced him, to relax, and to reflect. He always enjoyed his privacy, at least in his adult life. His affinity with privacy had influenced his never having given marriage a serious thought.

At thirty-two he was beyond the age when a woman could easily lure him into any permanent relationship. Physically he exhibited the qualities attractive to most women: five feet ten inches tall, one hundred sixty-five pounds, gently waving blonde hair, a medium build maintained by a commitment to conditioning, a tan complexion, dark intense eyes, small rounded nose, and full lips protecting sparkling white teeth.

In college he had no steady girl friends but did have dates, especially for the big social events, such as spring formals and fraternity parties. He even established a relatively long term relationship with a young elementary major who eventually graduated and headed to the Twin Cities to begin her teaching career. Justin stayed in touch with her for a couple of years after graduation. Their separate interests, their independence or whatever, gradually ended the relationship. Justin had neither heard from her nor seen her for more than five years.

During those five years, Justin dated very infrequently. Twin Pines did not attract young women, and those who grew up there by now already settled into a pattern or life style which long ago excluded having more than one partner at a time. Justin traveled extensively during vacations: Europe last summer, Hawaii at Christmas, the Bahamas the Christmas before that. He read widely while at home and enjoyed the minor tasks home ownership required.

He bought his small two bedroom rambler four years ago, having tired of apartment living and the restrictions that went with it. The investment, of course, was appealing, but more important, Justin desired the privacy and the independence that came with home ownership.

His house, located in the older section of Twin Pines, was only a short distance from the high school and only a little farther from the central shopping district of town. The house needed work: paint, a new roof, and improved plumbing, the major requirements. Justin welcomed the challenge of these improvements and devoted several hours to what he could do himself. He hired out the rest. After four years the house was evolving into a comfortable, valuable investment in which Justin took great pride.

Nearing the bridge, Justin thought he heard what sounded like the slam of a car door. He paused and listened more intently. He heard only the frogs. He came to a small clearing beside the creek, stopped, and gazed up at the moon just reappearing from behind a cloud. He sensed a sudden rustle and quick movement behind him. Before he could turn, his head exploded in pain. He felt himself falling. Then everything was blackness.

CHAPTER 25

Justin tried to move. His head pounded. He opened his eyes; the sky above blurred. He attempted to roll over on his stomach. The pain in his head forced him to stay on his back.

Trying to think about what happened, Justin could only remember looking at the night sky. He had to get back to the cabin. Raising himself on one elbow, he ran his hand over the back of his head. He winced as his fingers touched a large lump matted with dried blood and hair. He sat up; stabbing pain beat on the inside of his head. He had to get up and make it back to the cabin. He crawled to a nearby tree. Using the tree for support, Justin managed to lift himself slowly. He stood, dazed, breathing heavily, leaning against the tree.

The entrance road provided the only return to the cabin. Following the creek was too steep and irregular. Justin tried standing without the tree to support him. He swayed but regained his balance, the pain continuing but his vision clearing. Painstakingly, Justin moved toward the bridge and the highway. On hands and knees he inched up the embankment, stood up and walked haltingly to the entrance road a few yards away.

Following a near endless struggle, Justin stood before the cabin, lights glowing from inside. He headed to the bathroom where he suddenly felt sick. He threw up in the toilet. He wanted to wash the blood from his hair. His dissipated strength and dizziness prevented it. With what strength remained, Justin staggered to the sofa where he collapsed, unconscious.

Trees were just a blur on the sides of the highway. Shawn's hands gripped the steering wheel. He glanced inadvertently at the speedometer, eight-five miles an hour. Why was he driving so fast? He had no special destination. The need to go, to move, to flee consumed him. The image of his running flashed through his mind again, an image that recently occurred with increasing frequency. He would reach Twin Pines in a few minutes, and then what would he do? Confusion and indecision plagued him.

What was Justin Starling doing at Beaver Creek? Shawn was almost certain Justin knew nothing about the drug activities. What if Justin had seen the car? Everyone knew Shawn's car. It was the only one of its kind in town. If Justin saw it, he would surely have a good idea who hit him. Was Justin hurt badly? What if the blow had killed him? God! How he regretted having gotten entangled in this mess! How could he continue? How could he get out? Shawn's mind was cluttered; answers eluded him.

The lights of Twin Pines appeared in the distance. Shawn slowed. At four o'clock in the morning no one was out except the police. All Shawn needed was a speeding ticket.

Out of the confusion of his mind came the image of the small road, the small gravel road by the bridge, where he always parked when making his pickups. Shawn slapped his hand on his steering wheel. "Why hadn't I thought of that before?" He asked himself. That road must go somewhere Shawn assured himself.

In three years he had never seen another car near the bridge, anyplace. That where he always parked was a road leading somewhere never really occurred to him. A cabin, maybe there's a cabin in the woods. That's it. Shawn grinned.

Justin must be staying at some cabin. That would explain his presence at the bridge.

Shawn relaxed. Still, the possibility that Justin saw his car haunted him. What about Justin's condition? He had to find out. He had to find out now.

When Shawn finally returned to his apartment, it was only four thirty; not even the sun was up. He paced the floor. He could simply drive back to the bridge and investigate the gravel road. How could he explain his presence if he met up with Justin again, assuming Justin was still there? Shawn really hadn't swung that hard. Justin's condition began to take on greater urgency, not necessarily out of Shawn's compassion but out of his fear of the consequences of someone having seen him at the bridge.

Shawn sat down hard on the kitchen chair, gripping his head in his hands. "Think!" he commanded himself. "Who would know where Justin had gone?"

Shawn was unaware of Justin's friends. Assuredly, he was not one of them. Shawn knew very few of the teachers at the high school, at least not well enough to call and inquire about Justin. He knew Norma through negotiations. He would call her. Maybe she would know. Five in the morning. He stood up quickly to renew his pacing. He'd have to wait until at least eight or nine before calling.

CHAPTER 26

Justin opened his eyes. Where was he? He lay half on and half off the sofa. His first movement brought back quickly the memory of the blow to the head and the painful struggle back to the cabin.

Easing himself onto the sofa, Justin placed his hand on his head. His fingers gingerly traced a large, bulging lump. Dried blood and dirt matted his hair. It was still night, and the cabin lights remained on. He tried to stand up, but pulsating pain and dizziness prevented it. He sat for a moment, contemplating what to do next. A shower. If only he could get to the bathroom. I shower could likely clear his head. He thought about a concussion. He'd need medical attention. How could he get it? Driving was impossible in his condition. The remoteness of the cabin rendered useless a cell phone.

Justin forced himself to stand. He swayed while the room blurred. He steadied himself by placing a hand on the end of the sofa. The pain persisted, but his vision partially cleared. With careful, methodical steps, Justin moved toward the bathroom. The pounding in his head diminished to a steady, more even pain like a severe headache.

He groped for the bathroom light and switched it on. The mirror revealed a person Justin hardly recognized. Blood and dirt caked the side of his head, over his right ear and cheek. Traces of black from his previous beating accentuated the hollow gaunt look of his face. His hair stood up in clumps, stained with red and tangled with dirt and leaves. He checked the response of his eyes to rapid changes in light. They seemed to respond appropriately. Probably no concussion.

Justin turned on the shower. Leaning against the bathroom wall, he managed to take off his clothes. He stepped into the shower. Cautiously, he placed his head under the hot spray of the shower. At first, the water on the open cut in his head stung sharply. Gradually, the stinging disappeared. With shampoo Justin began the careful task of washing his hair. The hot water had a soothing effect. Justin started to feel better. The suds flowed from his hair over his face and down over his shoulders. Suds, leaves, and dirt floated at this feet before vanishing down the drain.

Justin stood in the shower long after he bathed, relishing the refreshing water. He began to feel quite good, considering the recent assaults to his body. The blow to his head apparently was not as serious as he first suspected. However, the bump remained painfully sore to the touch. At least in his shower, Justin no longer experienced the dizziness nor the throbbing sensation that crippled him earlier.

Having dried himself, Justin dressed in clean clothes and stood before the large front windows, looking out at the first traces of daylight. He tried to make some sense out of what was happening to him. Innately not the violent type, he rarely engaged in a fight with anyone in thirty-two years. Now, in less than a week, Randy Wilcox had savagely attacked him in the school parking lot, and a mysterious intruder had clubbed him on the head with who knows what?

Were these events related or were they mere coincidence? Only two people for sure knew he would be at the cabin. He was certain that last night's attack was a case of mistaken identity. He just happened to be in the wrong place at the right time.

As he reflected on the previous hight's incident, Justin remembered hearing the sound of a car door. Could someone other than Bob or Norma have known where he was? Could someone have followed him to the cabin? But why? Was Randy Wilcox intent on finishing the job? If so he definitely had his chance. The whole thing was a bit crazy, Justin concluded. He was caught up in a series of events that he couldn't understand, that really didn't make any sense.

CHAPTER 27

Squinting into the sun, Shawn troubled over the tenuous reason he gave Norma for wanting to know where Justin had gone. The tone of Norma's voice revealed her skepticism. The unfriendliness between Shawn and Justin was readily apparent at recent negotiations meetings. That Shawn needed to talk to Justin urgently did not seem sufficient justification to search him out at eight thirty Saturday morning. Why hadn't he gotten in touch with him earlier? Norma asked. Shawn admitted to some reluctance to apologize for his lack of cooperation, and he'd needed the time to decide exactly what to do. Having made his decision, he needed to carry it out immediately. With this explanation, Norma disclosed that Justin went to a cabin about forty miles east of Twin Pines. She knew no more than that.

The highway Shawn traveled so frequently at night looked strange in the daylight. The curves and the small hills were familiar, but the dense forest that lined both sides of the road was not. The beauty of the drive eluded Shawn. Tension and anxiety over his mission consumed him.

For a moment Shawn accepted what Norma said: Justin went to the cabin for relaxation. That Justin might suspect Shawn's activities with drugs remained a possibility but a highly unlikely one. Justin's condition concerned Shawn more than anything else.

Justin's suffering serious injury or maybe even death would engender a cascade of questions and a complete investigation. The whole area around Beaver Creek Bridge would probably be searched. The drop point would be located. Shawn didn't need those kinds of problems. He wasn't sure what he would do if he found Justin still lying motionless by the creek, but he was driven to find out. What he would do he would decide when he got there.

As the trees swayed in the morning breeze, Justin could catch glimpses of the highway and occasionally the turn off that led to the cabin. Breakfast revived him, and though his head was delicately sore to the touch, most of the dull, continuous pain ceased. He felt tired but grateful that the blow to his head was not any worse than it was.

Standing before the large window, he almost forgot the trauma of the night before. He delighted in just enjoying the view that spread before him. This afternoon he would try to read and perhaps catch up on his sleep. Tomorrow he would have to return to prepare for final tests and the frantic pace of the concluding days of the school year. His negotiating committee would also have to meet soon. Preparations would have to be made for the mediation sessions very likely occurring later in the summer.

Preoccupied with what the summer would bring, Justin stood by the windows, oblivious to the car that slowed and turned onto the small cabin road. He was startled when a car suddenly appeared almost from nowhere and pulled up behind his, parked in front of the cabin. Justin recognized the car instantly. It was Shawn Kelly.

Mystified by Shawn's presence, Justin stood frozen in the window, watching as Shawn slowly got out of his car to look cautiously around. Instinctively, Justin moved away from the window as if he did not want to be seen. "How the hell did he find this place?" Justin muttered to himself.

Before Shawn could knock, Justin opened the door, standing almost guarding the entrance to the cabin. At the bottom of the short flight of stairs that led up to the door, Shawn looked up examining Justin. Then with a smile and a peculiar sense of relief, he said, "Good morning, Justin. How are you?"

"Well, this is a surprise," Justin replied.

"Sorry to intrude, but I have to talk to you." Shawn sounded submissive and contrite.

"How'd you know I was here? How'd you find this place?" Justin asked in rapid succession.

"Norma," Shawn answered apologetically.

Justin stepped away from the door. "Come on it."

Shawn halted for an instant on the top step. He looked behind him, absorbing the view of the vast forest spreading out from the cabin. "Beautiful place. Is it yours?" He asked.

"No, a friend's." Justin motioned Shawn to enter the cabin.

"Come here much?" Shawn quickly surveyed the inside of the cabin.

"No. First time." Justin directed Shawn to the small wicker chair next to the sofa. "Could I get you something, coffee, soda, a beer?"

"No thanks."

Feeling uneasy about the situation, again Justin asked, "How'd you find this place?"

"Norma said something about forty miles east of Twin Pines so that's how far I drove. I saw the road so I tried it. Lucky, I guess."

Justin never before witnessed Shawn so subdued and so unsure of himself. He was puzzled by the whole scene.

Shawn moved restlessly in his chair, rubbing his hands together. "Justin, I've been a jerk," he confessed.

"What do you mean, a jerk?" The confession caught Justin off guard.

"You know very well what I mean."

"Negotiations?" Justin asked.

"Yes,"

"I know we've had our disagreements. Everyone is entitled to his own opinions, Shawn. I don't expect everyone to agree with me."

Shawn relaxed noticeably. "But my behavior has been unjustified. I got hung up on the money and . . . well, I think maybe some of the other issues are just as important."

Justin found difficult concealing the suspicion that cloaked Shawn's presence. 'I appreciate that, but you didn't have to drive way out here to tell me."

"It's bothered me the past few days. I decided I had to talk to you now. I'm sorry for the intrusion, but to be honest, it's a load off my mind."

Justin really couldn't believe in Shawn's sincerity. Shawn played the role well, but Justin was positive he knew Shawn better than that. Abundant evidence established that Shawn's entire life style revolved around money. Sudden feelings of guilt could not alter well entrenched habits.

Despite these misgivings, Justin joined in with whatever game Shawn played. They discussed subsequent steps to be taken in the negotiating process, Shawn displaying an intense and uncharacteristic interest in all that Justin had to say. Shawn finally inquired about what happened to Justin's face and head. Justin fabricated an unconvincing story about a fall, perplexed more by why Shawn said nothing sooner than concerned for the truth of his explanation.

They also discussed summer plans, and after about an hour of frequently faltering conversation, Shawn got up, announcing that he would have to leave. His mission was accomplished. Justin did not ask him to stay but thanked him for his consideration and change of heart.

Shawn left, confident Justin remained ignorant of his drug activities and thankful Justin received no life threatening injuries. For the first time Shawn drove the forty miles back to Twin Pines relaxed. It was such a refreshing drive.

CHAPTER 28

In retrospect Justin's weekend at the cabin included a mixture of nightmares, daydreams, and mysteries. Shawn Kelly's unexpected appearance continued to perplex him, but perhaps he had misjudged Shawn. Maybe he was sincere in his apologies. Justin reached for his briefcase, locked his car, and walked toward the familiar front entrance to Twin Pines High School.

Though the weekend at the cabin failed to resolve much of what troubled Justin, it allowed his mouth and nose to heal sufficiently. Barely visible was the cut on his lip, and though the bluish color under his eyes and around his nose was more evident than he hoped, student curiosity, he assumed, could be satisfied with some story about a household accident. Justin's head remained tender to the touch from the blow at Beaver Creek Bridge. To his relief, the bump was not visible.

Justin rarely went to the faculty lounge before school in the morning. Instead, he spent the time in his room making last minute preparations for his five classes. This week would be hectic, mostly review for final tests. Students typically did not take review seriously, and though Justin had spent time preparing review exercises and discussions, he knew for most of the students it was work done in vain. He really couldn't blame them for relaxing this last week of school. The semester had been a demanding one for both him and his students, especially those in his four writing classes. Nonetheless, the school year continued for another week.

Students entered Justin's classroom in a playful mood. A few looked at his face with interest. One of two bolder ones inquired about what happened and why he had been absent. Justin's hasty reply about a broken basement stairway quieted any more inquiries.

"Believe it or not we've almost made it." Justin stood before the assembled class. "But we're not done yet." Justin waited for the few isolated groans to subside before he continued. "As you know, this is the last week of regular classes." Again he waited for a spattering of cheers to die down. "The final test is next Monday at ten o'clock in the morning. There will be a special final test schedule. We will not meet first hour. I'll give you the final test schedule Thursday or Friday. If I hand it out any sooner, some of you will certainly lose it or forget it.

"This week we'll do a bit of review of some of the major writing skills that we have worked on this semester. These exercises are intended to help prepare you for the final test which will be an essay type." More groans. "Your last compositions I'll try to get back to you in a couple days. Any questions?"

"Yeah, when do we take our final in here?"

The class burst into laughter. Justin threw up his hands in surrender.

"Chuck, I just told you two minutes ago. Can't you hear or weren't you listening again? The final is next Monday at ten o'clock in the morning. Okay? Any other questions?" Justin paused long enough to let his eyes quickly survey the class. "All right, then, take out your composition books and turn to page eighty-three."

Justin explained the short assignment which he hoped would keep the class occupied for the entire period. He had work to do and could use the time. He concluded his explanation with, "Are there any questions? If not, you may get busy."

The class did get to work with only a few reluctant to get started. Justin knew that the assignment would receive only superficial attention from most of the students. He also knew that as the week progressed, the students would approach their assignments with less and less eagerness. Not just this class but all his classes had fallen victim to the end of year lethargy.

CHAPTER 29

During the interval between second and third hours, Justin assumed his usual position outside his classroom door. It was here that he, on occasion, talked briefly with Kitty Wilder as she headed for her next class, and he headed for the faculty lounge where he would spend part of his preparation period correcting composition.

"Hi, Mr. Starling," came the familiar voice.

"Good morning, Kitty," Justin smiled. "Have a good weekend?"

"No, just boring," Kitty frowned. "I told you nothing goes on over the weekend in this town." Kitty looked with alarm at Justin's face. "What happened to you?"

Again Justin used the feeble broken stairway story.

"Is that why you were absent last week?" Kitty asked.

"Yes."

Fortunately, Kitty did not pursue the topic but continued, "By the way, will you be around after school? I need your help in filling out an application for a counselor job at a summer camp up north."

"Sure."

"Good," Kitty replied. "I'll stop by your room right after seventh hour."

Justin nodded his head. "Okay, after school it is."

By taking his time, Justin had avoided the rush of teachers leaving the lounge for their third hour classes. As he entered the lounge, he noticed Norma Metcalf seated in her usual place by the window. She anxiously waited as Justin took the chair across the small table from her.

'How's your weekend?" She asked in a confidential tone.

"Fine. Great place."

"You've healed fast," Norma commented surveying Justin's face.

"Fortunately," Justin responded, stretching out in his chair and moving his papers to one side of the table.

After a pause, Norma asked hesitantly, "Tell me. Did Shawn Kelly show up at the cabin?"

"Yes, he did."

"I'm really sorry I told him where you had gone, but I felt I had little choice," Norma apologized. "What did he want anyway?"

"I'm really not sure," Justin frowned. "He seemed nervous and agitated. He apologized for his lack of cooperation on the committee. Strange he would go so far out of his way to do that. I guess he's kind of a strange guy."

Justin toyed with the idea of telling Norma about the attack by Beaver Creek Bridge but refrained from doing so. He wasn't much disposed to reveal the details of that event in the faculty lounge, even to Norma Metcalf.

Justin reached for his compositions which he intended to read and evaluate at the cabin. He never did. He rose from his place beside the small table, and with papers in hand seated himself in a cushioned lounge chair a short distance from Norma. Justin and Norma now shared the lounge all by themselves.

Norma tapped her pencil lightly on the table as she studied a student's paper before her. Suddenly, she asked, "How's this whole thing going to come out?"

"What?" Justin looked up from his work.

"How's this whole thing going to come out?" Norma repeated.

"What whole thing?"

"Negotiations, dummy," Norma joked.

Justin leaned his head back on the chair, looking up at the ceiling. "God, I wish I knew."

"You must have some idea," Norma persisted.

Justin sat up with his hands clasped between his knees. "It's going to take some risk, and it's going to take some sacrifice, I guess. Sadly, I seriously doubt if our staff has the guts to do either."

Norma pondered what Justin had just said. "You must understand, though," she cautioned, "that many teachers have more to lose than you do. If we were to strike or pursue some other drastic action, many of our people with families and other obligations would be hard pressed."

"I'm sorry, Norma, but I can't buy that argument. Security is wonderful except when it becomes an end in itself."

Justin stopped and took a breath. "When are we going to stand up and say, 'Look, we're teachers! We are important, more important than anyone else in this ungrateful world, and damn it we are no longer going to be content with the economic crumbs that are left over!'"

The discussion ended abruptly. Justin returned to his compositions but found he was reading them mechanically, without concentrating on what each said. He still surged ahead.

A few minutes passed before Norma almost apologetically asked, "Did you see the article about drugs in our schools? I think it was in last week's local paper."

Looking up from his compositions, Justin replied, "Yes, I read it. Frankly, I haven't thought much about it."

"I guess I haven't either," Norma confessed. "I feel rather guilty not taking more of an interest in a subject with such dire implications."

"How valid do you suppose the information is?" Justin asked, stretching and laying his papers aside.

"Supposedly some young reporter spent a lot of time talking with students in both the middle and the high schools."

"I don't know, but I sure as hell don't know much about the problem," Justin admitted. "God, I work here, and I know nothing about any drug problems. If there is a problem, that's a terrible admission to make."

"I know very little about it either," Norma agreed. "I can't believe the story's just sensationalism."

"I can't believe that either," Justin concurred as he returned to his correcting, not particularly interested in exploring the topic any further.

CHAPTER 30

Period seven dragged on endlessly. For the fourth time Justin assigned the same pages in the composition book. For the fourth period of the day he sat grading compositions. His eyes were tired, and he was tired.

As the final bell sounded marking the end of the day, Justin dismissed his class, leaned back in his desk chair, and closed his eyes. Placing his feet on top his desk, he relaxed. It was in this position that Kitty found him as she entered his room shortly after three o'clock.

"Don't fall asleep," Kitty laughed, standing directly in front of Justin's desk.

"Well, hello. No, I'm just recovering from a hard day at the office." Justin dropped his feet to the floor. "Okay, what is it you need to know?"

Kitty sat in a front desk. She thumbed through her notebook and extracted a form. "As I mentioned this morning, I've applied for a job at a camp near the Canadian border. I don't know much about it," Kitty explained, "but I think it's kind of a dumping ground for rich kids. Games, crafts, group activities, that kind of stuff."

"How did you find out about this job?" Justin inquired.

"In the guidance office down stairs." Kitty looked up at Justin, anticipating another question. Getting none, she continued, "A couple of questions ask about why I'm applying. I'm not sure what to write.

"I guess I would ask first, why are you applying?"

For the next ten minutes Justin and Kitty discussed why she would be interested in a camp counselor's job. He helped her mainly to identify three reasons that the application form called for. She would write these reasons in her own words. With this completed, Kitty collected her books and notebook. She gracefully eased herself out of the desk.

"Thank you, Mr. Starling. You're always such a big help. Someday I'll pay you back."

"I'll hold you to that."

Throughout the day, Justin was bothered by a peculiar sense of guilt, guilt about his ignorance of the alleged drug situation in Twin Pines High School and guilt about the obvious lack of interest in discussing the subject that he displayed earlier with Norma. Besides, he promised himself at the cabin that he would find out more about it. Students typically possessed more knowledge of what went on in the high school than anyone else. Kitty, if she did have any information about drugs in the school, would share it with Justin.

"May I ask you a question now?" Justin stood up, moved around to the front of his desk where he sat on the edge.

"Sure, what is it?"

"Did you read the article in the paper last week about drugs in this school and in the middle school?"

"No, I didn't. But I heard about it." Kitty set her books down on the desk.

"What do you think? Is what it said true?"

Kitty hesitated briefly. "I don't know about the percentages that I heard were used. I do know many kids use drugs of some kind, and I know of a few who use them all the time."

"Even here in this school?" Justin asked in disbelief.

"Yes, some kids are high often in school itself," Kitty stated with assurance.

"You're kidding." Justin slid off the desk to stand before Kitty, arms folded across his chest.

"No, I'm not," Kitty replied seriously.

"I feel ridiculous that I'm not aware of much of this happening."

"It does happen around here. Weekends are worse though."

"Do you think the problem has gotten out of hand?" Justin asked.

"With some kids I think it has."

"Where do they get the stuff, the drugs?" Justin pursued the subject.

"I'm not sure exactly from where, but they are certainly available for anybody who wants them."

Justin shook his head. "Hard to believe," he confessed.

"It's true, though," Kitty insisted, looking up at the clock. "I'd like to discuss this some more. But my ride home is about here."

"I would too. Maybe another time. Write up the ideas we've talked about on this job thing, and tomorrow show me what you've come up with," Justin advised.

The two of them walked to the classroom door.

"Thanks, again, Mr. Starling. See you tomorrow."

"Bye Kitty." Justin watched as Kitty walked down the hall and disappeared down the stairs at the end. His mind tumbled with thoughts about the conversation they just had. He turned back into his room, pausing to study the now empty rows of desks. How many of his students, minds blurred by drugs, occupied those desks each day? Pondering the question momentarily, Justin shook his head in ignorance, gathered a stack of papers, and stuffed them in his briefcase.

CHAPTER 31

Securing the outside door of the building, Justin headed for his car which now sat alone in the teachers' parking lot. Unlocking the door, Justin tossed his briefcase across the front seat, slid in behind the wheel, inserted the key into the ignition, and pressed the button that would roll down the driver's window. When he looked up at the windshield, he noticed the paper pressed under the wiper. "Now who's having a car wash?" Justin asked himself.

Getting out of the car, Justin pulled the paper from under the wiper. After unfolding it, he realized it was not any type of advertisement. He scanned the barely legible handwriting. After a moment he let his arm drop limply to his side.

"Holy shit!" Tension gnawed in his stomach as he leaned against his car, staring straight ahead at nothing.

He slowly raised the paper, studying it more carefully. It has to be just a prank, Justin reassured himself. Still, if his relationship with Kitty could so easily suffer misinterpretation to the person responsible for the note, it surely could suffer the same fate with others as well.

He read the note again. "Starling, if you want to keep your job, stay away from Kitty Wilder."

The initial shock of the note began to dissipate. More rationally, Justin analyzed the situation. Yes, he had established a relationship with Kitty as he had with other students. That carried with it no hint of indiscretion or improper, professional behavior. There was, in Justin's mind, nothing wrong with getting to know his students on a more personal level. By so doing, he violated no ethics of his profession, nor did he compromise his or Kitty's integrity. He found Kitty appealing, not for any perverted physical reason. He found her appealing for her intelligence, her personality and her charm. Somebody obviously was giving him a bad time. Just the same, he found deplorable the thought that someone played games with an honest, wholesome relationship with a student.

Justin jammed the paper in his pocket and got back into his car. As he drove home, he considered his alternatives. The only one that made any sense to him was to ignore the note for the time being even though events that he chose to ignore accumulated. Discussing the note with Kitty made no sense. He really didn't want to involve her. He would continue their relationship as though nothing happened to soil it.

Turning into his driveway, Justin was sure of only one thing: a special relationship between a teacher and a student had been defiled. No longer would it ever be the same. If the note was only a prank by some malicious student out for vengeance, it still tarnished a valuable relationship. If the note represented an attempt to destroy his career as a teacher, that was something else. In either case this was something more he had to worry about.

Justin stopped the car in the garage. He sat for a moment staring at the steering wheel. Kitty was a dynamic, energetic young lady who enjoyed a special relationship with most of her teachers. The note demeaned her while demeaning those relationships. The whole thing was disgusting. So disgusting that not for a moment did Justin even consider Connie Shetland's concluding remarks at the Pine Inn: "There are other ways to deal with the unreasonable."

CHAPTER 32

Connie dug through her purse, sure she had another twenty dollar bill. Randy would arrive in a few minutes to collect his fifty dollars. Why he waited so long to contact her for his money she didn't know. At least he had enough sense to come at a time when Vince would not be at home.

Where was that other twenty? Connie searched her memory to recall where she might have put it. She did not want Randy around any longer than necessary. Pay him the money and get rid of him. She dashed upstairs to her bedroom and another purse. There in the inside zip pocket was the twenty. The irritation subsided. More composed, Connie returned to the living room to wait.

Just before noon Randy arrived. As she approached the front door, Connie watched through the window. He was a handsome kid, well built and tall. Deep down Connie did feel sorry for him and regretted having offered little to assist him or her parents these past, few troubled years. For her, time for regret was gone. She had her own life and ambitions to attend to.

"Morning, Mrs. Shetland," Randy said in the sardonic fashion he usually used with her. "I guess you know why I'm here."

"Of course. Come in." They stood in the entry, Connie unwilling to invite him into her living room. Moreover, she felt very uncomfortable in Randy's presence. She detested the feeling but somehow couldn't control it. Worse, she knew that Randy was aware of it too.

"Here," Connie abruptly handed him the money. "It's all there."

"Oh, I wouldn't doubt that for a minute. Just making sure." As Randy examined the money, he commented softly, "Old Mr. Starling won't forget that parking lot for a while."

"I don't need the details," Connie interrupted.

"I thought you wanted a report."

"You did the job. That's all I need to know."

"Well, anyway," Randy grinned, "he'll have a good headache for a while." Randy's grin changed to a sneer. "I'd smash that bastard any day of the week. Maybe next time he'll think twice about running some kid out of school."

"Let's hope you did us both a favor." Connie locked her eyes onto Randy's. "Remember, you breathe a word of this, and I'll deny everything. You know who they'll believe. Keep in mind, assault is a criminal offense."

"Oh, you can trust me." Randy assumed an air of innocence and honesty. "Any other little jobs you have, just let me know. I'm always available."

"Now, leave," Connie demanded. "If anything comes up, I'll get in touch."

"Right." Randy left, closing the door behind him.

Relieved, Connie sat down. What would become of Randy rarely entered her mind. He continued living with her parents, his grandparents. The agony he had caused them would probably terminate that arrangement soon. Where he acquired his money was a mystery. A few thousand dollars of insurance money would become his when he reached twenty-one in another three years.

That he was now involved in drugs was possible. However, since his arrest for possession some months ago, there was no evidence to suggest that he persisted in either using or selling. Occasionally, he found short term employment around town. As far as Connie knew, he never maintained a permanent job.

Fully aware of the dangers of using Randy for her own purposes, Connie readily admitted that hiding her family relationship to him bordered on the impossible. Nonetheless, she was confident that save only the community old timers, few people knew Randy was her nephew. Furthermore, her status in the community would definitely shield her from any allegations made by Randy, who had firmly established himself as incorrigible and delinquent. With this reassurance, Connie directed her thoughts to the one o'clock luncheon date with Harold Baylor.

In recent months Connie became a regular customer at the Pine Inn. Several times each week she ate either lunch or dinner or both there. Today, she would share lunch with Harold Baylor.

Connie remained disturbed by the failure of the last negotiating session, and the set back caused by the teachers' rejection of the proposal she sponsored. Her future as a dominant force on the school board depended, she believed, on her directing negotiations to a successful conclusion. The last several months of negotiations convinced Connie that her leadership could guide negotiations to a contract settlement. From that settlement would evolve the board chair which would move her one step closer to her dream of influence, recognition, and success.

Harold did not desire to continue as board chair, even though another year remained of his three year term. Into his fourth three year term as a school board member, Harold had expressed reluctance to seek a fifth term. Problems that were beginning to face schools and school boards were more than he wished to tangle with. Besides, he intended to retire in another year and spend a portion of each year in Arizona.

Connie respected Harold's opinions. Despite the revulsion she felt remembering the last time they had lunch together, she needed his support. She had to regain the confidence of the rest of the board. Only through Harold could she accomplish this.

For over two hours Connie sat repulsed by the man sitting across the small table from her. She resented men who were incapable of handling their liquor. Harold Baylor was one of them. The more he drank the more talkative and irrational he became. Today was no exception.

Driving back to Twin Pines at the conclusion of her lunch, Connie concluded that despite the problems with the drinking, the meeting had been a success. Harold would support her. He gave his word, and if Harold could be counted on for anything, it was his word. Connie felt confident that Harold's support would ensure for her the chair of the Twin Pines School Board. She knew that none of the other board members possessed the least bit of interest in the position. She had made subtle inquiries.

The possibility of mediation Connie viewed with some ambivalence. Certainly, mediation suggested a failure of the board to entice the teachers into settlement by an attractive salary increase. Connie still recalled with bitterness and resentment the teachers' arrogant rejection of the board's proposal at the last negotiation meeting.

However, mediation would provide Connie the opportunity to display what she viewed as her increasing power and influence. Of course, there would be risks. The teachers could win the mediation decision. That would have some implications even though the decision would not be binding on either party.

Much remained that Connie could do to persuade the teachers, particularly Justin Starling, that to agree to the board's wishes would be in the teachers' best interest. She would soon assume the leadership. The contest between the teachers and the board would shortly be elevated to a new plateau. She relished the thought of establishing the board's authority. She would do it her way. She would permit no one to deny her this chance. The challenge was there. Eagerly, Connie would accept it.

CHAPTER 33

Though it was Friday afternoon, one of the busiest days of the week at the bank, Vince sat before the television in his family room slowly sipping a drink. He had left the bank early, complaining of a severe headache and upset stomach. The headache was real; the upset stomach was not.

The past few days had been hell for Vince. The money that he "borrowed" from the bank now totaled over fifteen hundred dollars. The deterioration of his relationship with Connie became more evident each day. There were moments when he thought he and Connie had recaptured some of the tenderness and understanding that once existed between them. Vince resented the loneliness and isolation created by Connie's growing obsession with school and community affairs. Her life was no longer a part of his. Knowing this hurt Vince profoundly.

Two drinks reduced the intensity of his headache. They did nothing for the frustration and desperation Vince struggled with. He did not know how much longer he could go on this way. The situation at the bank became more critical each day. From Vince's perspective everyone suspected him of manipulating his accounts. At least, that's the way he felt. He knew something would soon have to be done. His frequent deposits into checking without corresponding withdrawals from savings would inevitably be discovered unless he would repay the money shortly. With Connie's exorbitant spending habits, Vince did not know where that money was coming from.

Several times recently Vince pleaded with Connie to exercise more restraint in her spending. However, the result was always the same: an argument and more conflict in the house. She had her goals firmly established and nothing was going to interfere with the pursuit of those goals. How many times he heard those words, Vince did not care to calculate. How long he could continue to exist under conditions like those prevalent over the past few days, weeks, and months, he did not care to speculate.

Leaning back in the large chair where he sat for well over an hour, Vince closed his eyes, picturing those days so long ago when art, painting, and drawing occupied so much of his spare time. How delightful those hours were when he could escape the demands of the bank and his daily routine by simply holding in his hand a paint brush or a charcoal pencil. Now, there was virtually no escape. Nothing that he did helped ease the burdens that on this Friday afternoon created such anguish.

As Connie entered the garage, she was surprised to discover Vince's car already there. Vince did enjoy some freedom at the bank because of his position as vice president, but for him to be home on a Friday afternoon was highly unusual.

As she entered the family room, Vince appeared asleep with a drink clutched in his lap.

"What's the matter? You sick?" Connie asked.

Vince opened his eyes and sat up. "No." He sluggishly set the drink on the arm of the chair.

"Why are you home at this time of day?" Connie persisted, standing directly in front of her husband with hands on her hips.

"Had a headache so decided to come home early." Vince sounded vaguely apologetic.

"Do you think that drink's going to help your head?"

"I don't know about the headache, but it does help me relax," Vince replied quietly.

Connie turned to leave the family room, cutting short the brief interchange.

Vince stood up and motioned toward the sofa next to his chair. "Don't go. Come and sit down for a bit," he invited.

Connie turned to look at Vince. "I've had a long day. I'm going up to take a shower. You go back to sleep but don't spill the drink."

For a moment Vince wanted to beg Connie to sit down and talk with him, but what good would it do? Their discussions never resolved anything anyway. Vince said nothing. He just sat down, leaned his head back on the chair, and again closed his eyes. From above came the sound of the shower.

CHAPTER 34

Since the night of Randy's attack on Justin, the board and the teachers had not met. Justin's committee gathered briefly to prepare a counter proposal to the board's alleged final offer. The counter proposal essentially reasserted the need to adopt contractual language on the issues of class size and the limit of no more than six academic assignments in a seven period day for teachers in the middle and high schools. Justin also used the time to heal, eliminating the need to explain his injuries. To meet with the board during the final days of the school year added an enormous burden on Justin and his committee members. Nonetheless, the meeting was scheduled.

Now Justin studied the large crack in the window in a small classroom just outside the faculty lounge that served as a caucus room during negotiating meetings. It was six fifteen. Justin sat alone waiting for the other committee members to arrive.

All day Justin had been preoccupied with the note he found attached to his car. He tried to dismiss it as just another teenage prank. Something told him the note was more significant than that. The composition work he did perfunctorily, his preparation for the upcoming meeting with the board sketchy. He just couldn't focus his attention on one task at a time. Too many distractions intervened.

Leaning back in his chair, Justin stared at the ceiling of the small classroom. He ran his hand gently over his nose and around to the back of his head. The injuries had healed. The need to discover the truth about those injuries, and who was responsible for them had not. What part, if any, had Connie Shetland played in the recent events in Justin's life? What influence did Connie Shetland exert on other board members? Did they share her complete rejection of contract language on class size and the six hour teacher assignment? What recourse remained for the teachers if the board rejected their new proposal on these topics?

Justin tried to concentrate, to anticipate the problems he would face at tonight's meeting with the board. Unless some movement took place on either side, this meeting very likely would be the last for quite some time.

"What do you see up there?" Norma asked as she entered the classroom.

Justin, slightly startled by her sudden appearance, let his chair settle back level. "Just collecting my thoughts. Did you get the proposal written?"

"Yes, I did. Here, take a look and tell me what you think."

Justin took the single sheet of paper and scanned it quickly. "Looks good to me. Thanks for the typing."

As the other committee members arrived, Norma handed out to each copies of the revised proposal.

Assuming all had time to read the document, Justin said, "Tonight may be a pivotal meeting. I feel something has to give one way or another." He stood facing the other members of the committee sitting in desks in front of him. "First, I intend to give the board this proposal and explain that if they accept it, we would be willing to accept their latest money offer. Then it will be their play." Justin moved to one side of the room. "What that will be I can only guess so let's just wait and see. Does anyone have any questions or comments before we head into the lounge for the meeting?"

"What if they don't accept our proposal?" Bob Medford asked.

Justin hesitated then ran his fingers through his hair. "Of course, we would have to caucus again. I would say, though, that would put us at a complete impasse with the board. What we do from there is pretty well spelled out by state mediation laws."

"You mean we would set the strike wheels in motion?" asked Ruth.

"Yes, that's what I mean," Justin answered slowly.

The group sat quietly as each member assessed privately what that would mean for him or her. Not that they had not thought about strike before. The sobering reality of it now appeared more imminent.

"Any other comments?" Justin asked. He waited for just seconds for some response. "Well, then, let's go meet the enemy."

The three board members were already seated around the table when Justin and his committee entered the teachers' lounge. Members of the two committees exchanged friendly but superficial greetings. Justin sat directly across from board chair, Harold Baylor. Norma sat to Justin's right then Rita and Bob Medford. Shawn sat to Justin's left with Ruth between them. On Harold's left sat Charles Herman, the newest member of the board's negotiating team.

On his right sat Connie Shetland dressed immaculately as usual. Again, the thought passed through Justin's mind that she was beautiful despite her ambition and her unscrupulous tactics. In addition, she knew that she was attractive. At this moment she sat poised and sophisticated, smiling benevolently at those seated across from her.

"Well," Harold began, "tonight, I think, we'll make some progress."

Whenever Harold spoke, Justin found looking at him difficult. The bags under his eyes distracted Justin. Consequently, he had trouble following what Harold said. He forced himself to pay closer attention.

"At our last meeting," Harold went on, "we gave you what we thought was a generous offer of money. I said it would be our last. Since then we have reassessed our position. We admire our teachers here. We feel they are doing an outstanding job with our young people."

Justin moved restlessly in his chair. Connie, apparently, had accomplished something with her colleagues on the board.

"We have prepared another salary proposal," Harold pushed on, "that we feel does justice to your commitment as teachers in this community." Harold's eyes made contact with each member of the teachers' committee.

Justin's eyes moved toward Connie, who sat sedately, following Harold's explanation. Justin pictured Connie sitting at the Pine Inn, trying to make a bargain. He remembered the brief session he had with her not very long ago. He studied the table in front of him wondering just how much influence Connie had with the board. He also wondered for an instant what she did to get her way?"

"Therefore," Harold was still talking, "I want to give you this revised salary schedule which, I think, you'll find more than acceptable."

Harold handed Justin enough copies of the salary schedule for each teacher committee member. Justin distributed them to his committee then said, "We'll have to take a break to consider this proposal. Before we do, we also have a proposal which we want you to consider." Justin handed out his committee's proposal then watched as the board members perused it.

Connie's expression changed drastically. She sat more erect, folding her hands in front of her on the table. A hostile frown had replaced the gracious smile of earlier in the meeting.

Looking directly at each of the board members, Justin pushed back his chair and stood up next to the table. "Our proposal needs no explanation, but I am compelled to say that we feel an obligation to our membership to do whatever can be done to protect them from the burden of large classes and an unreasonable number of instructional assignments in a day. Please consider the proposal carefully." The board's new salary offer precluded any reference to the teachers' rejection of the previous one.

Justin surveyed the expression of anger, frustration, and resentment etched on the faces of the three board members. "Shall we take a break for, say, fifteen minutes to consider our respective proposals?" he suggested.

"I suppose," Harold grumbled.

CHAPTER 35

"That's more like it." Shawn had said virtually nothing all evening. Now he was the first to speak. "From what I can figure, this schedule comes awfully close to what we set as our goal early this spring. I think we should accept it."

The other committee members slowly seated themselves. No one responded to Shawn's comment. Waiting for some direction, all looked toward Justin.

Justin said nothing for several moments. He stood in the center of the room. Members of the committee moved nervously around the room, undecided about sitting down or standing up. Justin rubbed his temples, catching a glimpse of the cracked window he had studied earlier in the evening.

"The offer is more than I expected the board to come up with." Justin looked to each of his committee members. "Well, what do you others think?"

Norma was quick to respond. "We do have a proposal that the board must consider. What we do with this salary offer depends on what the board does with our proposal"

Shawn stood up and moved to the side of the room. He obviously was agitated. "Money is what is important right now. I think I speak for a significant number of teachers in this district. There's no guarantee that classes will become as large as we fear anyway. Let's just take the money and see what happens." Shawn stood firm with his arms folded across his chest.

"I don't know which teachers you have been talking to," Bob Medford, uncharacteristically challenged Shawn. "Most of us are concerned for our jobs. Money is scarce, and how does a district save money easiest? It cuts its most expensive commodity, teachers. With fewer teachers, large classes."

"That's your opinion," snapped Shawn.

"We have to consider what the membership will accept," advised Rita.

"I don't recall the membership ever rejecting the recommendations of the negotiating committee," Norma reminded the group.

Justin listened attentively to each of the comments, convinced in his own mind that the only alternative was rejection. "You all know my position. We did vote previously to submit the revised proposal to the board."

"Yes, but we didn't expect the new money," interrupted Rita.

"I know," continued Justin, leaning back on the desk in the front of the room. "I still don't believe we should let money blind us to more important matters. Unless the board accepts our proposal, I recommend we reject their latest salary offer."

"Does that mean strike?" asked Ruth.

"Damn right it does!" shouted Shawn.

With disgust, Norma looked up at Shawn, who stood defiantly facing the other members of the committee. "Not necessarily. The state has set up a whole series of steps beginning with mediation before an actual strike. So, let's not panic."

Justin failed to conceal a furtive grin, recognizing that Shawn's position and attitude had not changed. His apologies obviously meant little. His commitment to money remained.

Justin assumed that both Norma and Bob were on his side and would reject the salary offer if the teachers' proposal were rejected. The position of the two elementary teachers, Rita and Ruth, was difficult to determine. In Justin's opinion, their limits of concern did not extend much beyond the walls of their classrooms.

"Does anyone have any other comments?" Justin asked, looking carefully at each member of his committee.

"We need to vote again, I think," Bob suggested.

"I agree," said Ruth.

"As I see it, if the board does not accept our proposal on class size and teacher assignment, we reject the latest salary offer," Norma explained.

"Do you wish to put that into the form of a motion?" Justin asked.

"So moved," Norma answered.

"Second," Bob announced.

"Any discussion?" Justin asked.

"I think we are making a mistake if we accept the motion," Shawn declared as he paced before the windows of the room.

"Any other comments?" Justin asked with visible irritation.

Rita fidgeted nervously in her desk.

Justin observed her uneasiness. "Rita, you have something to say?"

Rita's face turned red. She cast a quick look at Justin then turned her eyes to the top of the desk where she sat. "I understand and support our position on class size. I'm bothered by this teacher assignment proposal."

Justin moved away from the desk where he stood through most of the discussion. "What do you mean 'bothered'?

Unsure of herself, Rita continued. "The board intends to assign secondary teachers six classes out of seven periods. At approximately fifty minutes a period that's three hundred minutes a day. I don't know, but that's what we in the elementary have been assigned for years."

Justin turned away from Rita and walked toward the door. He whirled around to again glare at Rita. "Look, I don't intend to waste time discussing who works harder, elementary or secondary teachers. Use your head. Adding one more instructional assignment increases each teacher's load by one-sixth. That's one more preparation; that's one more batch of papers; that's one more discussion. If you don't understand what that means to the quality of instruction or to the total burden of a secondary teacher's day, I'm sorry. Besides, it's too damned obvious to have to devote any more time to." Justin's face burned red; his breathing labored.

Rita sat rigid in indignation. She made no response.

Justin pushed his hands firmly into the pockets of his trousers. "This sixth hour thing, to me, is the most insensitive action this board has ever considered. For those of you who fail to see its implications, I suggest you defer to those of us who will suffer because of it." Justin's shoulders slumped as his arms hung limp at his sides. "Now, are there any more comments?"

All sat silently.

"Do you wish to vote by show of hands or secret ballot?" Justin asked.

"Show of hands is good enough," Norma offered.

"Any objections?" Justin looked at each committee member. "Okay, all those in favor of rejecting the salary offer unless the board accepts our proposal, raise your hand."

Ruth, Bob, Norma, and Justin raised their hands.

"All those opposed?"

Shawn and Rita raised theirs.

"Motion carried," Justin announced firmly.

"You people are nuts!" Shawn exploded. "I hope the hell you have fun carrying those picket signs, out there making asses of yourselves."

Justin turned to face Shawn. "God damn it. You've done nothing but oppose every sensible thing this committee has tried to do. If you don't like what decisions have been made, leave."

Shawn stood glaring at Justin, the rage in his eyes in sharp contrast to the contrition of the morning at the cabin. They faced one another for an instant. They both turned away. Hostility filled the room; silence prevailed.

"Let's get back," Norma urged.

As the teachers returned to the lounge, a heavy gloom pervaded the room. The teachers took their places at the table as before. The two committees sat across from each other saying nothing.

Finally, board chairman Baylor spoke. "We have examined your proposal and find it unacceptable. I have previously given you reasons why a board cannot give up its right to determine class size and to make teacher assignments."

"Our proposal does not deny you that right, Mr. Chairman," Justin said with composure. "It only asks that our curriculum committees have the chance to review class sizes and teacher assignments to make recommendations.

Harold moved restlessly in his chair. "I know what the proposal says. I said we read it. It is still an infringement on our administrative rights. We will have no part of it."

"Exactly, what are you afraid of?" No longer did Justin feel the need for diplomacy.

"We are afraid of nothing!" barked Harold, the bags under his eyes protruding even more than usual. "You teachers are not about to run this school. You are paid to teach. That's all you will do."

"Aren't you even a little concerned about the quality of that teaching?" Justin deliberately pursued the topic, adding fuel to Harold's growing anger.

"I don't want to talk about it any more." Harold breathed heavily, pounding his fist on the table.

Justin suddenly glimpsed some victory in defeat. Harold had almost lost control. "In that case, Mr. Chairman, I wish to announce that your most generous salary offer," Justin's voice, caustic and deliberate, filled the room, "has been rejected by my committee. You will not buy us off with a few extra dollars. I see no further reason to sit here tonight." Justin paused briefly moving his eyes over the board members across the table. "Unless you have additional proposals or suggestions, I suggest we adjourn."

The board members sat motionless, unable to believe that the teachers would refuse their generous salary offer.

"I don't see any reason for further meetings, Mr. Starling," Harold regained some control of himself. 'You had better contact the Bureau of Mediation because there is nothing else we can do here."

"We intend to," Justin said as he pushed his chair back and stood up.

Connie said nothing during the meeting and said nothing at its conclusion. She also stood up, collected her materials and with contempt for all, walked briskly out of the room.

CHAPTER 36

"Remember, do not write on the test itself. Answer the multiple choice questions on the answer sheet. Use the essay paper for the essay questions. You have your choice of essay questions. Pick only two. Pace yourself. You have an hour and a half to complete the test. Any questions?" Justin looked out over the more than one hundred faces that represented his four composition classes, all gathered in the school's multi purpose, lecture hall. "If there are no questions, you may begin and good luck."

Justin moved casually around the room, providing that halo of supervision the building administration insisted was essential to a good testing environment. Justin wasn't much concerned about cheating. Except for fifteen multiple choice questions, the test was an essay type. To cheat on an essay test was next to possible. Justin, still, made his presence known.

The aimless pacing around the room permitted Justin's mind to wander. For him, the end of the school year always came with some misgivings. A finality which he regretted accompanied the ending of the school year. It meant losing touch with the students he had spent so much time with the past few months.

Most of these students he found receptive to instruction and respectful of their teachers. Of course, the year included moments when some students created frustration and anxiety, but that was part of teaching. Justin simply liked the challenge young people presented him. Though he would miss their association, Justin still looked forward to the two and one half months which lay ahead.

In just over an hour some students were beginning to complete the test. Not until the end of the entire testing period would students be permitted to leave. Students leaving at various times would create a distraction for those still taking the test. Consequently, when they did finish, they turned their tests over on their desks, many placing their heads down and closing their eyes for a quick rest.

It was this position several students had assumed when a series of sharp explosions, from right outside the rear door of the lecture hall, shattered the silence of the lecture hall. Students jumped at this sudden intrusion. Justin, too, was shocked by the sharpness and volume of the blasts. He quickly ran to the door only to discover a blue haze and a strong odor of sulfur outside the lecture hall. Otherwise the hallway stood empty. A grouping of small burns etched the tiled floor with scraps of paper scattered a few feet away. Firecrackers, Justin concluded. He couldn't remember a year when something like this hadn't happened during the closing days of school.

Justin returned to the lecture hall where the students attempted to find out who had been responsible. Justin assured them he had no idea and reminded them they had only twenty minutes left to complete their test. With that, those who had not finished resumed their work. Those who had waited impatiently for their release.

At eleven thirty Justin announced that everyone would have to stop and hand in their tests and answer sheets. With all test materials collected, Justin dismissed the students. They made a rapid and noisy exit.

CHAPTER 37

Justin groaned as he looked at the enormous stack of tests he would have to correct in only two and one half days. Gathering the tests and answer sheets, he walked out the rear door of the lecture hall, again observing the burn stains on the floor where the firecrackers exploded.

He also noticed that discarded paper, notebooks, books, and whatever else the students had allowed to accumulate in their lockers over the past nine months littered the hallway next to the lecture hall. This, too, was an end of year tradition which Justin believed was getting worse each year. Jubilation, yes, at the conclusion of another school year, but this was irresponsible and indefensible.

Trying to ignore the confusion in the hallway, Justin slowly made his way to his room on the second floor. The second floor hallway was not in much better condition than the first floor. He reached his room and secured the tests and answer sheets in the filing cabinet next to his desk. Justin felt a strong urge to get started on the tests, but he also needed a cup of coffee and a few minutes relaxation before plunging into the task.

The teachers' lounge hummed with conversation and laughter, what a contrast from the recent, futile meeting with the school board's negotiating team. Teachers also looked with anticipation to the end of another school year despite the hours of work which most of them faced before grades were finally turned in at the end of the week. Justin greeted several of his colleagues and sat down next to Norma.

"Your final all done?" she asked.

"The easy part is. Haven't started the correcting yet."

"Do you know who's suspected of setting off the firecrackers last period?" Norma asked after a brief pause.

"No, but it scared the hell out of me."

"Your friend, Randy Wilcox."

Justin expressed little surprise at hearing Randy's name connected with the firecrackers. "What the hell is he doing around here?"

"I don't know, but I heard some students talking shortly after it happened. Someone had recognized him"

"No doubt they didn't catch him," Justin lamented.

"I don't suppose so. From what I could gather, it all happened so fast that not many saw anything."

"I wonder if he knew my classes were in the room?" Justin asked without really expecting an answer.

A phone call for Norma interrupted their conversation. Justin quickly asked if she would be available for a brief meeting with him later in the day. She agreed to three o' clock that afternoon and hustled off to her phone call. Justin finished his coffee, and after a few moments of idle conversation, much of it related to his recent absence, he returned to his room and the pile of final tests.

CHAPTER 38

At three o'clock Justin sat correcting tests. He had brought his lunch which he ate in his room. So, for almost three and one half hours, he read essay tests. Norma's arrival shortly after three proved a welcomed excuse to give up temporarily on the final tests.

"Almost done?" Norma asked jokingly as she entered Justin's room.

"Sure," Justin responded sarcastically. "Thanks for the excuse to quit anyway."

Norma sat in one of the front desks. In a serious tone she said, "I've been thinking. What have you decided to do about Randy Wilcox?"

"Nothing," Justin replied with a hint of resignation in his voice. "What can I do that would make any difference? He's after me obviously and won't give up easily. Look at the firecrackers this morning. I'm sure they were intended for my benefit."

"It just seems so unfair to permit this maniac to torment people, to beat them up and get away with it."

"I know," Justin agreed, "but what good would going to the police do? Do you think that would stop him from hating me? Probably, it would make matters worse."

"I suppose you're right," Norma conceded. "It has to stop someplace, though."

"God, I hope." My poor body has suffered about all it can take." Justin paused for an instant debating if he should discuss it with Norma. Leaning on his elbows planted on top his desk, he explained, "I didn't tell you about getting whacked over the head up by that cabin."

"You're kidding!" Norma replied in astonishment, eyes wide, mouth open. "What in the world for?"

"God, who knows? It's getting dangerous for me even to go outside anymore."

"I suppose you don't have any idea who did it?"

"No," Justin admitted. "I have really no idea. It was dark, and the area is heavily wooded."

"Was it in the cabin?" Norma asked, still puzzled.

"No, I was out for a walk. So I was quite a distance from the cabin. But something has occurred to me about that incident which may sound stupid."

"What's that?"

Justin leaned back in his chair, fixing his eyes on Norma. "Shawn Kelly's showing up the next morning. Maybe it was only coincidence, but it was almost as if he was checking on me."

"He did sound kind of strange when he called me that morning. Then much of what he has done seems strange."

"Strange or not, I simply can't figure out why he would be out looking for me in that wilderness."

"You're not suggesting he might have been the one to hit you over the head?"

"I don't know. His explanation for being at the cabin just doesn't make sense."

"Why should he want to attack you that way? I just can't imagine his doing that."

"I can't imagine it either." Justin closed his eyes. "His whole attitude, his appearance simply were not consistent with anything that I had previously known about him."

"Well, what did he say or do when he got there?" Norma asked.

135

Moving forward again and resting his elbows on his desk, Justin explained, "That's just it. As I told you before, he didn't say much of anything. He stared at me oddly for a few seconds then went into that phony apology about his behavior on the committee."

"He didn't sound very apologetic at our last meeting," Norma interrupted.

"That's what I mean. It appears to me that the apology was only an excuse for his being there."

"What other reason could he have had?"

"That's what intrigues the shit out of me," Justin confessed.

"Didn't he even come into the cabin?" Norma asked.

"Yes, he came in, ill at ease with very little to say.

"What did he say?" Norma persisted.

"Oh, as I said before some feeble apology for his behavior at meetings."

"I'm really sorry to hear about another assault. It's simply awful. I just can't believe Shawn had anything to do with it," Norma offered.

"You're probably right. Chances are I'll never know. I don't know where the hell I would even begin to find out who was responsible." Justin stretched and slouched in his chair.

A brief silence filled the air between Norma and Justin. Then Justin straightened up. "You know, something else bothers be a lot too."

"Boy, you do, indeed, have a busy mind. What else bothers you?"

Justin stood up slowly and walked to the row of windows making up most of one wall in his room. He turned facing Norma and sat awkwardly on one of the window sills. "Remember you told me that Connie Shetland is Randy Wilcox's aunt."

"Yes, I remember."

"Well, I just can't get that out of my mind. It seems incredible, but do you suppose she is, in any way, responsible for some of Randy's actions?"

"My God!" Norma exclaimed. "Why would she want to do anything like that?"

"It's only speculation," Justin confessed, "but so many unusual things have happened recently that I guess almost anything is possible."

"But a person in a position of responsibility like she is? What could she possibly hope to gain having people beat up?"

"Until she invited me to her little meeting at the Pine Inn, I would have said the same thing. Now I don't know."

"She must have been a real tyrant at that meeting."

"Perhaps not a tyrant but she apparently is accustomed to getting her way. When she doesn't, she can get nasty. She even said something about ways of dealing with people who are unreasonable."

"She did?" Norma pondered Justin's revelation briefly. "It's still hard to believe she would resort to physical violence."

Justin walked back to his desk and sat on the edge. With a shrug he said, "I guess you're right about that too. Whatever the truth, these past few days have been exciting in sort of a painful way."

Sliding off the edge of his desk, Justin seated himself in the desk next to Norma, saying, "Anyway, about this mediation thing."

"Exactly, what do we have to do?" Norma inquired.

"As far as I know, there are a few formal documents we must fill out and submit to the State Bureau of Mediation. After that we just wait until a mediator is assigned our case and the first meeting is set."

"Do we have the necessary forms?"

"No, but I'm getting them from our state office in St. Paul. Should be here any day."

"What then?" Norma asked.

"Our most important job is to prepare our case, justifying our requests and our rejection of the board's last offer."

Looking up at the clock, Justin got out of the desk. "Hey, let's get out of here. We'll have a committee meeting when I hear from the state office about precisely what steps we have to take."

"Just let me know what you want me to do," Norma volunteered as she squeezed out of the desk and walked toward the door.

"Thank you, Norma. Thank you for listening, and thank you for your willingness to help whenever needed."

"You're welcome. Thank you for your leadership." Reaching the door, Norma turned to ask playfully, "Do you think you can make it home without getting into trouble?"

"I'll try," Justin laughed. "See you tomorrow."

After Norma left, Justin gathered a stack of tests to take home. He had completed two sections already. He did not wish to leave too many tests for tomorrow.

As he strolled across the faculty parking lot, he recalled that just over a week ago he did the same thing with very painful results. He made a furtive look around for anything unusual. He saw nothing.

CHAPTER 39

Unlike most people, Mondays for Randy Wilcox differed little from any other day. He had nothing to do and nowhere in particular to go. His most recent job at a local service station ended abruptly two weeks ago following another argument with his boss. Randy did not like to be pushed around, especially by a two bit gas station owner. He expressed his feelings bluntly and was told he would no longer be needed. With the small amount of money coming from the station and the fifty bucks received from Connie, he had gotten by. Now his money was running out.

Randy lay in bed contemplating his status. He despised the thought of the meager jobs he found. The pay was poor, and he detested doing other people's dirty work. Any decent job always seemed to require a high school diploma. What was so magic about a damned piece of paper eluded Randy, but he boiled inside when he recalled that arrogant son of a bitch, Justin Starling, sitting there refusing to give him a passing grade in the chicken shit writing class.

That credit would have given him the damned diploma and a decent job. Because of that God damned Starling, he had neither. Oh, how he relished the thought of that asshole squirming on the parking lot blacktop. He'd almost do it again, for nothing, just to see Starling suffer.

Right now Randy needed money. Money was the answer to his problems. His expenses were increasing all the time.

He already was into Chip Overly for twenty-five bucks, and Chip wanted the money. Chip hadn't always been so persistent about payment, but recently he was edgy and impatient. Only after Randy assured him that he'd have the money on Monday would he agree to give him the stuff he required more urgently each day.

Six months ago Chip wouldn't have hesitated to advance him what he needed. At that time Chip was a good friend, and Randy admired him. Chip always seemed to have the things Randy wanted. He had an impressive car, dressed well, and handled himself with what Randy considered style and confidence.

They met casually several times at various hangouts around Twin Pines. Gradually, Randy got to know Chip and discovered that he was a reliable source for almost any kind of drug Randy desired. He learned that Chip hadn't graduated from high school either. At sixteen he dropped out of Twin Pines High School. After that he traveled to theTwin Cities to find work and just escape the constraints of small town life.

Chip believed the action was in the big city. He went there to become a part of it. He made the right contacts and returned to Twin Pines six years later, bringing with him what Randy interpreted as all the signs of success. What Chip had was what Randy desperately wanted. Sadly, for Randy, things had not turned out that way. All Randy acquired was an urgent need for what Chip could provide for him and practically no money with which to buy it.

Randy dragged himself from his bed and reached for his trousers tossed carelessly across the chair in the corner of his room. From the front pocket he withdrew a small packet of red pills, removed two, placed them in his mouth, and swallowed.

For Randy the effects the drug produced did not take long in arriving. His bitterness and disgust gradually diminished, replaced by confidence and a kind of swaggering arrogance. The world no longer appeared as an enemy but as an ally.

Randy felt he needed only aggressive determination to take advantage of what waited for him out there in the world. Nothing lay beyond his reach if he just didn't permit others to push him around. He could feel the strength of his own importance expand inside himself. He enjoyed what he felt.

Armed with this artificial courage and determination, Randy prepared himself a quick breakfast and decided he would pay his dear Aunt Connie a visit. She might be willing to supply him with the money he needed to maintain the style of life his habit established for him.

CHAPTER 40

At ten thirty in the morning the school looked quiet and almost empty as Randy drove by. Even with the strength that his pills had given him, Randy couldn't suppress the anger and resentment that welled inside him as he gazed at the school where he suffered some of his most agonizing moments. Justin Starling again appeared vividly in his mind as he relived the frustration and anger he felt at having been so close to graduating from high school only to lose to that stubborn bastard.

Randy believed he knew what was going on at the school during these closing days of the year. Not too long ago he was a part of it. He decided that creating a little confusion would add some humor to his day. Ideally, he would prefer to disrupt whatever Starling was doing. However, he wasn't sure if he would have the opportunity to go up to the second floor of the building where he assumed Starling's room was still located. Randy also knew that school officials would very likely stop him and ask him to leave the building if he had no legitimate purpose there. He'd have to take his chances.

As he parked his car about a block from the school entrance, Randy was in almost a playful mood. Secure in his jacket was a package of fifty firecrackers, each about the size of his little finger.

He entered the building quickly and unobtrusively. Not a person was in sight as he walked down the familiar hall passed the school offices. Randy determined that he might as well risk using his firecrackers on Starling even though his room likely was on the second floor. As he rounded the corner of the hall by the lecture room, he noticed three teachers emerge from the teachers' lounge just steps from the lecture room. To his relief they turned and walked the other way, apparently not even seeing him.

Not intimidated by the teachers, Randy still didn't particularly wish for a confrontation right now. So that not all was in vain, he quickly lighted the firecrackers and tossed them near the door to the lecture hall. He turned and ran as fast as he could to the front entrance through which he just arrived. As he passed the school office, the firecrackers went off, producing a violent succession of explosions that echoed throughout most of the building.

Racing for his car, Randy grinned with delight as he envisioned the confusion his little prank caused inside the school. It certainly didn't remove the bitterness that he harbored, but it did make him feel he was doing something to gain revenge on those who made his life so miserable and who deprived him of the damned diploma.

Back in his car Randy felt good about himself. Connie surely would listen to his plan which would give him a dependable source of money. The world, from Randy's perspective, looked far more attractive than it had earlier that morning.

CHAPTER 41

When Randy arrived at the Shetland house, there was no visible activity. Obviously, Vince would be at the bank, and since it was after eleven o'clock in the morning, even Connie should be up. It didn't make any difference as far as Randy was concerned. If she wasn't up, he would get her up.

Still energized by his earlier mood altering snack, Randy knocked loudly at the front door and waited. Nothing. He knocked again, this time even louder. From inside he heard a faint sound of movement. Shortly, the front door opened just enough so Randy could see that Connie still wore her robe.

"Good morning. Did I interrupt anything?" Randy greeted his aunt with an ingratiating smile.

"What are you doing here? I've told your not to come around here unless I asked you to. Now, what do you want?" Connie stood holding the door open only far enough for her to peer out.

"I just want to talk for a few minutes." Randy placed his hand upon the door frame and peeked through the narrow opening.

"We have nothing to talk about," Connie shot back angrily.

"Oh, I think we do," Randy replied confidently.

"What could that be?"

"Money," Randy shouted back.

"Money? Why should we talk about money?"

Randy leaned in closer to the slightly opened door. "Don't you think we could discuss this easier inside the house?"

"I don't want you inside my house!" Connie exploded. "Now get the hell out of here. We have nothing more to talk about."

Randy's confidence was fading, replaced by the old bitterness and hostility he felt toward others who attempted to push him around. He considered his aunt a snob and a bitch. He refused to accept any rejection from her.

Connie began to close the door in Randy's face when he lunged forward, smashing into the door and sending Connie sprawling on her back across the flagstones that made up the entryway floor. Randy slammed the door behind him and menacingly approached his aunt as she lay on her back on the floor.

Standing over her, Randy spoke in very measured tones. "Don't you ever shut the door in my face, you bitch! Who the hell do you think you are?"

At first frightened by the menacing look on Randy's face, Connie managed to regain some composure. Getting to her feet, she adjusted here robe and faced her nephew. "Now, exactly what do you want?" She asked as commandingly as she could.

Randy took two steps toward Connie and stood directly in front of her. "I want money," was his simple reply.

Intensity shown in Connie's eyes. "What makes you think I should give you money?"

"Simply because I'm your favorite nephew." Randy's tone was heavy with sarcasm. "Maybe you want me to let the town know that one of its leaders paid money to have the shit kicked out of that prick Starling."

Connie flushed with anger. Hatred danced in her eyes as she stared at Randy for several seconds. Then in a voice strained by outrage, she declared, "I told you that I would deny every word if you ever attempted to connect me in anyway with what happened to Starling. Whose word would people believe?

Certainly not that of someone who didn't even graduate from high school."

Randy exploded in anger and contempt. Not even the euphoric effects of the pills could restrain him. "You don't think some of those God damned, important friends of yours aren't going to ask questions if they hear rumors about paying for beatings?" Randy shouted in Connie's face.

"Don't you yell at me you good for nothing hoodlum!" Connie screamed, slapping Randy across the face.

Briefly stunned by the suddenness of Connie's action, Randy froze, glaring with intensity at his aunt. He then raised his hand and slapped her back, hard enough so that red marks appeared instantly on her cheek.

Connie yelled, "How dare you!" and threw herself at Randy, clawing and swinging and clutching for anything she could get a hold of.

Suddenly the front door burst open. Vince stood shocked by what he saw in the entryway of his home. He said nothing. He rushed to try to calm down Connie. He attempted to pull her away from Randy, who now simply tried to defend himself. Connie writhed in absolute fury as Vince fought to restrain her. She would respond to nothing he said. He finally got his arms around her shoulders, gradually pinning her arms to her sides.

Randy stood, lost in astonishment over the violence of his aunt's reaction. He quickly turned toward the open front door and ran to his car parked in the street. The screech of tires announced his departure.

Vince continued to hold Connie securely, waiting for her to calm down sufficiently to listen to reason. Slowly, Vince could feel a release of some of the tension that gripped Connie's body as she began to relax.

"You all right now?" Vince asked.

"Yes, I think so," Connie answered, breathing heavily.

Vince led Connie gently into the family room where they both sat down on the sofa.

"What in the hell was that all about?" Vince began.

Connie failed to answer as she sat staring down at the floor.

"Connie, what's going on? What did Randy want?" Vince asked. Still Connie said nothing.

"Look, Connie," Vince persisted, "something's going on. I want to know what it is. Now either you tell me, or I'll find out from Randy."

Connie slowly raised her head and looked at her husband. The marks remained where Randy had struck her. Finally she said, "It's really none of your business. It's a matter between Randy and me. I'd rather not discuss it."

"When I come home to a man attacking my wife physically, it becomes my business. Now tell me what he was doing here."

Connie's body stiffened hearing the authority in Vince's voice. He had not displayed that much command in months. She did not want Vince talking to Randy. Connie hastily considered the consequences of Vince knowing her involvement with Randy and with Justin Starling. She decided Vince would never understand her attitude toward Starling and her motive for what she paid Randy to do.

"He was here to try to get money from me." Connie responded calmly.

"Money? Money for what?"

"He has some distorted idea that we owe him something. We should help support him."

"Has he brought this up before?" Vince asked incredulously.

"Never before so violently but he has suggested it."

Vince looked at his hands folded in his lap. Then he looked up at his wife seated next to him. "How old is he now?" he asked.

'Almost nineteen, I guess."

"Why doesn't he get a job?"

Connie shrugged her shoulders in resignation. "He has had various jobs. He just can't keep one."

Vince trained his eyes on his wife. "Have you given him money before?"

"Oh, a few dollars here and there. Nothing significant."

Vince stretched out his legs and slouched in the corner of the sofa. "I suppose we have not really done our share with that boy," he admitted, "but he really has not been the type one wants to be very generous to."

Unwilling to pursue the topic any farther, Connie rose and walked toward the kitchen. "Let's not worry about it. What's done is done."

"What if he comes back and tries the same thing again?" Vince was not willing to drop the subject.

"He won't," Connie insisted as she poured herself a cup of coffee. "I don't think even Randy wants to face that scene again. But don't worry about it. I can handle him." Connie assumed she had satisfied Vince's desire to know the truth. She took another swallow of coffee. "By the way, what are you doing home at this time of day?"

Though not satisfied with what Connie had told him, Vince accepted her obvious refusal to continue the conversation. 'I thought I would come home for a light lunch rather than eating out. Good thing I did."

Connie sipped on her coffee, saying nothing.

CHAPTER 42

Vince completed his sandwich and returned to the bank. Connie ate a small combination breakfast-lunch then went upstairs to prepare herself for the day's activities. As she dressed, she considered Randy and what to do with him. He was becoming a nuisance. She didn't really fear what Randy might say about her and Justin Starling. Nonetheless, Randy was correct when he said that questions would be asked and suspicions would be aroused.

Nobody, Randy, Justin Starling, Vince, nobody was going to interfere with what she wanted for herself. For Connie, the beginning of a new phase in her life stood just around the corner, nearly within her grasp. She would not be denied the opportunity that this new phase offered her. Problems sprinkled the path on the way to the realization of her plans. These problems were not insurmountable.

She would have to maintain her relationship with Vince. She considered essential his continuing to provide her the means to achieve her ambitions. To alienate him would create a burdensome handicap. She also had to somehow persuade Justin Starling to compromise on his unrealistic demands at the bargaining table. Without success on the school board, Connie could not expect to attract the support and attention she needed to expand beyond the political limitations of school affairs.

Presently, Justin Starling was the most important reason Connie was not enjoying the success she strived for. If he would not deal rationally, Connie would not hesitate to employ any other means to accomplish what she set out to do. As far as Starling was concerned, she already demonstrated this commitment to gaining what she wanted. Still, other alternative measures lie within her grasp. If he didn't show more willingness to compromise, Connie again would feel no compunction about using other means of persuasion. This is where Randy might be useful.

Connie couldn't ignore the irony of her really needing Randy. She would have to prevent a recurrence of this morning's confrontation. She would have to pacify Randy somehow—money would likely do that—ensuring his availability when she needed him. When she would need him, she felt, would be very soon.

Connie looked at herself in her vanity mirror. The marks left by Randy's hand were scarcely visible now. As she studied her reflection in the mirror, she sincerely believed that she was looking at a woman whose name would soon become synonymous with power and respect.

CHAPTER 43

Shawn relaxed as he tipped back the can to let the cold beer flow down his throat. A beer hadn't tasted so good in months. Shawn sat down in the living room of his apartment and laughed out loud to himself. "School's out!" he uttered and raised his can of beer in a salute.

School wasn't exactly out. One more day remained, but the students would not return until September. They were done. To Shawn, a school building without students was unrivaled as a place of quiet and peacefulness. Though tomorrow he would return to school, students would not. That was the most exciting thought he had in days.

Since the article relating to drug usage in Twin Pines appeared in the local paper, Shawn was edgy and apprehensive. The one thing that frightened him most about his activities in the drug world was getting caught. Never a Puritan, he, nonetheless, always prided himself on possessing sufficient intelligence to avoid conflicts of any kind with the law. He certainly flirted with such conflicts but never faced one.

Now, he began to feel constant pressure to maintain his vigilance. First the article, then Justin Starling and the small cabin, then the frustrations of the negotiating committee all combined to make Shawn nervous and depressed, feelings he was not accustomed to nor ones he liked. Yes, he was aware of the risks when he started the drug connection three years ago.

The money was a greater lure than the risk was a threat. At least, that's what Shawn believed then.

He had never looked forward to the summer vacation more than this year. After tomorrow it would be a reality. Shawn took another long drink of his beer, lay back and closed his eyes. The last two weeks proved among the most unsettling he ever experienced. He valued this opportunity to relax and try to forget about those two weeks.

The sound of the phone shattered the silence. Shawn glanced at his watch. Typically, he received no calls at four o'clock in the afternoon.

"Shawn speaking."

The voice on the line sounded unfamiliar. Shawn listened as the caller greeted him and pointlessly inquired about school. Shawn answered mechanically, desperately searching his memory for the identification of the voice. Finally, he asked, "Who is this?"

"Fred Wyman," was the terse reply.

Shawn nearly choked at hearing that name. Flustered, Shawn mumbled, "I'm sorry. I just didn't recognize your voice. It's been a long time," Shawn stumbled on in a futile attempt to explain his failure to recognize his boss's voice.

"Forget it. It doesn't matter," Fred impatiently assured Shawn.

Three years is a long time in the drug business. Shawn had not spoken with Fred Wyman for at least that long. Shawn had seen Fred but once in those three years, when he met him to discuss an involvement in the drug market.

What Fred's current position in the organization was Shawn did not know. He did know that Fred most definitely held a position of importance. He also knew that this call was not a social call.

Shawn's hand on the receiver became hot and moist. Perspiration formed on his forehead and on his upper lip. His entire body tensed as if prepared to defend itself against attack.

"What does matter," Fred continued, "is that I see you as soon as possible. I'll be through Twin Pines tomorrow afternoon. Meet me at seven thirty at the same place that we met before. What's that place called?"

"The Oak Cafe and Lounge," Shawn blurted out much too eager to please.

"Whatever it is, be there at seven thirty tomorrow night," Fred commanded.

"Is there any thing wrong?" Shawn pleaded.

"That's what I want you to tell me. Be there tomorrow at seven thirty."

The phone clicked in Shawn's ear. He heard only the dial tone. Slowly and thoughtfully, he replaced the receiver. Trancelike, he walked to the fridge for another beer. Upon opening the door, he changed his mind and closed it again.

Fear, a powerful emotion, rarely posed a threat to Shawn. Right now, though, fear held him in its grasp. He tried to control himself. He considered what could happen. At worst, he assumed, he would be reprimanded. He contemplated exactly what he had done wrong? He expressed some reluctance to his phone contact because of the newspaper article. Was that wrong? Could anyone have found out about his run in with Justin Starling? Justin knew nothing. Shawn was convinced of that. What possible reason would Fred Wyman have for wanting so urgently to meet with him?

To his own satisfaction anyway, finding nothing that he had done wrong helped Shawn recover his composure. His fear slowly turned to anger. He slammed his fist on the kitchen counter, exclaiming, "Why did I get sucked in!" A mood of frustration and regret replaced his joyous mood of a few minutes ago when he thought about no more students. He cursed himself for getting trapped in a world over which he had little control. But trapped he was. Anxiety would fill the time until his seven thirty meeting tomorrow night.

CHAPTER 44

Shawn sat alone in a dimly lighted corner of the Oaks Cafe. Not an elegant restaurant but definitely a respectable one, the Oaks was frequented by those who didn't choose to drive out of town to the Pine Inn. Shawn checked his watch, seven twenty-five. He sipped his drink, his second since arriving at the Oaks shortly after seven o'clock.

Uncomfortably, Shawn waited for the arrival of Fred Wyman. He tried to picture Fred in his mind. The image only blurred. Nearly three years and countless late night journeys to Beaver Creek erased from Shawn's memory any vivid recollection of Fred Wyman. Shawn looked at his watch again. When he looked up, Fred Wyman stood by his table, accompanied buy the hostess.

Fred's appearance instantly refreshed Shawn's memory. A refinement, an immaculate appearance, and an air of superiority emanated from Fred. Shawn jumped to his feet, nervously extending his hand.

"Good evening, Fred, nice to see you again," Shawn said without conviction.

Fred shook his hand mechanically and took his place across the table from Shawn. A chill pervaded the atmosphere of the small table while both men busied themselves with their napkins and chairs. How different, Shawn thought, from their first meeting when Fred proposed that Shawn become a part of his organization.

"Have a good trip?" Shawn asked.

"Long and tedious but otherwise uneventful," Fred answered absently.

Another long silence ensued while the two men waited for the waitress to take their orders. Each ordered a drink, for Shawn his third.

"Shawn, I'll get right to the point," Fred began after receiving his drink. "I've had word that you have some problems here. What's the trouble?"

The drinks helped reduce some of the tension that traveled through Shawn's body. He started to regain some confidence. "An article in the local paper about the degree of drug abuse in our schools has put people on guard. Beyond that I'm not aware of any trouble."

"Have you maintained your pickups and drops?"

"Yes, I have," Shawn asserted, sure that Fred already knew the answer and relieved he had not refused the transaction shortly following the appearance of the article.

"That's good. Have you had any problems with the drop and pick up sites?" Fred drank from his glass, allowing the liquid to flow gradually down his throat.

Shawn's mind filled with a rush of questions: What did Fred mean by that? What did he know about Justin Starling and the cabin? Should he reveal the problem he encountered at the drop site? Shawn struggled with indecision. The opportunity to level with Fred was now. Later, telling the truth would be more difficult. Shawn remained convinced, however, that Justin did not suspect him. He was certain that Justin had no idea who hit him that night by the creek. Pressure stiffened Shawn's neck and shoulders.

"No!" He then blurted out, at bit too emphatically.

"That's good," Fred replied quietly, examining the drink before him. "You know this business is like a highly refined machine. Every part must do its job carefully and reliably or the machine cease to function at all. For this job, each part is well rewarded. Would you agree?"

Shawn only nodded his head in agreement.

"When one part of the machine functions reluctantly or poorly, that part jeopardizes the entire operation. Do you understand what I'm saying?"

Shawn again nodded his head but said nothing.

"If one part of the machine continues to interfere with the operation of the whole machine, that part must be disposed of and a new part put in its place. Do you still understand what I'm saying?"

"The operation here has run smoothly, hasn't it?" Shawn asked meekly.

"You should know that better than me."

"As far as I know it has." Shawn could feel his face turn red while perspiration dampened his under arms. Lying had never been so disturbing to him.

"I'll take your word for that for now." Fred took a swallow of his drink then placed his glass on the table. "I have heard rumblings of dissatisfaction and lack of cooperation which simply are not good for the organization. I'm here to discover the truth and to remind you of your commitment and responsibility."

"I don't have to be reminded of that. A deal is a deal," Shawn responded unequivocally.

"Wonderful, that's what I want to hear." Fred smiled for the first time since he sat down. "Now tell me, how has your year been going?"

CHAPTER 45

While Shawn and Fred talked more casually over their prime rib dinner, a specialty of the Oaks Cafe, they did not go unobserved. At the bar next to the dining room sat two young men who suddenly took an interest in Shawn and Fred, barely visible in the far corner of the dining room.

Chip Overly wanted to talk to Randy Wilcox. Following the violent confrontation with Connie, Randy returned to his grandparents' house and spent most of the day in his room. He tried to sort things out. No matter how hard he searched, the solution was always money. He needed money.

Chip called late in the afternoon to remind Randy of the twenty-five dollars. Randy assured him he'd get it. Chip insisted on immediate payment and demanded that Randy meet him a the Oaks at seven o'clock that evening.

Desperate, Randy scrounged through his drawers and his clothes, coming up with fifteen dollars. The remaining ten dollars he conned from his grandmother on the pretext that he needed gas for the car if he was to look for another job.

With the twenty-five dollars Randy arrived at the Oaks to find Chip waiting for him at the bar. The payment made, Chip assumed a much friendlier attitude toward Randy. After all, Randy was a good customer. Chip didn't want to alienate him completely.

"I don't mean to be unreasonable," Chip confessed, "but I run on a tight budget. My bills have to be paid too."

"Okay, you don't have to apologize to me," Randy grumbled.

"Another beer?" Chip offered.

"Sure."

As the bartender brought them the two beers, Chip turned to Randy and asked, "Found another job yet?"

"Hell no," Randy answered angrily.

"How many jobs have you had in the past few months?"

"I don't know. Two, three, I guess."

"What happened?" Chip pursued the subject.

"Not much," Randy grunted. "Can't get along with the boss. Who knows?" Randy took another long swallow of beer, avoiding eye contact with Chip.

Chip watched as Randy sat immersed in his own little world. "Do you think you could get along with me?"

Randy, caught off guard by the question, jerked his head around to stare at Chip. "What the hell is that supposed to mean?"

"Well," Chip placed his hand on Randy's shoulder in a gesture of companionship, "I can always use a good man in my business. I need someone who can take orders, do his job, and keep his mouth shut. Can you do those things?"

For a moment, groping for the right response, Randy said nothing. He tried to comprehend the full implication of Chip's question. After a brief silence Randy said, "Sure I can as long as I don't have to kiss someone's ass and do all his dirty work."

"Good. You do need to remember that sometimes doing the job or kissing someone's ass may only be in the way you look at the situation. To me, I have a job to do. I do what I'm told. That is definitely not kissing ass. That's doing the job."

Chip explained the advantages that Randy had for a job working for him: his age, his contacts with young people in the community, and his knowledge of the people who live in Twin Pines. Because of this, Randy would make an excellent street man and conceivably could make good money pushing the full line of drugs that Chip had access to. Randy, of course, was impressed with what he heard and already had visions of what the money would mean for him.

Chip paused in his explanation, gazing more intently at the table, dimly visible in the far corner of the dining room. "Say, Randy, do you know those two men sitting at the table in the corner over there?"

"Where?" Randy asked.

"There." With a nod of this head Chip indicated the direction in which he looked.

Randy studied the two briefly. "I'm not sure, but the one on the left looks like one of those shit head teachers. Can't remember his name, but I've seen him around. Why?"

"I think I know the other one," Chip continued. "Met him in the Cities a couple years ago."

"What's he do?" Randy asked.

"He's some wheel in real estate or something in the Cities. But I think he makes his real money doing other things."

"Like what?"

"My business contacts don't often get together. Last year I attended a party in Minneapolis. Some of the guys I work with were there. That man was at that party. The way everyone treated him he must be some big shot."

"What the hell does he have to do with some teacher?" Randy asked with obvious scorn.

"I don't know. It would be interesting to find out, wouldn't it?"

"I get what you're saying," Randy grinned. "To nail one of those smart ass teachers would make my day."

Chip turned to address Randy seriously. "One thing about this business, Randy, is caution. You won't last long by being stupid. At the same time, it doesn't hurt to know what's going on either."

They both sat silently, looking at the two men busily engaged in conversation.

"Well, I've got to run," Chip announced. "I'll get in touch with you soon. By the way, thanks for the twenty-five bucks."

"Sure. Thank you, too," Randy echoed.

In his car Randy's mind whirled with activity. His life suddenly turned for the better. The chance to get some of the things he wanted and needed finally arrived. He could live like Chip Overly lived.

Of course, there still was Connie Shetland. She would pay nicely for information about teachers. As long as there was money involved, that's all that mattered.

By the time he reached his grandparents' house, he already planned his next visit with Connie Shetland.

CHAPTER 46

The final three days of school passed without incident for Justin. Much too occupied with final tests, grades and year end details, he thought little about negotiations, mediation, Shawn Kelly, Connie Shetland, all of which had made significant intrusions into his life.

Even graduation on Friday night was free of much of the undignified behavior which characterized graduation ceremonies the past two years. The graduates were jubilant, of course, but no showers of Ping-Pong balls or marshmallows rained down on the dignitaries who spoke at the ceremony. The audience, with its frequent cheers and occasional cat calls, was more unruly than the graduates.

As Justin dried himself following his late Sunday afternoon shower, only a slight hint of the physical pain he suffered persisted around his nose. The discoloration around his eyes had nearly disappeared. For the first time in days, he felt rested, relaxed, and sure that he could deal with what the next few weeks would bring.

Though he did not find pleasure in attending graduation open house parties, he accepted them as an obligation. Besides, he like Ted Anders. Despite his feeling out of place in a strange environment meeting people he would perhaps never see again and talking aimlessly about nothing in particular, Justin always experienced some small satisfaction at having done his duty.

Nonetheless, Justin harbored misgivings about the Ted Anders' party. The Anders family enjoyed a great deal of wealth, though Justin had never met Ted's parents. As a junior, Ted developed a sincere attachment to Justin. An outstanding athlete and an above average student, Ted took his studies seriously. Composition II caused severe problems for Ted. Throughout the semester that Ted sat in Justin's Composition II class, Ted devoted considerable time discussing his writing weaknesses with Justin. During these discussions Justin discovered in Ted an earnest desire to improve in what he could not do very well—write. Rather than a passive acceptance of his inadequacy in writing, Ted aspired to overcome it.

At semester's end Ted had improved. Both Justin and Ted shared a feeling of accomplishment. This feeling endured through Ted's senior year. Even though Justin no longer had him in class, Ted commonly stopped to talk with Justin about the football season or about last night's basketball game or simply about nothing in particular. Ted also sought Justin's advice and assistance for his term papers in advanced composition. So for the past two years, Justin and Ted maintained close contact. For Ted to invite him to his graduation open house was only natural.

Ted and his family lived a few miles north of Twin Pines. Exactly where Justin did not know. Following Ted's directions took Justin north on Fox Avenue. As he drove, Justin was suddenly aware of the unfamiliarity of that part of town. He reflected on his ten years in Twin Pines, and how that should have been ample time for anyone to become completely acquainted with every aspect of a town its size, at last count about ten thousand people. Still he drove on streets he failed to recognize.

"Fox Avenue junctions with County Road 26. Turn right on number 26," Ted instructed. Justin started looking for the County Road 26 junction. He passed the city limits of Twin Pines and faced a flat expanse of recently planted fields, presumably sugar beet fields. Ted's father specialized in sugar beets. Sugar beets made Ted's father a wealthy man and at one time mayor of Twin Pines.

Turning right onto County Road 26 gave Justin a clear view of acres of carefully cultivated fields stretching on both sides of the road far off into the distance. Ted said about two miles on County Road 26, on the right side of the road. Within minutes, a large grove of pine trees came into view. Justin assumed it concealed the Anders' home. It did.

CHAPTER 47

If the Anders' home represented any measure of the family's financial status, they were indeed wealthy. The house, of contemporary design, spread over a portion of several acres of meticulously manicured lawns, shrubs, and trees, mostly large, graceful Norway pines. A long curving driveway brought Justin passed a four car garage and next to a long entry covered by a network of redwood and cedar.

A young, male attendant approached Justin's car, offering to park it for him. Justin thanked the young man who directed him to follow the sidewalk to the main entrance located at the end.

A dignified, slender woman in her mid fifties greeted Justin at the door.

Nervously, Justin said, "Good evening. I'm Justin Starling."

"Why, Mr. Starling, I'm delighted to meet you. I'm Ted's mother. I've heard so much about you. I regret not having the opportunity to meet you before."

"Thank you for inviting me," Justin replied.

"Ted has so much appreciated all you have done for him," Mrs. Anders spoke with refinement and confidence. "I want you to know that his father and I appreciate it too."

Justin could think of nothing else to say except "thank you" again.

"Please come in and make yourself comfortable," Mrs. Anders urged.

Justin stepped into a vast foyer that enclosed a large open stairway leading to the upper level of the house. Ahead, he observed a native stone fireplace surrounded in front by several plush chairs and small sofas in a conversational setting. To the left Justin glimpsed the kitchen dining area. To the right glimmered a large indoor pool. Patio furniture graced three sides of the pool with a dark oak paneled bar on the fourth. In front of the bar several large oak and leather stools served as resting places for a number of Ted's guests.

As Justin admired what he saw before him, Mrs. Anders, with obvious pride, stated, "Mr. Anders has provided well for his family. He enjoys the chance to give our children a comfortable home."

"It's beautiful," Justin agreed.

"Thank you. But follow me. The other guests are in the lower party room for now. Come, let's join them."

Descending the short flight of stairs off to one side of the pool, they entered the party room whose outside wall was entirely glass. Like the rest of the house, at least those parts Justin had seen, the party room featured richly decorated contemporary furniture made of polished oak and leather. Toward one end stood another bar, not as large, but equally as refined as the one by the pool. A dance floor of impressively polished inlaid wood graced a semi circular area in front of the bar. A thick, dark beige carpet covered the rest of the floor. Despite the presence of perhaps twenty-five to thirty people, the room appeared relatively empty.

Justin followed Mrs. Anders to the bar where most of the guests gathered. To his mild surprise, he saw several of his students and former students all enjoying plastic cups of beer. Not naive about young people and beer parties, Justin, nonetheless, felt uneasy when he confronted guests he knew only as students. Only rarely had he met any of them in a strictly social setting.

Casually, Justin greeted several of the young guests while Mrs. Anders disappeared briefly, to return leading a tall, well built man in his late fifties or early sixties.

"Mr. Starling, I want you to meet my husband, Arthur."

Extending a large hand, already tanned by the spring sun, Mr. Anders proclaimed in a voice accustomed to dominance, "My pleasure, Mr. Starling."

Justin grasped the large hand with, "I'm happy to meet you."

Mr. Anders studied Justin. "It's nice that you could come this evening. Not often do we have the privilege of entertaining any of Ted's teachers. You were his English teacher, weren't you?"

"Yes," Justin confirmed.

"I want you to know," Mr. Anders continued, "that you teachers do one hell of a job. Not very often do you receive the credit you deserve."

Justin smiled at hearing these comments. When he did, he always questioned the sincerity of the speaker. In his experience, platitudes directed at teachers and the job they do didn't cost anything. Providing funding so teachers could do their job did.

Mr. Anders persisted. "When I was mayor of Twin Pines, I made a special effort to acquaint the community with the outstanding work our schools did." He moved closer to Justin. "You know, Mr. Starling, taxes are a critical issue for the people in this town. Though they want to, people can't always afford the rising cost of public programs like education."

Justin listened out of courtesy. He resented hearing these misguided comments anytime. At social gatherings, they were particularly inappropriate. Everyone and anyone, it seemed, had something to say about the nature and quality of education. Few wished to accept the cost of quality educational programs. Still, the country teemed with experts on education. Apparently, Mr. Anders was yet another.

In a desperate attempt to change the subject, Justin asked, "Are all the fields around here planted in sugar beets?"

Obviously a subject of much interest to Mr. Anders, he embarked on a brief history of the sugar beet in the Twin Pines area. Justin listened politely to the answer to his question, never expecting the near dissertation Mr. Anders delivered.

"Hey, Mr. Starling. Good to see you. Thanks for coming." To the rescue, Ted Anders waved from across the room where he was engaged in conversation with other students. Immediately, he made his way toward Justin and Mr. Anders In the two years he'd known him, Justin was never so happy to see Ted.

"I see you have already met my dad. I hope he hasn't been boring you with his predictions for this year's beet crop," laughed Ted.

"Yes, your father and I have met and yes, our discussion did have something to do with sugar beets," Justin agreed. "By the way, I haven't had the chance to congratulate you on your graduation."

"Thank you, Mr. Starling, and thank you for all the time you spent trying to teach me to write."

"If all students were as eager to learn as you, our job would be a lot simpler."

Ted noticed Justin stood with empty hands. "Hey, Dad, haven't you gotten Mr. Starling a drink yet?" He asked.

"We were just on our way when we got involved in our conversation," Mr. Anders said apologetically.

"You'll have to forgive my dad. He likes to talk. Anyway, what would you like?"

Though drinking with young people so recently his students made Justin uneasy, he replied, "A beer would be fine."

"You wait here. I'll get you one," Ted announced, turning and heading for the bar.

Ted shortly returned with two large, plastic cups of beer. As he handed one to Justin, he quipped, "Here, have one on me."

"Thank you. I will," Justin responded. He took a swallow of the cold, foamy beer then asked Ted, "What are your plans for the fall?"

"Nothing definite." Ted looked down at his plastic cup then back up at Justin. "Probably the university in Minneapolis."

Justin nodded his head in confirmation. "I'm sure you'll like it there. A lot of people but still a good school."

CHAPTER 48

Though Justin was not much of a beer drinker, it was cold and refreshing. His cup emptied quickly. Ted volunteered to get him a refill, giving Justin the first opportunity to move around. He walked toward the bar. His attention ranged over the large room. Several groups of people clustered here and there talking and enjoying the beer.

On one of the three or four small sofas stationed in front of the bar sat George Matson, the physics teachers. From what Justin knew of George, he spurned parties of any type. Seeing him at this one created a mild surprised for Justin. Not one of Justin's favorite colleagues, George did not represent someone with whom Justin wished to become trapped in a conversation.

"Here you are, Mr. Starling," Ted announced as he handed Justin a full cup of beer. "From now on you're on your own," Ted laughed. "Talk to you later." He then drifted away toward a small group of his classmates.

George caught Justin's attention and motioned him over. Reluctantly, Justin acknowledged and moved slowly toward the sofa on which George sat.

Justin assumed that George's first comment would be, "How are negotiations going?" Justin had become accustomed to that question and had developed some good evasive answers. Being too specific about details from the bargaining table could be misleading to those not very familiar with the give and take

169

of the negotiating process. Besides, George should know by now that they were applying for mediation.

As Justin approached, George, with a wide smile, asked, "How are negotiations going?"

"Not very well."

"Oh, really. Why not?"

We are submitting a request for mediation this week," Justin answered.

"You don't say, I thought I heard some talk about that last week." George moved to one end of the sofa. "Here, take a load off your feet. This furniture is first class, not like the faculty lounge, I tell you," George chuckled. George chuckled often but usually by himself.

Justin understood that George was an excellent teacher. However, removing him from the classroom and his physics experiments rendered him a complete bore. He perpetually attempted to dominate any conversation and frequently flavored that conversation with uninteresting and equally unsuccessful bits of humor. Students did respect him, however, Ted Anders showing his by inviting George to his open house.

More serious, George asked, "What does applying for mediation mean?"

"Very simply it means a third party agreed upon by the two sides hears the arguments. He then renders his decision which is not binding on either side."

"What good does that do?"

Justin drank another swallow of beer, searching for an escape from this conversation. Finding none, he answered, "Sometimes very little, but it does introduce a neutral point of view which hopefully will be acceptable to both parties."

"And if it isn't?"

"Then we go to arbitration." Justin assumed the conversation would end there and started to get up.

Before he could, George asked, "What's the big problem between you and the board?"

Justin looked down at the rich carpet, studying the imprint his feet made, getting out of this conversation gracefully his immediate goal. Nonetheless, he did have to answer the question. "Class size, how many classes we teach each day, who gets first priority in filling vacancies, things like that."

Again, Justin started to get up in a desperate hope that George would ask no more questions. Again, George forged ahead with "Don't administrators get paid for making decisions like that?"

Justin's shoulders slumped; he set his cup of beer on the small table next to his seat; his hands squeezed his knees as he sat on the edge of the sofa. "I suppose they do. That doesn't mean we can't have something to say about the decisions they make." Justin tried to conceal his irritation. He hesitated, debating whether to go on. "You know, George, education is more than dollars and cents, desks and rooms. It's people, people working with other people. Creating the best working conditions requires more than merely manipulating numbers or moving people around at the whim of some administrator."

George refused to give up. He slid closer to Justin, adopting a more intimate tone. "Sometimes, I think, we get involved in things we should leave to others. I have taught for twenty-eight years, and I think my students have learned something about physics. During those twenty-eight years I haven't had any serious complaints about class size and stuff like that. Why not just stick to the money in negotiations? Friction between the administration and the teachers or between the board and teachers doesn't do anyone any good."

Justin suppressed the urge to say, "Why you dumb ass. Don't you see what's happening?" He controlled his temper and replied brusquely, "Changes are happening. They are happening rapidly in this town and across the state. Enrollments are declining and people are demanding a reduction in taxes."

Justin paused, breathed deeply, and folded his arms across his chest. "The public is insisting on cost reductions and at the same time expecting schools and teachers to take on greater responsibilities for kids with wider varieties of problems. School districts are responding to these demands by indiscriminately cutting programs, cutting staff, increasing class size and generally ignoring educational quality."

Justin turned to face George directly. "What happened twenty-eight years ago doesn't apply any more. There are new problems facing us now, and though you may not perceive them, they are here. If addressing them creates friction, then so be it."

Justin stopped, slightly embarrassed over his vehemence. Despite his intense feelings about these issues, a graduation open house was not the place to discuss them. Better, somehow, to have evaded George's questions. He smiled, saying, "How about a beer, George. I'll get you one."

George, sensing the end of the discussion, declined. Somewhat offended, he said, "Well, anyway, good luck in your mediation."

"Thanks. Have a good summer."

Relieved, Justin got up this time, reached for his cup of beer, and walked toward the bar. He hoped he could avoid any more controversial discussions. One more beer might help to wash the bad taste from his mouth. Then he would leave.

CHAPTER 49

Justin ambled inconspicuously around the small groups of guests now scattered in several places in the party room. What lay beyond that massive glass wall of the party room intrigued Justin. Before he left, he wanted to investigate.

With a fresh cup of beer, Justin opened the sliding patio door which gave him access to the spacious patio. The sun had set. Already several stars sparkled in the northern sky. An enormous deck, tastefully furnished with redwood chairs and tables, extended beyond the house.

Justin walked to the edge of the deck and viewed the vast lawn that in the near darkness was alive with the sounds of the night. He sat down in a nearby chair, relaxed, and looked out into the twilight.

He thought about tomorrow, next week, three weeks, and what those days would bring. The mediation request and subsequent meetings hadn't occupied much of his attention the last two or three days. Now that the rush of the end of the school year had concluded, mediation once more became the dominate concern.

What of Shawn Kelly and Randy Wilcox? His violent clash with Randy, now only two weeks ago, seemed much longer ago than that. Was Shawn Kelly really serious about his apologies at the cabin? Justin had no definite answers, only feelings. His feelings told him not to trust Shawn Kelly.

Even as critical as these events were, Justin thought little about them in the past few days. In the solitude of the Anders' deck, they all came rushing back.

Justin took a long shallow of beer. As he did, someone said, "What are you doing out here all by yourself?"

Having heard no one approach, the sudden question startled him. For an instant he choked on his beer. Coughing lightly, Justin turned and said, "Just enjoying the night."

Realizing that the voice belonged to Kitty Wilder, he got up and offered her a seat next to him.

Kitty sat down, apologizing for her apparent intrusion. "Sorry if I scared you. I didn't think I was that quiet."

"I really wasn't paying attention to what was going on," Justin confessed. "Just enjoying the beautiful evening."

Kitty gazed out over the sprawling yard. 'It is pretty tonight, isn't it."

Justin stretched his legs out in front of him. He turned to face Kitty. "Well, next year at this time you'll enter what is affectionately called the real world," Justin joked.

"I know," Kitty acknowledged, "but I have to get through this summer and my senior year first."

Justin nodded in agreement. "Say, by the way did you get that job, counseling at a camp wasn't it?"

"Haven't heard yet. I should hear soon. Camp opens in the middle of June. Thanks again for helping me with the application,"

"Think nothing of it. Always willing to help a pretty girl."

Neither said anything for a few brief moments. Kitty turned to face Justin. "May I ask you a question?"

"Sure, go ahead."

"I heard some rumor about your getting attacked and beaten up in the parking lot a couple weeks ago. Is that true?"

"Yes, I'm afraid it is."

"You said something about a fall down the stairs."

A furtive grin served as Justin's response.

"Why on earth would anyone do a thing like that?" Kitty asked.

"That's a good question. I wished I had the answer."

"Do you know who did it?" Kitty asked with sincere interest.

"Yes. Randy Wilcox. Do you know him?"

"Vaguely, I think." Kitty shook her head. "My God, I can't believe anyone would do something like that."

"Believe me. It was a shock to me too, literally," Justin agreed.

Silence settled over the two. Kitty spoke again, changing the subject. "Sometime ago you asked me about drugs in our school."

"Yes, I asked you about the article that appeared in the local paper."

"Kids do talk about these things, more than you teachers think. Do you know whose name comes up often in these discussions?"

"Randy Wilcox?"

"You're right. His name is mentioned often." Kitty spoke definitively.

"That doesn't surprise me one bit," Justin admitted. "Though I have no proof, he certainly would be a person I would suspect, even if he hadn't assaulted me."

Justin finished his beer and true to his earlier promise, he was going home. Slowly, he stood up, dropped the empty beer cup in a trash container next to his seat, and looked out over the lawn. The shrubs now appeared as black shapes with shadows dancing around them as the moonlight filtered through the pine trees. "It really is a gorgeous night, but I've a big day tomorrow so I think it's time to get home. Thank you for the conversation, Kitty."

Kitty also stood up. "Thank you for all the good conversation we have had and for all the advice and help you have given me." Kitty stepped forward, placed her hands on

Justin's shoulders and kissed him gently on the cheek. "You're really a neat guy and teacher." Kitty spoke softly.

Justin stepped back, grasping Kitty's hands. He exhaled audibly, "Thank you, Kitty. You are a wonderful young lady."

He dropped her hands. Taking Kitty in his arms, he held her tightly for an instant then whispered, "Walk with me back into the house."

Kitty looked up at Justin, smiled, and quietly said, "Sure, let's go."

As they turned to face the sliding glass, patio door and the bright lights emanating from the party room, Justin stopped abruptly. On the inside of the patio door, a familiar face and a familiar pair of eyes stared intently at him and Kitty.

Connie Shetland stood clearly visible with the party room as her background. Elegantly dressed as usual, she flashed a smile of victory as she greeted Justin with, "A marvelous night out there, isn't it, Mr. Starling."

"Indeed it is," Justin replied tersely while he walked with Kitty at his side toward the bar and the stairway that would take him to the main level and the front entrance.

CHAPTER 50

Mondays were typically slow at the bank. Mondays in the summer were remarkably dull. The people of Twin Pines didn't seem to have much need for bank services on Monday. Perhaps the rush that occurred on Friday carried the customers over until the next Friday. Maybe people, concerned about getting back into the groove of work following the weekend, precluded the worry about money.

Vince Shetland didn't mind the slow pace of Monday except the day did tend to drag. There was always paper work to attend to, and without the frequent interruptions that marked most days, he could with greater leisure complete the approval of several loan applications that lay before him on his desk.

This morning, though, his mind refused to concentrate on the loan applications. Rather, he found his attention diverted to other matters, only his eyes perfunctorily reading the application data.

The spring had been an unsettling one for Vince. Hardly a moment passed, particularly while he was at work, that his conscience did not remind him of his abuse of bank funds. The amount was not yet large, eighteen hundred dollars, but the amount wasn't the only critical factor. That he surrendered to the pressure and the temptation was even more difficult to accept. That he violated not only the law but also his father's trust and confidence overwhelmed him with guilt and remorse.

Was it really worth it? Vince asked himself this question countless times in recent weeks. He loved Connie deeply. After all, only for Connie did he violate his father's trust as well as the law. Having convinced himself of this made the guilt and pain a little easier to bear.

He admired Connie's ambitions. Surely, he did not wish to stand in the way of her accomplishing her goals. Still, what he did was wrong. At times, Connie responded coldly and harshly to him. This he couldn't understand. At other times, she displayed the warmth and love that had so captivated him early in their relationship.

If only this negotiations battle were over, Vince thought, perhaps Connie would be more herself. Then together they could work out their financial problems before someone discovered the manipulation of his accounts. Maybe at the end of July when his vacation arrived, they could leave Twin Pines for a three week escape from the bank, from negotiations, from board leadership and attempt to recapture some of the understanding and warmth they once shared.

In the midst of these thoughts came a soft knock on his office door. The loan applications remained virtually untouched in the pile before him.

"Yes?" Vince responded to the knock while pretending to give his full attention to the papers on his desk.

"Do you have a minute?" his father asked as he opened the door and peered in.

"Of course, Dad, come on in and have a seat."

Vince's dad seldom came to Vince's office. When they did have matters to discuss, they usually did so in his father's office. At the bank, their relationship remained at a professional level. Personal and family concerns only infrequently entered their discussions.

Since Vince started padding his accounts with bank funds, he experienced a tension and insecurity in his father's presence. Now was no exception.

"What's on your mind, Dad?" Vince leaned back in his desk chair.

His father slowly lowered himself into the client chair positioned in front of Vince's desk. "Oh, nothing really. A slow day. I haven't had much of a chance to talk to you lately. How are things going?"

"Fine, I guess," Vince replied, curious what his father was getting at.

Mr. Shetland paused as if searching for what to say next. "Vince, you haven't been yourself in recent weeks. You've been withdrawn. You look pale. Are you feeling all right?"

"I feel fine. I've never felt better," Vince asserted feebly, attempting to hide the anxiety that gripped him.

"If there is something bothering you, I hope you know you can always discuss it with me."

"I know, Dad. I appreciate that. Really there is nothing that needs discussing."

Mr. Shetland leaned forward in this chair then leaned back, crossing his legs. "How's Connie?"

"Busy as ever." Vince pretended to relax by moving his chair back and clasping his hands behind his head. "This summer hasn't been good for her. You know, the teachers are seeking mediation, and that bothers Connie a lot. She so much wanted to conclude the contract talks without having to resort to that."

"Yes, I'm sure that's a big worry. No doubt a little of that burden falls on your shoulders too."

"Naturally, it's difficult to avoid getting involved to some extent," Vince admitted. "Connie's a tough girl. She can handle her responsibility without much help from me."

"I'm sure she can." Vince's father hesitated, aimlessly brushing a piece of lint from his trousers.

Silence settled over Vince's office. Something troubled Vince. His father knew it. Vince's evasive answers only concealed what it was, which thwarted his father's efforts to find out. Finally Mr Shetland asked, "Does she still intend to seek the board's chair?"

"Oh, yes. She wants that position, and from the looks of things she'll probably get it."

"If that's what she wants, then I hope she does. A big job, thankfully there are people like Connie who are willing to take it."

Vince nodded his head in agreement. "She does well in positions of leadership. I'm proud of her and don't want to stand in her way. Her commitments do consume much of her time," He paused. "Time that we obviously can't spend together."

"Son, I understand that. I hope that you are willing to share your wife in that way."

Vince removed his hands from behind his head and placed them, folded, on the desk. "I hope I can. Up to now there have been only minor inconveniences. I suppose that situation could get worse. If it's what Connie wants, then it's what I want too." Vince looked down at his hands clasped tightly in front of him, fully aware that what he just said was an unmitigated lie.

"Good, that's what counts." Vince's father slowly stood up. "Well, I'll let you get back to work now. Just remember, if you ever do need someone to talk to, I'm always here."

"Thank you, Dad. I know that."

Vince's father stopped at the door saying, "Why don't you and Connie stop over for dinner soon. Your mother and I haven't seen you two for quite some time."

"We'll do that. Thanks again."

CHAPTER 51

Alone, Vince reached for a tissue and wiped his face. He felt confident that his father did not suspect him of anything illegal. Right now, guilt threatened to destroy that confidence. Knowledge of his embezzlement would be devastating to his father. Unless he stopped and repaid the money he owed, he was sure he would be discovered, eventually. It was only a matter of time.

What would Connie do? She valued his position in the community. What would news that the vice president was embezzling money do to Connie's future? Vince refused even to think about the consequences for her and ultimately for their relationship.

Vince slumped in his chair and stared into the empty space of his office. He reflected on what the past weeks meant for his career and his marriage. Ironically, Vince had done the manipulation of his accounts only for Connie. Because her life style required more money that he could provide, Vince had jeopardized his reputation and his career to ensure she could maintain that style.

The price required by his actions was high. How much longer he could continue this alone, Vince wasn't sure. Each new day brought only more anguish. If only Connie would understand, Vince thought. Maybe if she knew the truth, she would understand. Vince floundered. His indecision only expanded his agony.

Vince forced his attention away from his personal problems to the work on his desk. It was almost noon, and he had accomplished almost nothing. He completed the examination of the loan applications and for the remainder of the day occupied his time with a few customers, phone calls and idle moments which he spent inside his office; the door closed securely.

The day stretched interminably. Though not typically a part of his afternoon routine, Vince felt a strong need for a drink after leaving the bank at five o'clock. The closest bar was the Oaks Cafe and Lounge.

As Vince entered, the Oaks Lounge was almost deserted. Four people sat at one table and three people sat by the bar. Besides the bartender, Vince saw no one else. However, one of the three people seated at the bar was Randy Wilcox.

Randy's presence annoyed Vince. He came to the bar to get away from his problems, not face more. He recalled vividly the quarrel he interrupted between Randy and Connie. Connie had been evasive about the cause of that quarrel, and Vince hadn't pursued it. Despite the fight, Vince simply did not like Randy. He regretted the sorrow Randy experienced as a young boy. However, Randy's behavior in the past five or six years erased any compassion that Vince might have felt for him.

Vince sat on a stool at the bar, debating whether even to acknowledge Randy's presence. He was certain Randy saw him, but Randy ignored him. Vince ordered just a beer. While he sipped it, he sat studying the rows of bottles shelved behind the bar and reflecting on what had transpired that day. As he did, he decided that he would buy Randy a drink.

Perhaps something good would come out of this day with a friendly gesture. He would try to avoid any arguments with Randy; just buy him a drink and have a friendly talk. When Vince prepared to move next to Randy at the end of the bar, Randy got up from his stool apparently to leave. Vince grabbed his beer and quickly walked to where Randy had been sitting.

Standing in front of Randy, Vince asked, "Buy you a drink?"

Randy stood for a moment saying nothing, just looking at Vince in the same sinister way he looked at Connie last Friday. "Yes, I suppose. I'll have to make it quick."

"Got a heavy date?" Vince grinned.

"No, I have to meet a guy," Randy replied, unimpressed with Vince's attempt at humor.

They both climbed onto a bar stool. Each ordered another beer. Vince paid the bartender.

They sat silently, sipping their beer. Finally Vince broke the silence with, "What are your plans for the summer?"

Randy looked over at Vince, puzzled by the sudden amity. "Got a couple things in mind," Randy answered. "Nothing definite." Privately, the prospects of Chip Overly's offer excited him. He wished to tell someone about it, but he knew he couldn't, especially not Vince.

The image of Randy and Connie screaming at each other crowded into Vince's mind. That Randy struck Connie still ignited Vince's anger. Here at the bar, he controlled himself. He intended to forget about the incident but couldn't resist the present opportunity.

Cautiously, Vince asked, "What was the argument about between you and Connie last Friday?"

Randy displayed no particular emotional response to the question. "You ask her," was his simple reply.

"I did."

"Well, then why bug me about it?"

"I just wanted to hear your side."

"No one has given much of a shit about my side before. Why start now?"

"Randy, that's not true, and you know it."

"Bull shit! All you people give a shit about is your own good time."

Vince wished to avert a scene. At the same time he knew his natural passiveness, in part, produced the problems that now plagued him. He refused to permit Randy to get away with his blatant rejection of his family. "Sure, you've had it tough, but you can't go around blaming everybody all your life."

"What do you know about tough?" Randy's voice sounded throughout the bar. "All you ever had to do was ask Daddy, and it was there."

Vince moved nervously on his bar stool. "I've worked for everything I have," he quickly defended himself. "My life is not the question here. It's yours."

"My life and what I do with it is none of your God damned business anymore. So stay out of it."

"When your life involves my wife, it is my business."

"If you're so fucking concerned, ask her, like I told you before. If she doesn't tell you, that's your problem, not mine." Randy took a swallow of beer then turned to face Vince. "All I've got to say is she's Miss Big Shot around here. Someday she's going to get her ass in a sling."

"What do you mean?" Vince asked, making no attempt to hide his irritation.

"That's for you to figure out. Gaining confidence with each swallow of beer, Randy barked, "Talk to your damned wife. She has all the answers. I've said all I'm going to say. Thanks for the beer." With that, Randy wheeled around on his stool, stepped down and walked briskly out of the bar.

Vince sat alone, more troubled than ever. He sipped his beer slowly, trying to make some sense out of what Randy said. What was he getting at? Was there something between Connie and Randy that he didn't know about? Was Randy only attempting to create hostility between him and Connie? Certainly, Randy was not known for his honesty. Why would he deliberately suggest some collusion with Connie if there wasn't some truth to it?

Vince drank the last of his beer. Depression weighed more heavily on him now than before. What should he do? If only he felt more confident in discussing with Connie what was tearing him apart. Recently, Connie frightened him with her all consuming ambition. She ignored that he had a life to live too. Living that life was becoming an increasing burden.

Vince slowly walked out of the bar, resolved to do something to confront the vicissitudes of his life. Exactly what, he wasn't sure, just something.

CHAPTER 52

Randy waited as the phone rang repeatedly. He supposed that at eleven in the morning even Connie Shetland should be out of bed. Disconnecting the line, he dialed again. Three rings brought a breathless and irate voice on the line, "Shetland's."

With last week's scene in the Shetland foyer still fresh in his mind, Randy wisely dispensed with his customary sardonic manner, determined to discuss his proposal rationally with his aunt. "Connie, this is Randy."

"Of all the nerve!" Connie shouted into the phone. "What in the hell do you want?"

Not accustomed to apologies, Randy groped for the appropriate words and struggled to express them. "Look, I'm sorry about the other day. No hard feelings."

"Let me remind you," Connie threatened, "you pull anything like that again, and I'm going to the police." In a calmer but even firmer voice, she pronounced, "Whatever you might say, the truth is on my side. Don't you forget it."

Randy did not intend to argue with Connie this morning. What she would or would not do didn't concern him at the moment. He had information his aunt, positively, would want, maybe even willing to pay for. To antagonize her would only jeopardize his chance for a few bucks and his chance to cause embarrassment or worse for teachers.

"Okay, Okay, I said I was sorry, didn't I?"

"What do you want this time?" Connie asked with less animosity in her voice.

"I think we should talk."

"What do we have to talk about?"

"I don't want to discuss it over the phone. I think I have some information that might interest you."

With curiosity aroused, Connie asked, "What kind of information?"

"I said I couldn't discuss it over the phone. Can I meet you someplace?"

"I don't have time to go running off to meet with you or with anybody else unless I know what the meeting is about."

"All I'll say is that it has something to do with the teachers. I can't say any more right now."

Indeed, information about teachers concerned Connie. Any information about her adversaries enhanced her advantage. Right now teachers were her adversaries. "What's your plan?" Connie asked in a much more conciliatory tone.

Randy spoke with renewed authority, proud of the manner in which he cooled Connie's antagonism. "You know where Lion's Park is?"

"Of course, I do."

"Can you meet me there sometime this afternoon?"

"What time?"

"Your schedule is tighter than mine. You name it." Randy suggested.

Silence filled the phone line as Connie thought about her schedule for the day. "How about three o'clock?" She suggested.

"Fine. See you in Lion's Park at three."

Randy hung up the phone. From his bed he reached for his trousers and the small packet of pills, his constant companion.

CHAPTER 53

Randy reached Lion's Park early. He had little else to do anyway, especially on a summer afternoon in the middle of the week. A few children played around the swings and the bars. Lion's Park offered no competition for the city pool and park facilities located several blocks away. During the summer, the pool area was the first attraction while Lion's Park slowly slipped into disuse and disrepair. Because it did, it served as a relatively secure place for Connie and Randy to talk for a few minutes without arousing suspicion.

Wandering around the small park, Randy enjoyed the summer day while feeling the effects of the last three pills he had taken. Right now, he stood at the top of the world.

His new association with Chip Overly would certainly work out. Nothing much yet had happened since he started his new job as street man for Chip's local operation. His job assured him a continuous supply of the pills that made his life so much more bearable and of the money to satisfy his other needs. Chip talked at length about caution. Randy listened carefully to that talk, determined to avoid the consequences of carelessness. He had responsibilities which made him answerable to Chip. Slip ups could cost him his future.

Connie soon would join him in his personal campaign to disgrace those damned teachers. He knew she would be more than willing to pay for the information he possessed.

Her potential value to him required that in the future he avoid provoking her.

Randy continued his slow, purposeless walk through the park. Shortly after three o'clock, he saw Connie's car pull into the small parking lot. She parked. Getting out of her car, she carefully surveyed the area until she spotted Randy seated on a bench about fifty yards away.

Approaching the bench on which he sat, Connie had misgivings about this meeting with Randy. She simply didn't trust him. She stopped in front of him.

He got up, reflecting some courtesy and said, "Good afternoon. Glad you could make it." His purpose and the latest dosage combined to give him a sense of assurance and cordiality.

"You'd better make it worth my time," Connie replied with lingering bitterness.

"Sit down?" Randy asked.

Connie sat as far away from Randy as the bench allowed. "Now," she began, "what's this fantastic information you have for me?"

Randy turned to face Connie, resting his arm on the back of the bench. "Not quite so fast," he advised. "I think we should discuss a little business first."

"You bastard! I might have known there would be some strings attached."

Staying calm, Randy replied, "What do you expect? Information isn't cheap."

"You're wasting my time," Connie said with disgust as she got up to leave.

Randy also stood up. "Wait a minute. How much is it worth to you to nail a teacher?" He stopped, waiting for a response. Looking intently at Connie, he repeated, "Well, how much?"

"I'm not sure. Depends upon who the teacher is, and what you mean by 'nailing a teacher'."

"I mean getting rid of him for good," Randy announced with sneering enthusiasm.

Randy now had Connie's undivided attention.

"What's your price?" Connie asked, eager to find out what Randy had to say.

"Maybe two hundred dollars."

"Two hundred dollars! You're out of your God damned mind! Nothing you have is worth that much money to me."

Realizing he was getting nowhere, Randy decided to chance it. "Suppose we negotiate the price after you hear the information. I trust you, and you trust me. Okay?"

Sitting down again on the bench, Connie only grinned in response to Randy's proposal. She really had little to lose. She agreed to his suggestion. "Okay let's hear what you have to say."

"Do you know a teacher by the name of Shawn Kelly?"

"Yes, I do."

"What do you know about him?" Randy asked.

"Look, I didn't come here to play question games. If you have something to say, let's have it. Otherwise forget it."

"Okay, okay," Randy said, waving his hands in a downward gesture to calm Connie.

Randy sat down on the bench and turned to face Connie. "I saw these two guys in the Oaks Lounge the other night. I thought I recognized one of them as a teacher but had never seen the other one before. I found out later that the stranger may be some big wheel in the drug traffic from the Twin Cities."

Connie paid much closer attention at the mention of drugs.

"Don't ask me how I know that. I just do." Randy plunged ahead in his story. "I went to the library. Yes, I went to the library and looked at some high school year books. This teacher's picture wasn't in any of them. I was positive he was a teacher anyway."

Connie asked, impatient for more information. "Does it really make any difference how you knew it was Shawn Kelly?"

"It was a clever bit of detective work on my part," Randy bragged, "and I'm proud of it. Anyway, I asked the lady in the library if she had any other types of yearbooks or anything on the schools.

"She then brought out this big folder which had some old copies of school papers and things from both the middle school and the high school. In the second or third paper I looked at, there was that face. A bit younger but there it was. His name is Shawn Kelly, and he teaches social studies in the middle school." Randy gleamed. "Now, aren't you proud of me?"

Connie was. Randy hadn't in years showed such diligence about anything. "Yes, I'm impressed," Connie replied sarcastically. "Shawn Kelly is also a part of the teacher negotiating team."

"Well, son of a bitch. I hit the jack pot!"

"Don't get too excited too quickly," Connie interrupted. "That does sound interesting, but just because you saw Kelly talking with this guy who may have some contact with the drug world doesn't make him guilty."

"Maybe not, but it could be worth looking into, don't you think?"

Connie considered the effect information like this, if true, could have on her bargaining strength with Justin Starling. Wouldn't it be sweet if it were discovered that a teacher, a negotiating committee member, engaged in drug dealing. Connie's revealing this conspiracy would definitely strengthen her position on the board as well as enhance her reputation in the community.

Connie looked at Randy, smiled benevolently, and asserted, "Yes, Randy, I think you may be right this time. This does warrant some looking into."

"Didn't I tell you I had information that would be worth your while? Maybe you'll listen to me in the future," Randy said with evident self satisfaction. "Now what about the money?"

"I don't know anything for sure yet," Connie advised. "Look, I'll give you fifty dollars now. If you can bring me proof of what you are suggesting, I'll give you the other hundred fifty."

"It's a deal," Randy answered eagerly.

"Remember, though," Connie reminded, "the situation is the same. If you open your mouth about this to anyone, and I mean anyone, I'll deny every word of it. You know whose word people will believe."

"Don't worry," Randy assured Connie. "You cooperate with me, and I will cooperate with you."

"Good. Now when you have further information, call me. We can't meet here very often. Maybe at mother's house would be better."

"That's all right with me. She doesn't pay much attention to what I do anyway. What I intend to do is snoop around a bit. When I find out something, I'll call you."

"Make sure Vince isn't around when you call. He's not going to put up with you around the house after what happened last week."

"Gotcha," Randy concurred.

Connie rose to leave.

"By the way," Randy spoke tentatively, "did Vince tell you about our discussion Monday afternoon at the Oaks Lounge?"

"No, he didn't," Connie answered, puzzled by Randy's disclosure.

Randy stood facing Connie, hands on hips, "He could be a problem."

"In what way?"

"I think he suspects something is going on between us," Randy picked up where he left off. "He pushed me about what I was doing at the house last week and what the big fight was about."

"What did you tell him?" Connie displayed an urgency as she pressed Randy for details.

"I told him nothing, but he didn't seem satisfied with that. Funny, he didn't insist on more answers from you."

Connie's initial anxiety over the meeting between Randy and Vince diminished. With a tone of assurance typical of her voice, she said, "You leave Vince to me. I can handle him. You look out for Shawn Kelly. That's your job. Just stay away from Vince and stay away from the house."

With that she walked toward her car, leaving Randy by the bench fifty dollars richer and with an exciting challenge to occupy his time.

Pulling out of the parking lot, Connie began to sort out the implications of what Randy had told her. She would have to wait further word from him before confronting Justin Starling. She had time. Believing she had the advantage increased her patience and her methodical approach to achieving her goals.

Perhaps the mediation hearings could be avoided after all. She knew the delays associated with mediation proceedings. Both the teachers and the board had submitted preliminary documents. The scheduling of the first meeting, however, awaited submission of detailed arguments from both sides. That could take days, even weeks. She had time.

Connie turned her concentration to Justin Starling. Persuading him to meet with her privately might prove difficult. Nonetheless, she did feel certain she could arrange such a meeting. He would respond to a renewed suggestion that his relationship with some of his students was less than professional.

Though she was unaware of the repercussions of the note Randy attached to his car, both from Randy and from her personal observations at the Anders' house, she possessed evidence of his affection for Kitty Wilder. Maybe it was innocent enough, but innocence could be distorted into something incriminating for a person in Starling's position.

Vince posed a different problem. Connie grimaced considering the conflicts that had grown between them the past few months. His sharing her drive for accomplishment, her desire for status other than that of just another wife of a small town bank, vice president would likely resolve these conflicts. Sadly, Vince had shown no desire to share her ambitions.

She must exercise caution. He could ruin all her plans. For Connie, appearance defined the person. A breakup of their marriage now would erode the influence that she worked so long to establish. Her strategy would require brains and discretion. Connie believed she possessed both. She would exploit them to achieve what she wanted.

CHAPTER 54

Justin Starling spent the entire morning working on the documentation for the mediation sessions. He carefully outlined the agreements which had been reached and the issues which remained undecided. All this material required discussion with his committee. Always, before meeting with his colleagues, he insisted on his own preparation.

Despite the work on the information for mediation, Justin enjoyed the first few days of his summer vacation. The last two or three months of school always brought a rush of hectic activity. This year was even more so for Justin with the added responsibility of negotiations, the mystery surrounding the behavior of Connie Shetland and Randy Wilcox, as well as the incident at the cabin with Shawn Kelly. Furthermore, Justin still hadn't dismissed completely the note he found attached to his car in the school parking lot. Though not absolutely sure, he generally concluded the note represented an innocent prank.

Freedom from specific, daily commitments, an escape from the rigid routine of the previous nine months refreshed Justin, giving him short periods of relaxation. He even gave renewed attention to his bike.

Not a serious cyclist, Justin delighted in short rides of five to ten miles. The rides offered excellent exercise as well as a perfect way to enjoy the sights and smells of early summer. Unfortunately, Justin had little time for such activities before school ended. Now he promised himself that he would make time.

Justin rode leisurely passed lawns, green and rich, nourished by the warm summer sun. Spring and summer were times of renewal, houses painted, fences repaired, trees trimmed, streets cleaned. Everywhere he looked, people engaged in fixing, cleaning, repairing, and renewing.

His ride took him within one block of the school. He had no real desire to ride any closer. The traffic of downtown Twin Pines was not excessive on a Tuesday morning. Still, Justin wished to avoid the downtown. Biking surrounded by traffic, light or not, had little appeal for him. Besides, the community offered several other more desirable places to ride.

He would have to pass Lion's Park if he intended to gain access to the highway that went west out of town. Riding a couple miles on the highway would give him a chance to extend himself and to clean out his lungs.

Lion's Park, so named because the Twin Pines Lion's Club built and partially maintained it, occupied exactly one square block. Though not large, it provided attractive playground equipment and space for the young children of the neighborhood. A few large maple and pine trees dominated the park, placing it in sharp contrast to the concrete and asphalt that surrounded it.

Justin coasted as he neared the park. Looking for nothing or nobody in particular, he simply slowed to observe the activity happening in the park. As he did, he thought he recognized two people seated on one of the benches near the small off street parking lot. A more careful look confirmed that one of the two persons was Connie Shetland. He could see only the back of the other person and, at first, could not identify him.

Justin gradually slowed his bike. He didn't want to be conspicuous. Though he wished to avoid recognition by Connie, he was curious why she sat talking with some man in the middle of Lion's Park. Then that man turned his head, attracted by two small children racing after a ball. To Justin's alarm, the man was Randy Wilcox.

Though tempted to do so, Justin did not stop. As far as he could tell, Connie and Randy did not see him. He preferred they didn't.

Justin pedaled slowly, questions rolling through his mind. Why would the two meet in a park? Why wouldn't they meet at her house? From what he understood of their relationship, why would she wish to meet with Randy at all, especially in public? What could they have going between them that would require such an unusual meeting place? They were related, Justin reminded himself. They could have any number of reasons for meeting in the park.

Seeing Connie and Randy together awakened Justin's memory of recent events. As he rode his bike, the image of Connie sitting across from him at the Pine Inn floated in and out of his mind. Why would a woman so beautiful resort to intimidation and aggression? Justin would never forget the look of hatred and vengeance etched on Randy's face and evident in his strained, harsh voice that night in the parking lot.

Did a connection exist between Randy's behavior and Connie's desire to control the negotiations? Justin previously entertained such a connection but dismissed it as too improbable. What he just witnessed in Lion's Park compelled him to reconsider. Now, he refused to dismiss the possibility too hastily.

Justin pedaled easily on the very edge of the highway. Only a few more yards and he would turn around and head home. Before crossing the highway, he glanced back to see a car rapidly approaching. He decided he'd best wait until the car passed. Pulling onto the shoulder of the highway, he stopped his bike and placed one foot on the ground, resting the other on the pedal.

The car came closer, obviously traveling at an excessive speed. About fifty feet in front of Justin, the car glided off the highway with one wheel on the shoulder. For an instant, Justin couldn't believe what he saw. The car speeded right for him.

He froze, staring at the grille of the approaching car. Justin suddenly realized the car aimed directly at him. He dropped his bike and dived for the shallow ditch bordering the highway. In a blur the car raced by, catching the back of Justin's bike. Glass and gravel flew in all directions. The bike, smashed on impact, crumpled into the ditch some twenty yards beyond Justin.

He lay in the ditch, stunned by the suddenness with which everything had happened. He was almost afraid to move, not knowing if any part of his body would hurt. He tried. Nothing hurt. He was all right, just unable to control the shivering. He forced himself up to look around. The road stood deserted, not a car in sight. A few yards away his bike lay bent and broken partially concealed by the tall grass.

Justin sat down by the side of the road. My God! Someone had tried to kill him! He could see again the dark car that raced around the school parking lot that night now several days ago. He could still see the sneering contempt on Randy Wilcox's face. Could the car that had just tried to run him down belong to Randy? Justin was in no condition to verify that. He wasn't sure he could even remember the make of the car. It all happened too fast.

He stood up. Though uneasy in the knees, Justin's strength and stability started to return. He'd have to rescue his bike later. Neither he nor his bike was in any condition for a ride. He started walking back toward town, feeling puzzled and vulnerable.

CHAPTER 55

Shawn nervously wandered around his apartment. Since his meeting with Fred Wyman, he couldn't relax. He couldn't figure out what was happening to him. Though he tried, he couldn't escape the fear and anxiety which had taken hold of him. Besides that encounter with Justin Starling and the article in the local paper, nothing had disrupted his drug activities. Still he felt nervous. What happened to that confidence with which he always attacked what he did? Three years in drugs should have prepared him to deal with the pressures and potential dangers of his second job. They didn't.

Shawn went to the fridge for a can of beer. He switched on the television to catch the six o'clock news. He watched but didn't comprehend what he saw and heard. The extra money always served as a source of comfort and justification for his drug involvement. Lately, even that didn't seem to make any difference.

He wondered what his life would be like now if he hadn't accepted Wyman's offer. No doubt he would be planning a trip, perhaps to London, beautiful and exciting in the summer time. Since his days in the Army, he planned to return to London. Maybe he still could. His spirits brightened for a moment as he recalled the weekend he spent in London, enjoying the sights, the girls, and the pubs. He deserved some time away from Twin Pines.

Getting out of the mediation sessions would present no problem. The committee could function very well without him. They agreed with little he said anyway. His drug routine, however, presented a much greater problem. Why hadn't he discussed with Wyman a short vacation from his drug courier responsibilities? Wyman would have understood. It would be good for both of them. The next time his phone contact called, he would suggest it.

More relaxed, Shawn walked to the fridge for another beer. With the first swallow still in his mouth, the phone rang. Shawn gulped, choked, and coughed violently to catch his breath. He spat the beer into the sink. The phone continued its intermittent ringing.

Shawn considered letting it ring. He couldn't do it. He reached for the receiver and taking a deep breath, placed it to his ear. Weakly he answered, "Yes."

"Catch you in the shower?" the familiar voice asked.

"No, no, I was just having something to eat," Shawn lied.

"Got another shipment for you."

Shawn battled to conceal the fear in his voice. "Okay, when?"

"Tomorrow night."

Shawn's earlier thought of requesting some time off never even occurred to him now. He gripped the receiver tightly and with a voice barely audible uttered, "Right."

"Till next time." The phone clicked, leaving only silence.

Shawn stood unmoving, the phone still clutched tightly in his hand. Slowly he replaced the receiver and stared blankly into space. He walked into his bedroom, opened the bottom drawer of his dresser, and placed his hand under the neatly folded sweaters. As he withdrew his hand, he gripped a thirty-eight calibre revolver.

CHAPTER 56

Hardly anyone was around at one fifteen Saturday morning in Twin Pines. Most taverns and bars closed at one a.m. on Saturday. The last movie ended at twelve thirty; the A & W closed at midnight; one or two service stations accounted for the only evidence of life in Twin Pines so early in the morning.

Randy relished this time of the morning. He was more alert, he thought. The freshness of the early morning air stimulated him. He loved the feeling of mastery the early morning gave him. He was in charge. No one else was around. Even the police made only occasional appearances on the streets.

This also was when Randy transacted most of his business. Working with Chip Overly kept Randy busy. The article in the local paper about drug use in the Twin Pines schools captured the truth.

Randy turned to drugs long ago. Shortly after his parents died, he had his first exposure to the release that various stimulants gave him. At times, he faced an unbearable life, no one to talk to and no place to go for help. He valued what the drugs did for him, then, while anticipating what they would do for him now.

Particularly during the summer, kids roamed the streets of Twin Pines searching for companionship, excitement, or simply looking for something to do. Randy promoted and sold his products on the same streets and places where the kids congregated. He realized the need for caution, but it all seemed so easy.

Tonight was a good night. Randy grinned while he patted the roll of money that bulged in his front pocket. Though Chip Overly would get most of it, some was his. Randy smiled with pride. He believed his chance finally arrived. He would make the most of it.

Several places Randy frequented he considered perfect for the exchanges he made. The A & W drive in was especially lucrative tonight. Though it officially closed at midnight, the owner didn't mind if customers talked in and around their cars until the completion of the necessary cleaning. The A & W represented only one place where Randy was rapidly becoming an important friend to many young people in Twin Pines.

A one fifteen a.m. Saturday, Randy started for home. He was tired. Not only did his duties on the street keep him busy, his commitment to Connie and his own curiosity made him constantly alert for insight into Shawn Kelly. Despite the money his aunt had yet to pay him, his detective role intrigued him.

During the preceding two days Randy discovered where Shawn lived. He even observed his entering and leaving his apartment. He discovered what type car he drove. For those two days he monitored Kelly's every move.

Randy realized quickly that Shawn did not do much. He spent most of his time in his apartment, only occasionally making short trips in his car. While Randy tracked him, Shawn met with or scarcely talked with another person. Exactly what he did during all those hours in his apartment remained a mystery to Randy.

Now as Randy prepared to head home to some much needed sleep, he caught a glimpse of Shawn Kelly's car about a block away. He knew it was Kelly's car, one of those expensive foreign models, the only one of its kind in town. Randy immediately changed his mind about going home. Instead, he followed Shawn Kelly.

Randy turned left at the Second Avenue intersection where he saw Shawn turn. Sure enough, there he was about two blocks ahead. Randy regretted now the absence of traffic. He would have to be careful. His car and Kelly's shared the street together, the only cars in sight.

Determined to find out where Shawn was going, Randy kept a good distance behind. Not to arouse Shawn's suspicion, Randy made a quick maneuver involving a right turn for a half block, then a left through an alley, another left at the next street for a half block, then right onto Second Avenue, the street he started from. Ahead glowed the same pair of tail lights.

The only traffic light on Second Avenue was at its intersection with Highway 14 which ran east and west out of Twin Pines. Randy watched as Shawn turned right at the traffic light and drove east.

Maybe he's just leaving town for the weekend, Randy thought to himself. He debated whether or not to follow him. He didn't wish to embark on a wild chase that resulted in nothing. He, likewise, didn't wish to miss an opportunity for specific evidence confirming Shawn Kelly's narcotic involvement. Randy turned right onto Highway 14, committed to following Shawn regardless of where it might lead him.

CHAPTER 57

Shawn's hands perspired as he held the steering wheel of his Porsche. He told himself this was going to be the last time. The agony just wasn't worth it. After this pickup and drop, he would decide how to sever relationships with people like Fred Wyman.

Shawn checked his jacket pocket for the third time, ensuring his gun was still there. The dashboard clock showed one thirty A.M. The night was clear and mild. Shawn almost preferred clouds on these nights. However, in another hour or so weather wouldn't matter. He would be on his way back to Twin Pines. He recalled how he used to enjoy these early morning rides. The freshness, the calm, the sheer beauty of first the flat fields then later the hills and pine trees captivated him, almost making him forget the real purpose of his journey.

Tonight he had no difficulty remembering why he was there. His hands began to tire from the firmness with which he held the wheel. His head began to throb as the gazed at the highway illuminated by his headlights. Oblivious to everything but the road in front of him and his growing desire for freedom from all of this, Shawn never noticed the headlights that followed him.

Wisely, Randy maintained a good distance between himself and Shawn. The highway was not heavily traveled this time of the morning. Randy was concerned with missing Shawn if he should turn off on some side road. Other than that, only an occasional glimpse of the familiar tail lights satisfied Randy that Shawn had not slipped away from him.

For nearly forty miles Randy played hide and seek with that pair of tail lights. He started to wonder where this was leading him. Suddenly, Shawn's brake lights flashed. Randy prepared to watch for what would happen next.

Shawn's car gradually slowed then disappeared over the crest of a hill. When Randy approached the crest, he noticed the sign identifying Beaver Creek. He pulled to the side of the road and shut off his lights and engine. Several hundred yards ahead, he could see that Shawn stopped near a small bridge, turned off the lights, but sat in the car.

Randy knew he would have to get closer but dared not use his car. His lights would be clearly visible from the bridge below. He got out of the car. On foot, he made his way toward the bridge, keeping to the trees that lined the road. Nearing the bridge and Shawn's parked car, Randy stopped, crouching behind a tree. Shawn still sat in his car, lights out. More cautiously, Randy inched closer and closer.

Then the car door opened. The interior light shown brightly on Shawn's face. He moved very deliberately. When Shawn walked across the highway toward the bridge, Randy crept as close as he dared. Shawn paused on the bridge and looked carefully in all directions. He then ran around the end of the bridge. He emerged a few minutes later clutching a small package in his hands.

"That son of a bitch," Randy whispered to himself. He shivered with excitement as he envisioned Connie's reaction to the information he would bring to her. To get hold of that package would be the ultimate proof. At this time, he couldn't risk trying to grab it. The information he had would more than make Connie happy. It would also make him one hundred fifty dollars richer. After all, if he didn't have to risk getting hurt, he definitely didn't intend to.

Shawn made his way furtively across the bridge and to his car. Randy raised slightly, moving to his right for a better view. His foot struck something, perhaps a tin can. A sharp, hollow crack broke the silence of the night. Randy instantly fell to the ground, motionless.

Shawn stopped and reached into his jacket for his gun. He raced for his car, searching the darkness in the direction the sound came from. His hand was moist on the gun handle. In desperation, he again peered into the darkness while trying to control the panic that surged through his body.

Shawn's hand trembled as he used the top of his car for support. He aimed the gun in the direction of the sound. He heard movement. Without another thought he fired, one, two, three times. The shots echoed in the calm night. He waited, almost paralyzed by what was happening. He heard a groan, a thrashing movement. He fired again and again until the gun clicked. Then he jumped into his car and raced across the bridge, not looking at what he left behind.

Randy lay twisted in pain, his chest burning up. One of Shawn's wild shots had ripped through his back. He could hardly breathe. The pain was excruciating. He tried to stand up. He had to stand up. Everything went black. He slipped to the ground. He tried again, clinging to a small tree. More shots zinged near by. He fell to the ground, stunned. A door slammed shut; an engine roared, then silence returned.

Randy struggled to clear his head. His breathing came in short gasps. The taste of blood filled his mouth. He spat. Again, he attempted to get up. He had to get to his car. He couldn't die here in the ditch.

Finally, he stood, dizzy and weak. He must get to his car parked what seemed miles away. Everything was blurred. The burning raged in his chest. He started slowly at first, then faster. He couldn't get air. He stumbled and rolled in the grassy ditch. He lay unmoving. He must get to his car. He urged himself to his feet. In the haze before him he could see the car's dim outline. He could make it. His shirt felt wet and sticky. With each breath his chest burned like fire.

Randy staggered out of the ditch onto the shoulder of the road. Going was easier there. With each labored step, he moved closer to the car until, at last, he fell exhausted against the hood. He grasped the metal of the hood to keep from slipping to the ground. Using the car for support, he inched his way to the driver's side, opened the door, and collapsed on the front seat.

He fought the urge simply to lie there. He reached for the steering wheel and pulled himself up. He coughed. His mouth filled with blood. He learned over, spitting through the open door. He fumbled for the key still in the ignition. The engine burst into life. With all his energy, Randy put the car in gear and slowly turned it in the direction of Twin Pines.

Randy pulled the light switch, but the road still floated before him in a dim haze. He battled the steering wheel to keep the car to the right of the center line. His foot pressed harder on the accelerator. The trees passed faster and faster. He coughed again, the pain tearing at his chest.

The car swerved and slipped onto the shoulder. Hopelessly, Randy fought to control the car. It was too late. The front wheel caught the edge of the ditch, pulling the car farther off the shoulder. All was confusion.

The car tipped wildly onto its side, throwing Randy against the opposite door. Weeds, dirt and grass flew as the car plowed through the ditch. For an instant it tipped back on four wheels. A large rock caught the left front wheel and fender, hurling the car end over end.

Randy felt nothing when the door ripped open and his lifeless body tumbled under the demolished car.

CHAPTER 58

Six o'clock Saturday morning was an unusual time to drive to the hospital. Connie pondered this idea along with numerous others while she drove to St. John's, Twin Pines' only hospital. She received the call at about five fifteen A. M. A highway patrolman spotted Randy's car, battered and ripped practically beyond recognition. Randy was pronounced dead at the scene.

The suddenness of Randy's death, at first, overwhelmed Connie. She became concerned for the reactions of her mother and father. Since then Connie regained her composure to consider more rationally the tragic event.

What had Randy been doing out there at two or three in the morning? Had he found out something about Kelly or Starling? She did feel a sense of loss. Randy could have become a real ally for her. On the other hand, his tortured life, at least since the death of his parents, conflicted with most who knew him. Now, that would end.

Since Connie's parents refused, the officials asked Connie to make the official identification. Dr. Collins, who pronounced Randy dead at the scene of the accident, would meet Connie at the St. John's Hospital morgue.

Entering the hospital, Connie went directly to the main desk. Hospital staff escorted her to Dr. Collins' office just down the hall.

For the previous six months, Dr. Collins served as a resident at St. John's. Tall with a dark complexion and black hair, he smiled compassionately as Connie entered his office.

"Mrs. Shetland, thank you for coming." The doctor came around his desk to offer his hand to Connie. "Please accept my condolence on the death of your nephew, I believe. Let me assure you that everything possible was done under the circumstances." He paused, expecting some response. None came. "Please take a seat. Is there anything I can get for you?"

"No thank you. Let's just get it over with."

"Yes, of course. Please come with me."

Connie followed Dr. Collins to the morgue. She shivered in the clammy coolness of the room. When Dr. Collins pulled back the sheet covering Randy's body, she cringed. At that moment Connie felt a sincere regret over having done so little to help Randy adjust to life after the deaths of his parents. Nothing she could now do would change that. Randy's had truly been a pathetic life.

Connie nodded in recognition after which Dr. Collins replaced the sheet over Randy's head. The morgue attendant would take care of the rest. Dr. Collins directed Connie out the door then stopped.

"Mrs. Shetland, do you have a few minutes?"

"Well, yes, I guess so,"

"Could you come back to my office? Just a few things I want to clear up with you."

"Sure," Connie agreed as she followed Dr. Collins back to the first floor and his office.

Please be seated, Mrs. Shetland," the doctor directed. "Again, I am sorry about the death of your nephew. I don't wish to detain you at a difficult time like this, but I must ask a few questions. If you would rather wait, I understand."

"No, no, go ahead," Connie insisted.

"Mrs. Shetland," Dr. Collins began, "What did Randy do?"

"Please, you may call me Connie." Connie smiled. "Very little," she replied tersely. "He had several odd jobs over the past months. Keeping a job was difficult for him."

"Did you know his friends?"

Connie shifted restlessly in her chair. "I'm not sure he had very many friends. He was sort of a loner."

The doctor rose from the chair behind his desk, walked around the desk, and sat on a chair next to Connie. "Do you know where he spent his spare time?"

Connie turned to face the doctor. With obvious irritation she said, "Look, doctor, I really don't see what good these questions are going to do. What difference does it make who his friends were or where he spent his spare time? He's dead and that's that." Connie folded her hands in her lap in a gesture of finality.

"I'm not sure about that, Mrs. Shetland."

"You're not sure about what?" Connie retorted.

"I'm not so sure his death doesn't make a difference," the doctor continued elusively.

Connie frowned in confusion. "Dr. Collins, what are you getting at?"

The doctor turned to face Connie. "Mrs. Shetland, Connie, there is strong evidence that the accident did not kill your nephew. I think he was dead or nearly so before the accident happened."

Connie sat up straight, "What are you talking about?" she demanded.

The doctor calmly replied, "Randy was shot, shot through the lung."

With eyes wide and arms spread in front of her, Connie exclaimed, "Shot! Why?"

"I thought maybe you could shed some light on that."

Though Connie did not intend to reveal them to the doctor, several reasons why someone might wish to shoot Randy occurred to her. Innocently, she confessed, "I have absolutely no idea who could have done something like this. We really didn't see Randy that often. We really were not that close." Connie began a brief explanation of the tragedy of Randy's young life.

"I'm sorry to hear that," the doctor sympathized. "For whatever reason, you nephew was shot. It is my opinion from the condition of his right lung he probably would not have lived much longer even if he had not attempted to drive."

The doctor returned to the chair behind his desk, sat down, then continued. "It's difficult to tell, but it appears that he lost a considerable amount of blood before the accident. His shirt and trousers were heavily soaked with blood, most of it dried before the patrolman found him."

Connie slumped back in the chair, "I have no idea who could have done this or why."

"You realize," Dr. Collins rested his elbows on his desk, "we'll have to report this to the police. I'm sorry but they, too, may inquire as to Randy's recent activities."

"I won't be much help," Connie shrugged.

"I just wanted you to know what to expect."

Connie stood up. "Is there anything else?" she asked.

"No, I guess not, for now at least." The doctor stood behind his desk. "Thank you for the time and the help you have given. Again, I'm sorry."

"Thank you," Connie answered mechanically.

Walking to her car in the hospital parking lot, Connie pondered what she would do next. Now that she needed Randy or could use him, his death eliminated his availability. She counted on him and the information he could possibly obtain.

She wondered if maybe he discovered something or gained new information about Kelly or Starling. If true, how could she, now, find out what he knew? Perhaps, she would have to go to Justin Starling with something less than concrete evidence against Shawn Kelly.

"Damn it!" she muttered to herself. The circumstances demanded a new strategy. One thing for sure, she was now on her own. She could handle that.

CHAPTER 59

For Justin, summer, Saturday mornings differed little from any other morning. The days of the week also blended, one not readily distinguishable from another. Justin savored the freedom of his summer schedule, a direct contrast to the rigidity of his school year routine that began at five thirty each morning and ended sometimes passed eleven at night.

Sleeping later than eight or nine o'clock in the morning was sheer heaven for him. On several occasions this summer he did just that, this Saturday morning one of them.

Justin lay in bed thinking about mediation and the committee meeting planned for Monday when the ringing of the phone interrupted his thoughts. He let it ring, three, four, five times. Since his involvement in negotiations, he never knew who would call next.

Finally, he reached for the receiver, "Hello."

"Hope I didn't get you up," were the first words he heard.

"No, I'm up," Justin answered tentatively.

"Bob Turner here."

Justin raised up with one arm resting on his pillow. "Oh, hi, Bob. Couldn't place that voice at first. Probably should get that caller I D thing."

"I didn't really wake you up, did I?"

"No," Justin assured him. "Just staying in bed is a rare privilege."

"Enjoying your vacation?"

"Couldn't be better."

"Say, Justin, the reason I called has to do with this Wilcox kid." Bob paused, cleared his throat. "He was killed last night."

"He was what?" Justin threw back the sheet, got up, and stood beside his bed.

Bob explained, "He was killed in a car accident last night east of town, out near my cabin."

"Anyone else along? Anyone else involved?" Justin asked, shocked by the news.

"No, he was alone in the car. It rolled a few times. I saw the car when it was towed in. What a mess."

Justin ran his fingers through his ruffled hair while sitting down on the bed.

Bob went on, "Knowing something about the problems you've had with him, I figured you'd be interested."

"Yes, indeed, thanks. When did it happen?"

"Well, that's another reason I called. I happened to be at the cabin last night. Had to install a new well pump. Well, anyway, about two or two thirty, something like that, I got up to use the bathroom. You know how my cabin overlooks the Beaver Creek Bridge."

"Yes, I remember."

"I looked out the front window. I was sure I saw a car parked off to one side of the road near the bridge."

"Did you recognize the car?" Justin asked.

"No, I didn't. I thought I'd go down to look around. Maybe someone was in trouble or something. I stepped out the door when, my God, I heard gun shots."

"Gun shots!" Justin repeated.

"Yes, gun shots, five, six of them. Then a car roared away. I think across the bridge."

Are you saying that Randy Wilcox had something to do with the shooting?" Justin asked.

"I don't know. Shortly after the shots, I heard another car farther up the road, start, and apparently head back to Twin Pines."

Justin sat on his bed shaking his head. Could all this happen in quiet Twin Pines? "Have you contacted the police?" Justin inquired.

"Haven't had the chance to yet. I intend to. I can't figure out who would be out in the middle of the night shooting at each other. Almost like TV."

"I can't either, Bob. If Randy Wilcox was one of them, who was the other?"

"Good question."

"Look, Bob, thanks for calling. If you find out any more information, please let me know. I'd better get myself organized this morning."

Justin's mind buzzed with possible explanations for Randy's death. Surely, he did not enjoy wide popularity in Twin Pines.

Justin walked to the bathroom. How, he thought, could one kid make such a difference in a teacher's life. Randy caused him more grief than any other student in recent memory. Justin recalled clearly the scene Randy caused in the conference room when he learned he would not pass the critical composition course and would not graduate from high school. Justin vividly recalled the hate in Randy's eyes as Randy pounded on him in the parking lot. The nature of his association with Connie, the meeting in Lion's Park, all of this churned in Justin's mind while he showered and dressed.

CHAPTER 60

Randy's death was a relief for Justin. The teaching profession encouraged Justin to capitalize on the good in young people, helping to mold them into mature, responsible adults. Justin simply couldn't find anything good about Randy Wilcox. It reminded him of the morbid joke which really contained little humor: like doctors, teachers, too, could bury their mistakes.

As he prepared and ate his breakfast, Justin couldn't get Randy Wilcox off his mind. Even after his burial Randy's Wilcox would continue to haunt Justin. Too many unanswered questions remained. Could Randy have been responsible for the earlier attack on Justin at Beaver Creek? As for last night, perhaps Randy stumbled onto something at the bridge, much as Justin had earlier.

Justin stood staring out the window over his kitchen sink. What about that bridge that caused so much violence? Though he couldn't generate any sincere sympathy, Justin acknowledged that the bridge and whatever secrets it guarded provided the scene where a young person met his death.

Shawn Kelly, also, had some connection to that bridge. His visit to the cabin still puzzled Justin. From what Justin knew of him, Shawn apologized for very little. Certainly, he would not drive out of his way to do so.

Justin stacked the dishes in the dishwasher. Already he wasted too much of the day. He needed to complete mediation materials as well as make preparations for the committee meeting planned for Monday afternoon.

He tried to forget Randy Wilcox and all the rest that swirled around the news about his death. Someday he might find out the truth. Just how, he didn't know. Right now he faced more pressing matters. He vowed, early in his summer break from school, to reserve Sunday for more enjoyable activities than negotiations. Unless he started with what he needed to do, that would never happen.

CHAPTER 61

Shawn sat wearily on the edge of his bed. He couldn't sleep. Yet, he was tired; his head ached; he fought a persistent nausea. Since Friday night, he scarcely slept or ate. The trauma of his latest pickup proved nearly more than he could handle.

He never intended to use that gun. He now wished he had never bought it. Nonetheless, he used it. He hit someone. He had no doubt about that. Who, he had no idea. The sound of pain he clearly heard. To flee was his only consideration, to get away from that bridge, to hide someplace. After he completed his job and drove home, he hid in his own apartment, alert to every sound and suspicious of every car that drove by.

Shawn heard about the Wilcox death. Amazed that he hadn't seen the accident, Shawn never made the connection between the person he shot at and Randy Wilcox. Randy Wilcox plainly did not register with Shawn. He was just another former student who caused the school district headaches.

"No more!" Shawn vowed out loud. "I'm getting out." Living the way he did he viewed as not living at all. Fear fed on him constantly. The culmination occurred Friday night at the damned bridge. No matter how much money he made, he wanted no part of it any more. He would inform his phone contact the next time he called. That didn't ease the fear and confusion he suffered, knowing almost certainly he shot someone. It did give him a sliver of hope he didn't have before.

Duane A. Eide

He would have to face Justin, Norma, Rita, and the rest at ten o'clock that morning. He had no choice. He could feign illness. Ultimately, though, he needed to face reality. Hiding in his apartment, pacing the floor and staring at the walls drove him crazy. He considered it very important to give the impression everything was as it should be. He needed to avoid behavior that created suspicion.

CHAPTER 62

Justin welcomed Norma at his front door, the first of the committee to arrive for the meeting. Not since school ended for the summer had they seen each other; however, they spoke on the phone several times.

"How's the vacation?" Norma greeted Justin with a smile.

"Fantastic. If I could just get out from under this mediation thing."

"What would you do with your time if you didn't have that?" Norma joked.

"You name it. I'd do it."

Justin guided Norma into the living room where she found a seat while he remained standing, waiting for the others to arrive.

Norma settled into a large stuffed chair. "Say, wasn't that just terrible about Randy Wilcox."

"Yes, it was. I didn't have a whole lot of affection for that character. You're right, though. It was a tragic thing to happen."

"What do you suppose he was doing out there?" Norma pursued the subject of Randy Wilcox.

"Who knows?" Justin replied, unwilling to share with Norma, at least at this time, some of the questions he asked himself.

"Maybe it's rather stupid to say," Norma continued philosophically, "but I think it was for the best for everyone."

"I'll buy that," Justin concurred. "He didn't make very many people very happy."

Before they could continue the conversation, Rita and Ruth arrived together, followed by Bob. They exchanged the usual greetings. They also brought up the topic of Randy Wilcox. Neither Rita nor Ruth ever had Randy in class. They were, however, will aware of the problems he created during his years as a student in the Twin Pines schools.

As usual, Shawn arrived late. When he did arrive, he attempted to act natural, as if nothing out of the ordinary had happened. He greeted everyone while contributing nothing to the conversation regarding Randy Wilcox.

Justin waited patiently while the others discussed the Wilcox death then suggested they get to the mediation documents. He made sure his committee members were comfortably seated before he explained what the Bureau of Mediation expected from them, and how they needed to prepare for the first mediation session.

Justin stood so that he could establish eye contact with each member of his committee. "Essentially, we have done all the hard work." He explained. "It's just a matter of getting on paper our justification for our demands and identifying those we refuse to compromise on. Of course, money is one of them. I think you understand that some controls on class size and some means of limiting a teacher's instructional assignment are the real critical issues in our dispute with the board. We have discussed them before. I don't see any need to do so again."

Heads nodded in agreement. Even Shawn Kelly voiced no opposition to what Justin said.

Justin went on, "I don't wish to be presumptuous, but I have written some preliminary justification for our position. What I want to do this morning is give you the chance to read what I have done, suggest revisions, and agree on a final copy.

"Sounds good to me," Norma declared.

"Any other comments?" Justin asked.

For the next two hours the committee poured over what Justin had prepared, stopping here and there to discuss potential weaknesses in their arguments or in the reasons supporting them. Ultimately, they all agreed on the final form of the documents. Ruth would type them that afternoon, making them available for the monthly school board meeting scheduled for that night.

That he faced little opposition from any committee members over what he had written relieved Justin. He really hadn't anticipated much resistance except perhaps from Shawn, who said very little about anything. By twelve thirty, except for the final typing, the committee completed its work.

"I have a few sweet rolls and related goodies which I have saved until now," Justin smiled as he rose and walked toward the kitchen.

"I was wondering when you were going to come through with something," joked Norma. "I'm starved. I ate breakfast at six o'clock this morning."

"Six o'clock," Rita repeated in mild shock. "You're up at six o'clock when you don't have to be?"

"Sometimes. That really is the best time of day."

Justin served the committee the small lunch he prepared. Conversation focused mostly on plans for the remainder of the summer and, of course, the committee's chances in the forthcoming mediation sessions. The name, Randy Wilcox, did not come up again.

Shawn ate his lunch slowly, picking at his food. He listened to the conversation but said virtually nothing. In Justin's mind, Shawn behaved like a new kid on the block, shy, inhibited, and compliant.

Before the committee members left, Justin urged them to attend the board meeting that evening at eight o'clock. A regular school board meeting that would consider agenda items not necessarily related to negotiations, attendance was not mandatory but advisable. After the evening meeting, Justin would deliver to each committee member copies of what they completed that morning. He wished to determine first if the board might entertain some compromise at the last minute. He really didn't expect any. He merely held to some remote chance.

Norma said she would attend. The others expressed a reluctance to commit themselves. Justin didn't expect to see them at the meeting.

Chapter 63

Justin was right. Of his committee, only Norma attended the school board meeting. Justin never blamed anyone for avoiding a school board meeting. He missed only a few over the previous five or six years. With minor exceptions he found them boring and uneventful.

The number of hours school board members could discuss which parking lot to resurface or which roof to repair amused Justin. Ironically, decisions relating to educational policy or school curriculum rarely required more than a few minutes' discussion.

Decisions arrived at this way, typically, were poor decisions. Over the years Justin lived with a few of those official "mistakes." From his point of view, the board's rejection of controls on class size would constitute another mistake. To Justin, mistakes of this kind threatened to erode the quality of the educational program in Twin Pines.

As the meeting began, Connie Shetland sat resplendent at the board table, exhibiting no signs of regret over the recent death of her nephew. Justin hadn't expected Randy's death to overwhelm her with grief; nonetheless, a part of her family had died an apparent violent death. To present herself radiantly attired, Justin considered crass and insensitive.

Several routine items took up nearly an hour in some of that needless discussion that Justin had become used to. Even the board's passing, without discussion and without a dissenting vote, the critical resolution to submit to mediation failed to alarm him. Though this action was a formality since the board by law had little choice, Justin expected some discussion of unresolved bargaining issues. None happened.

Since this was the board's annual meeting, committee assignments, elections of officers, and other organizational matters dominated the discussion. The board formally inducted two new members. Justin knew neither. One, Charles Langley, a local contractor and the other, Mitchell Johnson, a farm implement dealer, ran unopposed for the two positions on the board vacated by the retiring Harold Baylor and Richard Drews, who simply chose not to seek reelection. Justin did not regret the departure of Harold Baylor.

The election of officers concluded the board's agenda for the night. This agenda item intrigued Justin. A favorite for the position of chairperson, Connie lost face in her futile attempt to reach a conclusion to negotiations by convincing fellow board members that money could buy off the teachers. That she still wanted the position was no secret to Justin or to anyone else connected with the board. How the new members would vote remained speculation. That speculation injected some excitement into an otherwise dull meeting.

Justin waited with growing interest as the board turned its attention to the election of its officers. The anticipation that the election may have generated lasted only briefly. When retiring chairman Baylor opened nominations for the position of chair, he received only one nomination. Connie Shetland was elected new board chair by an unanimous vote.

Justin shifted uneasily in his seat as Baylor called the vote and announced the decision. Her ambitions and her manipulative power made Justin apprehensive about future relations between the board and the teachers. What one person could do was limited. However, that one person choosing to ignore both ethics and law could make the months ahead difficult. That Connie would choose to function this way remained conjecture. From experience, Justin believed for Connie Shetland the ends justified the means.

Chapter 64

Justin sat before the television in his living room while the late movie dragged on. More occupied with other matters, he stared at the TV, oblivious to what played there. What happened at the board meeting was no surprise, unfortunate perhaps, but no surprise. He didn't linger after the meeting, as frequently happened, to engage in casual conversation with colleagues, acquaintances, or even board members. He thanked Norma for taking the time to attend and went directly home.

No matter what the agenda, board meetings invariably produced an unsettling effect on Justin. Though he was tired and it was after eleven o'clock, he just didn't feel like going to bed. The repercussions of Connie Shetland's securing the board chair bothered him. He perceived some of her activities as less than honorable or well-intentioned. Whatever happened, Connie sitting as the board's chair would not make any easier his job as leader of the teachers' negotiating team.

Justin's thoughts wandered freely over the contract and over previous conversations with Connie Shetland. He chuckled to himself, remembering when he first met her. He recalled her beauty and her confidence, almost arrogance. What warmth she had exuded then, several months ago, as she expressed her extreme pleasure at meeting him. How easily we can be deceived, Justin thought to himself.

Justin had drifted into a slight sleep when the doorbell rang. Startled by the sound, he sat up and looked at his watch.

It was after midnight. The doorbell sounded again. This time he jumped up and walked to the front door. When he opened it, Connie Shetland smiled, saying, "Good evening, Justin. I hope I'm not intruding."

Justin didn't know what to say. He fumbled for some reply, coming up with only, "No, you aren't"

"Sorry for this late visit. You left the meeting tonight so quickly I didn't have a chance to talk to you there."

Justin moved to one side of the door. "Come in. Have a seat." He closed the door and gestured for Connie to sit on the sofa.

"Thank you," Connie replied in her most gracious tone of voice.

Justin remained standing, perplexed by Connie's presence in his house at such an odd hour. He then sat across the living room from her so they looked directly at one another. Connie smiled with her patented charm.

She leaned forward with eyes fixed on Justin. "I think there are matters we should discuss."

"Such as what?" Justin prepared himself for a renewal of her private bargaining.

Clasping her hands on her lap, Connie spoke slowly and precisely. "I'll get right to the point. I would like to avoid the tedium of mediation sessions if possible. I'm really not convinced they will help us that much anyway."

Justin's body tensed. He rubbed his hands nervously on the upholstered arms of his chair. He felt cornered. She knew as well as he that state statutes precluded the type of discussion she was leading to. At the Pine Inn, he previously faced this situation. That he wanted no part of it he made abundantly clear then. "I don't want to either," Justin agreed. "But, Mrs. Shetland, as I told you before, these are matters not to be discussed in dark corners between you and me."

"Mr. Starling, I know what the laws say. I also know the laws are not intended to inhibit progress toward a settlement. Look, we're not Minneapolis or Duluth or one of those big suburban schools. We're just little, old, Twin Pines. What we can do to hasten this process of negotiations, which, as I see it, has gone on far too long already, would not be objectionable to anyone on my side."

Justin refused to be coerced by the simple logic Connie employed.

Not deterred by his failure to respond, Connie went on, "Why don't you relinquish some of your class size demands, and I still think we can reach a settlement that will appeal to your membership,"

The anger he felt weeks ago at the Pine Inn threatened to return. Justin resented her attempts to buy him off. The resentment echoed in this response. "I can't do that. I don't want to do that. The people I represent don't want to do that."

"Are you sure about that, Mr. Starling?" Connie sat rigid on the sofa, her mood changed. No longer gracious and soft spoken, she persisted, "Are you sure your people want to risk the entire contract for issues which really are administrative prerogatives anyway?"

"They did before."

As if plotting her next maneuver, she studied Justin carefully. "You undoubtedly heard about Randy's death over the weekend." Connie began again.

Surprised by the abrupt change in the conversation, Justin sympathized, "Yes, I did. I'm sorry."

"Thank you, but you needn't be. He was not a very successful human being," Connie replied bitterly. She moved closer to the edge of the sofa. "Did you know that what probably killed him was not the car accident but a bullet wound in the lung?"

"A bullet wound!" Justin repeated in alarm.

Yes, a bullet wound. The doctor at the hospital explained to me that conceivably Randy was dead or nearly so before the accident happened."

"That's horrible." Justin recalled his conversation with Bob Turner. He resisted the temptation to convey to Connie what Bob told him. She was not the person to confide in. He wanted some escape from this conversation. "Again, I'm sorry, but what does that have to do with me or with negotiations?"

"I thought maybe you could tell me something about that?"

"Me?" Justin asked in consternation.

"Let's stop kidding around." Connie rose up with hands gripping her knees. "Like you, there are things I want. I don't like to be frustrated in my attempts to get what I want. You have done a good job of doing that, and I don't like it." While she spoke, her face reddened and her eyes glowed with intensity. "I want this contract settled now. I don't particularly want to go to mediation to do it." She left no doubt that she meant what she said.

Justin sat unsure of what to expect next. He prompted Connie to outline her wishes. "Exactly what do you want?" he demanded.

"I want a settlement. If I don't get it, someone's going to suffer."

"Who's going to suffer?" Justin asked with derision.

"Some of your committee members are involved in some suspicious activities, Mr. Starling. Without a settlement these people are going to pay the price." She sat back and crossed her arms over her chest.

"I don't know what the hell you're talking about." Justin breathed deeply. "If you think you're going to bribe me into giving in to your demands, you're nuts." Justin exploded, jumping from his chair and confronting Connie sitting on the sofa. "If you have information about me or anyone else on my committee, you tell any God damned person you want to. We've nothing to hide."

"You sure about that?" Connie sneered.

"Damn it! If you have something to say, say it."

Connie stood as if ready to defend herself. "Maybe you'd better check on what Shawn Kelly does in his spare time. I think he's into the drug business."

Stunned by her accusation, Justin stepped back. "I don't know where in the hell you got that information, but you damned well better have something to back it up. That you think he's into drugs is not good enough, even for you, Mrs. Shetland."

Unfortunately, Connie did not possess the evidence she wished she did. She was certain that Randy knew something about Shawn. The hundred fifty dollars was sufficient stimulation for him to move in on Shawn as quickly as possible. However, she did not have nor did she know how to acquire information about Shawn's activities. Still, she had planted the seeds of suspicion.

"Don't worry. I will," Connie said with lofty confidence. "Furthermore, Mr. Starling, if I were you, I'd be a little more careful about my conduct with young female students."

Justin's mouth dropped open. He stood speechless. The note was more than a prank. He stared at Connie, overwhelmed. Words then came, "My God, are you crazy?" he shouted. "You can't be serious."

A sinister smile curled Connie's lips. "I could make life very uncomfortable for you, Mr. Starling. Negotiator and experienced teacher involved with his students in an unprofessional way would make good gossip in Twin Pines, wouldn't it?" she threatened.

His boss and a respected member of the community mattered little to Justin anymore. "You do whatever you wish. I've nothing to hide. Nothing you say will even tempt me to change my mind on anything. Now, please get out of here."

Connie stood defiant with hands on hips. "You'll regret this Mr. Starling," she snarled. "We'll see who comes out on top. You've rejected the chance I've given you to avoid some embarrassment. Now the consequences are your responsibility."

Justin walked to the front door, opened it, and stood aside, waiting for Connie to leave.

CHAPTER 65

Justin trembled with anger and disgust as he stood before the door he just slammed behind Connie Shetland. He breathed deeply, controlling the compulsion to push his fist through the door. He turned and walked to the kitchen. Waiting for the rage within him to subside, he leaned against the counter. He reached for a glass, filled it with water, and drank it all without stopping. Feeling some calm returning, he reentered the living room. As before he sat down in front of the television, the screen now black.

The claims, the accusations, and the threats Connie made tumbled through Justin's mind. What about Shawn? Was he really engaged in narcotics? Would he really do something like that? Justin put his head in his hands and pressed his temples. Some of Shawn's unusual behavior, his apology, his reticence at recent committee meetings, surfaced. Though Shawn had his faults, Justin refused to believe that he would entangle himself in a world of crime and violence. Justin shook his head in disbelief. And now Randy's death.

Justin exhaled deeply, running his fingers through his hair. He rubbed his eyes. What about Kitty Wilder? More rationally, he considered the note attached to his car in the high school parking lot. Connie Shetland had no way of knowing about that unless she somehow shared involvement. What about Randy's vicious attack? Could Connie have been complicit in

Duane A. Eide

that too? From Justin's perspective, she was capable of doing almost anything.

The question that troubled him as much as any was what would he do? He couldn't permit her to get away with bribery, with threats to his integrity, the integrity of the committee, and the integrity of the teachers in the district.

To Justin, the solution to most problems required getting to the source. Shawn Kelly, very likely, was that source for the present problem. He had to talk with Shawn. How Shawn would respond he didn't know. He could think of no other way to uncover the truth. Justin lay back in the chair, sighed, and began planning his approach to Shawn Kelly.

In the morning Justin awakened with resolve and determination. Gone were some of last night's misgivings. Connie Shetland's abuse of her position and complete disregard for any code of ethics still disturbed him. He would have to ignore that in his search for the truth, ending the violence and confusion that promised to disrupt the entire community.

As he dialed Shawn's number, Justin still harbored doubts about how he would introduce the topic of drugs. The phone rang in his ear. Deep down he almost hoped no one would answer.

After four or five rings a surprisingly weak, hallow voice answered, "Hello."

"Shawn?"

"Yes."

"This is Justin."

Shawn emitted a barely audible sigh. With more assurance, he said, "Good morning. What can I do for you?"

"Well," Justin hesitated, selecting his words carefully, "there are just a couple things we need to talk about. If you intend to be home later this morning, I could perhaps stop over." He waited for Shawn's reply.

"Anything the matter?" Shawn's voice sounded apprehensive.

Of course, there was something the matter, something drastically the matter, but Justin wished to avoid conveying any sense of urgency. "I don't think so. I just would like to talk with you if you don't mind." In the silence that followed, Justin detected reluctance. Since he simply had to talk with Shawn, he pushed a little harder. "Look, Shawn, it'll take only a few minutes. How about if I stop by in about an hour?"

"Sure, in about an hour," Shawn agreed.

"Fine. See you then." Justin replaced the receiver, his fingers lingering on the phone. The difficult part awaited him at Shawn's apartment. He slumped. His sense of urgency reinforced his determination.

Justin had visited Shawn's apartment once or twice on matters dealing with negotiations. Only minutes from Justin's house, the apartment joined several others in the largest apartment complex in Twin Pines. That gave him a little more time to think about Shawn's reaction to Connie's allegations.

Though they had been together numerous times during negotiations, Shawn was still an enigma, making difficult any predictions of his reaction to what Justin would say. At times, Shawn displayed forcefulness and impatience. At other times, he appeared timid, withdrawn, and scared. Despite his doubts, Justin was committed to doing what he knew he had to do.

CHAPTER 66

Walking up the two flights of stairs leading to the third floor, Justin noted the worn carpet. Though the building wasn't more than three, maybe four years old, already the carpet looked terrible, Justin thought. The walls of the hallway also showed evidence of wear and abuse. Tenants moving in or moving out or simply carrying boxes or groceries obviously exercised little care. Scratches and dents on the walls attested to that.

Justin stood before Shawn's apartment door, breathed deeply, straightened his shoulders, and rang the doorbell. Immediately, the door opened. Shawn, dressed in jogging shorts and a sports T-shirt, greeted him tentatively and asked him to come in.

"Have a seat," Shawn offered. "Can I get you anything? Coffee? Pop? Beer?"

"Nothing, thanks." Justin eased himself into a large chair in the corner of the small living room.

I need some coffee. Excuse me for a second." Shawn disappeared into the kitchen to return balancing a steaming cup of coffee on a saucer. He place the saucer on the end table next to the sofa, then sat down, resting his elbows on his knees and folding his hands in front of him.

In a voice calm and unsuspecting, Shawn asked, "Now, what are these matters you need to discuss with me?"

Justin clasped his hands together then looked up at Shawn. "Last night after the school board meeting I had a visitor."

Shawn sat expressionless, seeming almost uninterested.

"My visitor was Connie Shetland," Justin continued. "She said some things that absolutely shocked me and implied some others that angered me." His voice came smoother and more even. The initial tension of this confrontation with Shawn passed. He now dwelled on his real purpose for being there.

A puzzled look crossed Shawn's face, his brow wrinkled, his eyes slightly squinted. "What does that have to do with me?" He asked, folding his arms across his chest in a more defensive posture.

"I'm not sure. That's why I'm here."

"Well, what did she say?" Shawn insisted.

"For one thing she suggested that you somehow were involved in illegal drugs." Justin found no other way to broach the subject than simply to say it.

For several seconds Shawn sat almost paralyzed. He stared directly at Justin with a look that Justin interpreted as a mixture of fear and anger. Suddenly, a faint smile brightened Shawn's face. He relaxed and leaned forward, saying sarcastically, "You must be kidding."

The panic Shawn experienced over the weekend marked his lowest emotional level. Fear threatened to overcome him for several days even before the last weekend. He clearly could not go on like that. Since then he made a decision. Regardless of the wisdom of the decision, he would have to live with it. Succumbing to fear and panic would not help.

Shawn had desperately tried to get hold of himself, to reclaim some of the old confidence. The other alternative, he determined, was suicide. In the past few days he reached a decision that excluded suicide. He was getting out. In the meantime he refused to permit what had happened to overwhelm him. His response to Justin's question indicated that he was regaining control of himself.

Justin studied Shawn's reaction. He waited for an explosive response, a denial. Surprisingly, Shawn displayed relative calm. "I'm afraid I'm not kidding. This is really nothing to kid about."

"I'll say it isn't. But this is ludicrous," Shawn laughed artificially. "Where in the hell could she have gotten such a wild idea?"

"That's what I'd like to know. She's trying to use it as a lever to force us to concede in our bargaining."

"Holy shit! I can't believe it. Will the son of a bitch do anything to get what she wants?"

"I think she would," Justin concurred.

"I tell you, Justin, it's the biggest God damned lie I've ever heard. Are we going to let her get away with this bullshit?"

"That's why I'm here. I've got to know the truth. I thought this would be the best place to start."

Shawn got up and walked aimlessly around the living room. He turned and threw up his hands in frustration. "I can't believe it! Out of the fucking air she accuses me of dealing in drugs."

"What do you know about Randy Wilcox?" Justin asked bluntly.

Shawn wheeled to face Justin. "I know he was killed Friday night," he blurted out.

"He may have been murdered."

Murdered!"

"Yes, Connie told me he suffered a fatal bullet wound to his chest."

Every muscle in Shawn's body tightened. The noise by the road, the shots he fired again rang in his ears. Could he have shot blindly at Randy Wilcox? The thought burned in Shawn's mind. Murder he never contemplated. His color faded and his mouth opened as if he wanted to say something. Nothing came.

"I don't know any details, but apparently police will investigate," Justin advised.

The situation forced Shawn to say something. He just couldn't stand there, dumb and unspeaking. With feigned indignation he bellowed, "Don't tell me she accused me of that too!"

Justin quickly waved his hands in denial and said, "No, no. She only discussed the accident and what the doctor told her."

Sensing Shawn's increasing agitation, Justin elected to drop the subject of Randy Wilcox. Instead, he slowly got up from the chair and stood facing Shawn. "I don't know what the next move is, but I don't intend to let it drop. I appreciate the chance to talk with you. I don't trust Connie Shetland any more than you do, but we have to get to the bottom of this before she destroys everything and everyone connected with this school."

Shawn remained, unmoving, in the center of the room as Justin walked to the door.

"Thanks again. I'll be in touch."

"Sure. Let me know anything else you hear," Shawn requested mechanically as he closed the door.

Justin move quickly through the hall, down the stairs, and out to his car in the apartment complex parking lot. Certainly, Shawn was innocent of Connie's blatant allegations, but why would she have fabricated such a total lie? Shawn's mysterious behavior at the cabin and at recent committee meetings hovered over him. He refused to believe that a teacher could possibly resort to anything as devastating as drugs, but then teachers were only human. Though Shawn's reaction to the accusations seemed sincere and natural, Justin reminded himself that he lacked the qualifications to assess that.

Still something deep in Justin's mind refused to accept Shawn's vehement rejection of the alleged drug activities. Only his own investigation would allay his misgivings. The whole mess began, at least as far as Justin was concerned, at

Bob Turner's cabin near Beaver Creek, as good a starting point as any.

Justin started his car, relieved that though he failed to uncover any answers, the confrontation with Shawn was over for now. In the afternoon he would drive to Beaver Creek.

CHAPTER 67

Driving out of Twin Pines, Justin vividly recalled the conditions which resulted in his earlier drive to Bob Turner's cabin. The series of events which preceded and followed that trip dramatically altered his life. It resembled a bad dream he hoped would dissolve. It hadn't dissolved.

On the quiet drive north, Justin remembered wistfully the placid summers of the past: three weeks in New England, a week at Lake Louise, camping in the Boundary Waters area. Even those many summers he spent in hot classrooms at the university in Minneapolis seemed attractive in contrast to what he now experienced. Another short trip away from all this offered a compelling option with increasing appeal.

After the flat land outside of Twin Pines came the gradually thickening forest of pine and oak trees Justin admired a month ago when he first used Bob's cabin. He was amazed at how quickly the landscape changed, as if some prehistoric force pushed rocks and dirt into large hills then suddenly stopped.

Stretching north out of Twin Pines, the road became increasingly marked by curves and small hills. Sooner than the last time, Justin saw the sign indicating Beaver Creek and signaling the long hill descending to the small bridge.

Justin slowed the car, searching for the partially concealed entrance road to the cabin. Locating it, he turned off and stopped a few yards from the highway, just far enough to reduce his car's visibility. He turned off the engine and rolled down the window to enjoy, for a moment, the sounds and smells of the forest. He found himself absorbed in the peacefulness and the tranquility of the area. Ironically, he thought, how could so much violence take place surrounded by such peace and beauty? He slowly got out of the car, stretched, and decided the cabin offered the best place to start his search; for what, he really didn't know.

The walk up to the cabin proved strenuous. When Justin finally arrived, he breathed heavily. Apparently, Bob Turner had mowed the area immediately around the cabin and had attended to the flowers growing in two flower boxes under the huge front window.

Attempting to detect the unusual, he casually walked around the cabin, looking first in one direction then another. He discovered nothing. He stood staring at Beaver Creek, by the cabin a small stream gently spilling its way downhill to the bridge below. Nearby he saw the path he took that horrible night when someone clubbed him over the head. He followed the path downward toward the bridge, with each step he took observing carefully the area around him. Still, he saw nothing that looked the least bit suspicious.

The bridge was now in view. Justin walked toward it, remembering he had been struck from behind near the bridge. The bridge itself was concrete, likely rebuilt recently. It appeared in excellent repair. Only a double-lane bridge, Justin assume examining it would require only a few minutes.

He walked slowly under the bridge, inspecting the concrete beams that served as the foundation for the road above. Except for an occasional bird's nest and an accumulation of cob webs and spiders, he saw nothing out of the ordinary.

He would have to cross the creek to take a look at the other end of the bridge. Directly under the bridge, the creek reached eight to ten feet in width, too wide for him even to attempt a leap across. Retracing is steps along the edge of the creek, he located a spot narrow enough to allow him to cross without getting wet.

Back at the bridge, Justin continued his inspection, again looking carefully at the concrete beams and the end supports. Almost to the other side of the bridge, he looked up. Concealed at the point where a concrete beam rested on the end support was a small container shaped like a rural mail box. He stopped and looked at the box. Some bridge worker left his toolbox behind, Justin speculated. When he reached for the small container, he noticed it was not just an ordinary box. Instead, it appeared much heavier than that and was securely fastened to the bridge support. Attached to one end was a bracket. A heavy duty lock dangled from the bracket.

Justin tried to remove the container from its shelf. It wouldn't budge. He tried the lock. It was secure. Leaning against the concrete end support, he contemplated the purpose of the container. Maybe the highway department placed some monitoring equipment there to determine traffic volume over the bridge. Maybe some nearby cabin owner made some use of the container. Did he dare to dislodge it? What if it were somehow wired to a controlling device located in the nearest highway department headquarters or the nearest police station? That's all he would need.

His curiosity aroused, Justin ignored his better judgement when he walked to his car to find something either to open the container or to dislodge it. He rummaged though the trunk to find only a jack handle. Back at the bridge, he began prying at the container with the jack handle. No sooner had he started when he heard an approaching car. Quickly, he pressed himself tightly against the bridge support, making him nearly invisible from the road above.

The car gone, Justin resumed prying and poking to loosen the container. He failed. Presumably, bolts on the inside held it securely to the concrete. Next, he examined the lock. The bracket did not appear that durable. Placing the jack handle under the bracket, he pushed, lightly at first then harder and harder. The bracket gave. Then with a clang it popped, freeing the small door at the one end of the container. He stepped back to listen for any sounds that might come from inside. Nothing. Still, he had visions of red lights flashing on some emergency board in a police station near by.

Justin laid the jack handle aside and reached up to open the small door. Though the bracket proved fragile, the door itself was solid and heavy. It opened easily, however. He reached up to place his hand gingerly inside. Pushing his hand in farther and farther, he touched nothing but the hard steel of the container. Disappointed, he withdrew his hand, inadvertently wiping it on his trousers.

Again he leaned against the end support of the bridge, even more perplexed by its mystery. He raised his hand to his nose to brush aside a spider. His hand smelled. He looked. Traces of a white powder lay in the creases of his fingers and around his nails. He glanced down at his trousers. There too the white powder gathered where he wiped his hand only moments earlier.

He reached into the container a second time. He moved his hand around inside, searching in each corner and along the edges. This time he scraped together a large pinch of the unfamiliar while powder. He tapped his fingers on the edge of the box, adding to the powder accumulation. From his billfold he extracted his fishing license, always issued in a miniature envelope. Into this envelope he scraped the powder from the edge of the container.

Excited by his discovery, Justin hastily picked up his jack handle and returned to the car. There, he smelled the powder again, concluding it represented a drug of some kind. It had to be. He stared absently into the space in front of his car. He frowned. Resting against his car, he looked at the small envelope he held in his hand.

Some of the violence that occurred near this bridge would possible make sense if the bridge served some drug related purpose. The sudden realization he might have interrupted such a transaction that night of his attack made him shiver.

It could have been worse, he thought. People involved in that kind of thing could fall victim to desperation.

In his mind Justin tried to fit the pieces together. Randy Wilcox was shot. Apparently, his accident occurred only a few miles from the bridge in the direction of Twin Pines. As Justin had earlier, Randy could have come across some drug transaction in progress. Desperate people will do most anything. Perhaps, Randy got in the way of a desperate person.

Justin stopped himself. His imagination ran wild with speculation. Speculation or not, he reminded himself that the drug connection at this bridge was possible and definitely worth investigating. The small envelope of white powder he placed in the glove compartment of his car. The jack handle he returned to the trunk. A car whizzed by on the highway, nothing more than a blur through the thick foliage. He stood thinking of what to do next.

With resolve, he walked back to the highway, thinking if Randy was shot near the bridge, surely some evidence would confirm it. He paced around the upper portions of the bridge and the roadway itself. He retreated passed the cabin entrance road into the shallow ditch beyond. Dense and entangling, the growth in the ditch made walking difficult. He climbed to the inside bank of the ditch, looking carefully at the ground and surrounding trees.

In a few more steps he stood before a large oak tree that literally blocked his way. A brief examination of the tree revealed two recent chips from the bark. Thought he wasn't certain, stray bullets could have caused those chips. To get around the tree, he had to use the ditch or struggle through the underbrush. He took the ditch.

On the other side of the tree, Justin searched the bark and the ground below. Something had obviously trampled the grass and weeds. Embedded in the grass he saw a circular stain, black now but strangely thick. Justin's mind weaved the evidence into a plausible explanation of what must have happened. With conviction he determined that someone was shot at this spot and that the circular stain was blood. That someone who was shot could have been Randy Wilcox. That someone who did the shooting . . . Justin interrupted his reconstruction of the scene. He shook his head in a refusal to believe the picture his imagination created. That someone who did the shooting, his thoughts irresistibly pushed on, could have been Shawn Kelly.

Despite its sobering implications, Justin took pride in his investigative work. Not sure what he would do with the information, definitely he vowed to avoid any premature conclusions. Though he might not possess all the facts, he felt confident the container he discovered under the bridge was in some way connected to drug operations. Precisely how, of course, remained the crucial question. Justin fully intended to find out.

Returning to Twin Pines, Justin still could not accept the possibility that Shawn Kelly was guilty of drug activity as Connie alleged. Things like that just didn't happen in small, remote towns like Twin Pines. But Shawn's recent behavior combined with the evidence uncovered by Justin's investigation offered compelling justification to believe the allegations. If true, that would give credibility to Connie Shetland's claims, including the one against him and his unprofessional conduct with young girls. He shook his head and turned on the radio as he completed his drive back to Twin Pines.

CHAPTER 68

Justin pushed the lawn mower, not particularly aware of the job he did. He regretted more and more the death of Randy Wilcox, not out of compassion but out of a realization that now determining exactly how much Randy and Connie worked together would be much more difficult. That they did conspire to influence the course of negotiations and, worse, to destroy the careers of two teachers he was convinced. How to prove it was another matter.

Turning the corner so that he headed in the direction of his driveway, Justin looked up to see a police car parked there. He stopped the mower and walked across the front yard to the waiting car. When he approached, a young, dark haired policeman in his early to mid thirties emerged from the car to introduce himself as Officer John Shier of the Twin Pines Police Department.

Justin couldn't help notice the officer's immaculate uniform precisely creased. The standard police gun, hand cuffs, and small radio were arranged meticulously around his belt.

They quickly shook hands with Officer Shier getting right to the point.

"Mr. Starling, I'm sorry to intrude on your work, but I do have a few questions I'd like to ask you." The officer's eyes never strayed from Justin's face.

"What kind of questions?"

"Questions about Randy Wilcox." Shier still stood stiffly in front of Justin.

"I'll do my best to tell you what I know," acknowledged Justin, who began to feel uncomfortable with the formality of the man before him.

"You, of course, know that he was killed last Friday night."

"Yes."

Officer Shier positioned his hands on his equipment belt. "I believe you had him as a student, didn't you?"

"Yes, I did. Most of one semester." Justin shifted from one foot to the other.

"What was he like as a student?"

Justin failed to comprehend the purpose of these questions or what difference they made, but he cooperated. He turned slightly and rested his arms against the top of the police car. "He was not a good student. He had the ability, I think, but he stubbornly refused to use it."

"Stubbornly refused? Could you explain that?"

"Well, he had every opportunity for help with his assignments. I even gave him extensions on some of them. It made little difference."

"What kind of assignments?"

"Writing assignments. He was in my writing class." Justin felt a growing irritation with the questions and the arrogance of the officer.

"He was a dropout, wasn't he?" The officer pushed on.

"Yes, he was."

"Did your class have anything to do with that?"

"Mr. Shier, I think you know the answer to that or you wouldn't ask." Justin's irritation increased.

"I want you to tell me."

"Yes, he failed my class, and yes, he did not graduate."

"Do you feel, Mr. Starling, that Randy resented you or held you responsible for his not graduating?"

"I suppose he did."

Shier placed his hands on his hips and expanded his chest. "Did he ever show this resentment in any concrete, specific way?"

Justin was sure that Shier already knew about the parking lot incident. This staid, highly polished officer annoyed him with his deceptive questioning. With increasing reluctance to cooperate, Justin asked, "What do you mean?"

"Was there ever an incident or a direct run in between the two of you?"

Justin shifted his weight against the car. "Look, is this some kind of game? You know damn well there was."

Shier dropped some of his formality. "Mr. Starling, a young man is dead. No, this is not a game. I'm after the truth. Anything you can tell me may help me find that truth. If you won't willingly cooperate, I'll have to ask you to come to the station."

"Okay," Justin relaxed, "there was. In fact there have been two or three such incidents." Justin described his beating in the parking lot. He also related his suspicions about the firecrackers during test day and about what happened when he was on the highway riding his bike.

Shier listened attentively as Justin told of his experiences with Randy. His eyes followed Justin's every move and every gesture. Yet, he said nothing when Justin completed his brief story. He shuffled his feet, placing his hand on his well shaved chin, the image of a man in deep thought. Justin stood patiently waiting for the next question.

"Do you know, Mr. Starling, that Randy Wilcox had been shot?"

"Yes, I know that."

"How did you know that?"

"Mrs. Shetland told me."

"Do you have any idea why anyone would want to kill Randy?"

"I really don't know. He was notoriously incorrigible during most of his school days, though I didn't have any serious discipline problems with him in class."

"Exactly how did you feel about him, Mr. Starling?"

"I just told you. He was incorrigible and indifferent about school." Justin's reply was blunt, reflecting his impatience with Shier's persistence.

Again Shier waited before asking his next question. "Where were you between midnight and five A.M. Saturday?"

Justin pushed himself away from the car and stood erect, facing Shier. Anger boiled inside him; his face turned red. With all the control he could muster, he squared off in front of Shier and spoke directly into his face. "I don't know who you've been talking to, but let me tell you one thing. I don't like being implicated in a murder case. If you have questions to ask me, ask me directly. Don't beat around the bush." Justin breathed hard, wiping away with his hand the saliva that had formed at the corners of his mouth. He stared at Shier; Shier stared back, unflinching.

With contempt in his voice, Justin uttered, "By the way, I was sleeping from eleven Friday night until eight thirty Saturday morning. Now, do you have any more questions? I have a lawn to finish."

More of the formality disappeared from Shier's manner. He realized he had gone far enough. "Don't be offended. We have to check out every possibility. When a murder may have been committed, nothing must be left unchallenged."

With his hands in his pockets, Justin stood silently next to the police car. He said nothing.

"Thank you for your time, Mr. Starling. If you can think of anything else that might shed light on this case, please give us a call."

Justin nodded but said nothing.

After Shier left, Justin felt a little embarrassed by his own display of anger. Nonetheless, he deeply resented the implications of Shier's questions. Restarting his lawn mower, he wondered how long Shier had talked with Connie Shetland.

The cold beer tasted good. Nothing was better than a cold beer after mowing the lawn. Justin raised the can high, letting the beer flow freely down his throat. He lowered the can, wiped the foam from his lips, and walked out the back door. With the beer in his hand, he sat in one of the webbed lawn chairs on the patio he constructed next to the back step. Looking over the lush green lawn pleased him. Freshly mowed, it was, indeed, a lawn to be admired.

Resting on the patio, he wondered how extensively the police investigated the circumstances surrounding Randy's death. The accident site, yes, but had the authorities considered the Beaver Creek Bridge area? He toyed with going to the police with what he discovered there, but he was reluctant to. Having to explain why he even searched the area, which he undoubtedly would be compelled to do, would require revealing his suspicions about Shawn. Right now he was not prepared for that revelation. He would simply continue his own investigation.

His mind carried him beyond the Beaver Creek bridge. Connie remained a serious problem. What she told the police already or what she might tell them, Justin feared. He would have to move quickly in his search for the truth.

His beer can empty, he went to the kitchen for another before returning to his lawn chair. Perhaps Shawn's apartment would tell him something. He considered the risks of being caught in Shawn's apartment without an invitation. It would make him even more vulnerable to police suspicion. He shook his head. What was he getting himself involved in, an involvement that could jeopardize his career as well as that of others.

He slumped lower in his chair, absently studying the clear, blue sky above. He balanced the can of beer on his stomach and closed his eyes, thinking that breaking into an apartment couldn't be that hard.

CHAPTER 69

For over a week, Justin's adamant rejection of her attempt to bargain nourished Connie's contempt for the teachers' group in general and Justin Starling in particular. That they would not accept what she considered a generous board offer infuriated her. Even more antagonizing for Connie was the arrogant presumption inherent in the teachers' rejection, an arrogant presumption that the board would relinquish its authority to determine class size and teacher assignments, an arrogant presumption fostered by Justin Starling.

Connie seethed as she recalled his righteous indignation when confronted with her accusation of Shawn Kelly and of Justin himself. Adding to her anger was her belief that not once but several times Justin thwarted her efforts to facilitate the settlement of the teacher contract.

Frustrated by her indecision, Connie sat alone in the den. Vince would spend the evening at the club's weekly men's night. At least, she'd have time to think, to devise some way to capitalize on what she was absolutely convinced Randy had discovered about Shawn Kelly.

Since Randy's accident and death, the police had made little progress as far as she knew. They knew no more about who shot Randy than they did the night she was called to the hospital to identify Randy's body. Still, she was convinced he was gathering evidence against Kelly when the bullet fatally wounded him. She knew and understood Randy. The chance for real money awakened his determination and his reliability. He worked hard and completed the job quickly. For Randy, two hundred dollars was real money. Furthermore, he could work on his own, be his own boss. That inspired him.

Connie felt certain that after their conversation in Lion's Park, Randy would unselfishly devote himself to finding out whatever he could about Shawn Kelly. Randy, moreover, she believed, would not venture out in the country in the middle of the night for nothing.

Despite her conviction about Randy and the circumstances surrounding his death, she lacked concrete evidence about Kelly's drug trafficking. Obviously, Justin Starling did not intend to accept her offer to reconsider the board's proposal. The futility of her recent late night visit at his house confirmed that. If he would not cooperate, she desperately wanted to expose her suspicions about him as well as those about Shawn.

Still, she wavered. Since her case against them lacked convincing evidence, time for Connie was critical. To bring charges now involved some risk. As she pondered what to do, she envisioned the headlines in the local paper. Conceivably, the story would receive much broader coverage, maybe even national attention. If she were responsible for insisting that justice be served concerning these two men, the publicity would enhance her political career. She couldn't resist the temptation to smile at the thought of what this could mean for her future.

She would submit a resolution to the school board with accusations against both Starling and Kelly. Whatever the risks connected with such a resolution, she would accept. She gave Justin Starling a chance. He rejected it. The resolution must be written.

By twelve thirty in the morning when Vince came home from the club, Connie had completed the resolution outlining the charges against Shawn and Justin and recommending termination for both. What the legal authorities might do to them was not her problem.

As far as Justin was concerned, not much more would likely happen. His transgression, from Connie's perspective, involved a violation of professional ethics. Nonetheless, without his stubborn, uncompromising leadership negotiations would conclude quickly. Shawn Kelly was another case. If all she suspected proved true, he would spend much of the rest of his life in prison.

With satisfaction, Connie reread the resolution, then placed it safely in the bottom file drawer of the desk, the drawer reserved for her special material. Having reached her decision gave her a sense of relief and removed any misgivings. Her course was irrevocably set. As she prepared for bed, she enjoyed a marvelous feeling of accomplishment, of certain victory.

This feeling of excitement and adventure kept Connie awake. Any desire to wait up for her husband played no part. For the past weeks, maybe even months, Connie and Vince really weren't husband and wife. They merely lived in the same house and slept in the same bed. They rarely conversed. When they did, the conversation invariably ended in depressing contention.

Connie considered Vince's addiction to the weekly men's night just another weakness. To her, Vince was slipping toward the pathetic in his inability to control his own life. In the past weeks, he was more moody than ever and more withdrawn. At one time Connie considered Vince's unaggressive nature a sign of quiet strength. Now she resented it, seeing only weakness and an inability to make decisions.

CHAPTER 70

Vince made his way quietly up the stairs and to the bedroom. Men's night at the club no longer offered the escape it once did. It had become a drudgery like everything in his life. Depression shadowed him constantly, leaving him alone and isolated. Though he didn't expect to find Connie awake, his need to talk to her grew stronger each day. Perhaps, he thought, if they made a special effort, they could avoid another verbal battle.

Vince began undressing in the darkness of the bedroom. He developed skill in doing that. At least once a week, his night at the club gave him a chance to practice. Connie stirred in the bed.

"Are you awake?" Vince asked in an apologetic tone.

"I guess so," Connie answered sullenly.

Vince stood in the darkness, uncertain of what to say next. He'd drunk less than usual at the club. The few drinks he had afforded him a degree of courage he otherwise lacked when dealing with his wife.

"Heard any more from the police about Randy?" Vince asked quietly.

"No," came Connie's blunt answer.

"I heard at the club tonight that the police questioned Mr. Starling about the whole thing."

Connie paused in the midst of changing her position in bed. "Is that so unusual?"

"Well, I can't imagine what connection he might have."

Raising herself on one elbow, Connie said, "He was responsible for Randy's not graduating."

"I realize that. But that doesn't make him any kind of suspect in his death, does it?"

"The police must think so."

"What do you think?"

With the completed resolution still fresh in her mind and the excitement over the repercussions of that resolution leading her on, Connie was eager to discuss her plans with someone, even Vince. In a few days the entire town would know anyway. She would call a special board meeting where she would present her resolution. To discuss it with Vince would make little difference.

Connie reached up and switched on the small table lamp positioned next to the bed. Now in his pajamas, Vince looked with surprise as Connie sat up in the bed and leaned back against the headboard.

"Vince," she asserted, "no, I don't think he had anything to do with Randy's death. But he's not as pure and professional as he would like everyone to believe."

"What do you mean by that?" Vince stood before the bed puzzled by Connie's willingness to talk as well as by the meaning of her comment.

"Starling likes the young girls."

"He what?"

"I have evidence that his relationships with some of this students are less than professional."

Vince eased himself into a sitting position at the end of the bed. "What kind of evidence?" His eyes locked onto Connie's face.

"For one thing, I saw him embrace some young girl at the Anders' open house."

"So what does an innocent embrace mean? Do you think he is stupid enough to fool around with a young girl at a party attended by parents, teachers and students?"

"It doesn't matter to me what his intentions were. All I know is that there he was out on the patio with this girl in his arms, kissing her," Connie said with satisfaction in her voice. "I think Mr. Starling has taught his last year in Twin Pines."

"What are you planning on doing?"

"I've already done it," Connie answered with finality.

"Done what?"

"I have scheduled a special board meeting for next Wednesday evening. The sole purpose of that meeting is to present a resolution, which I have prepared, outlining Starling's unprofessional and unacceptable behavior and recommending his termination."

"My God, you're kidding, aren't you?"

"Connie raised her hand in a quieting gesture. "There's more. You may as well know the whole truth. The resolution also names another teacher, Shawn Kelly, who is suspected of trafficking in drugs. Of course, the board will demand his resignation and turn his case over to the police. Something else, which I have chosen to leave out of the resolution but which I strongly suspect, is that Mr. Kelly may be the one, at least in part, responsible for Randy's death."

Vince stared in disbelief at Connie, who sat with her hands neatly folded in her lap, beaming with pride.

"How in the hell did you find out all this?"

"I have ways."

"Do the police know any of this?"

"I doubt it."

"Are you going to tell them?"

"They'll find out after Wednesday's meeting."

Vince sat perplexed. He started to ask another question, then stopped. He hesitated then started again. "Where did you get all this so called evidence?"

"I already told you. I have ways."

"What ways?" Vince sounded more demanding in his questions.

"It doesn't matter. What matters is that two bad influences in our district will be removed. The contract maybe then can be settled, and we can get on with the business of education in this district. Just as important, the action will eliminate a source of the destructive power of drugs."

"And you will bask in glory as the community shares your victory," Vince said bitterly.

"Don't be stupid, Vince. The opportunity is there, and I'm going to take it."

"That's great for you, Connie, but these are serious charges. My God, you're suggesting that this Kelly fellow is guilty of murder! You'd better know what you're doing before you plunge into this."

"Don't worry. I know what I'm doing."

In deep concentration Vince remained seated on the end of the bed, attempting to assimilate what he just heard. Suddenly, he sat more rigid. "Randy," he gasped.

"What did you say?" Connie asked.

Vince ignored her question. Rapidly, several incidents flashed through his mind: the struggle between Randy and Connie in the front entry, the conversation with Randy at the Oaks Bar, the occasional mysterious phone calls.

Vince turned again to face his wife, who slumped more deeply into the bed. "Connie, were you using Randy as a source of information?"

Connie raised herself, supported by her elbows behind her back. She displayed absolutely no alarm at Vince's question. Shaking her head slowly from side to side, she answered calmly, "It doesn't make any difference. Evidence is evidence."

More agitated, Vince countered, "If he was fifty miles out of town in the middle of nowhere at three o'clock in the morning under your direction, you're as responsible for his death as anyone."

"Nonsense!" Connie replied.

"Connie," Vince pleaded, "there are laws against collusion, invasion of privacy and things like that." In frustration Vince threw up his arms. "What about Randy's attack on Starling a few weeks ago? Did you put him up to that too?"

"I'm tired. Good night." Connie switched off the light, slid fully under the sheet, and turned away from Vince.

He sat in the darkness, aware of the futility of continuing the conversation. He walked into the bathroom where he perfunctorily brushed his teeth and took two aspirins. To him, what Connie did was wrong, just plain wrong. She was asking for trouble, serious trouble with her wild accusations and her questionable methods of obtaining information. He could not let her do it.

When he returned to bed, Connie was already sleeping. He rolled and turned restlessly before drifting off into a shallow sleep.

CHAPTER 71

Since Justin's visit, Shawn scarcely left his apartment, desperate in his struggle to figure out what he would do. He confessed to himself that Justin knew more than he admitted. He probably even determined who attacked him near the Beaver Creek Bridge. Shawn was ready to believe most anything. Clearly, his association with Fred Wyman and the rest had to cease. Even more devastating for Shawn was the strong possibility that one of his bullets struck Randy Wilcox.

In the days since that horrible Friday night at the bridge, Shawn suppressed most of his sheer panic. He now tried to control the wild speculations of his own imagination. Realizing that he couldn't function that way, he urged himself to think rationally. The job involved taking risks. He accepted that when he agreed to work for Wyman. Simply, he would now have to face the consequences of that agreement. Panic and fantasy did him little good.

To devise some means of severing ties with Wyman, leaving Twin Pines, and hiding out for a while demanded his immediate attention. Just to leave would make him a marked man. His connection to Randy Wilcox's death posed another problem. Apparently, Justin suspected he might have had some role in that. Regardless, Wyman was his pressing concern. After him, he'd have to deal with Starling.

Normally, the thought of Fred Wyman generated fear for Shawn. For the past few months, despite infrequent contact, he was very apprehensive in Wyman's presence. He wasn't now. He exhibited nascent courage in his refusal to make the last pick up, a midweek one. As a result, he expected Wyman to contact him personally. Naturally, Wyman did. He was coming to Shawn's apartment, a drastic departure from established practice, but Fred insisted.

Determined to level with Fred about everything: Randy, Justin, everything, Shawn made himself believe that Wyman was a reasonable man. Just possibly he would understand. He anticipated Wyman's reaction; at first objection but with an honest appraisal of the circumstances, he would accept Shawn's proposal, a reassignment someplace.

Obviously, he could not stay in Twin Pines as a teacher or as anything else. Fred would concur with that. Shawn intensely wanted to believe he would. Facing the man with the facts seemed to him the only sensible approach, his only chance.

Fred Wyman would arrive at five o'clock. At four forty-five, Shawn paced the floor, gathering strength to face his future.

CHAPTER 72

Though he waited for what seemed like hours, Shawn jumped when the knock at his apartment door finally came. Without delay, he went to the door and with less than honest cordiality invited Fred to please come in.

In his gray, three piece suit, white shirt and dark blue tie, Fred could easily have been mistaken for any business executive. Fred, very deliberately, entered Shawn's apartment, for a moment surveying the small living room and the adjoining kitchen. Shawn requested him to sit down and offered him a drink. Fred accepted the seat but declined the drink.

Tiny beads of perspiration formed on Shawn's upper lip and on his brow. Some of the confidence he felt earlier in the afternoon began to fade. He sat opposite Fred, much as he sat opposite Justin only a few days before. The two men said nothing, Fred staring at Shawn and Shawn trying to avoid the stare. Finally, after several tense seconds Fred broke the silence, "Shawn, tell me what the hell is going on around here."

Shawn groped for the words he rehearsed. They weren't there. He had to say something, but he felt utterly helpless in his inability to express anything. Instead of answering the question, he sat rubbing his hands together childishly.

"If there is a big problem, I want to hear about it." Fred could sense the near paralysis that took hold of Shawn. He softened his tone to help Shawn relax. Under his obvious stress, they would accomplish nothing.

Suddenly Shawn exploded, "I can't do this anymore! I don't want to do this anymore!" All his planning, all his preparations for Fred's reaction vanished. He felt only a compulsion to release the words that churned inside him.

"Don't want to do what?" Fred asked almost as if he and Shawn shared some clinical therapy session.

"I can't make the pick ups at the bridge any more," Shawn's voice cracked. He looked away from Fred.

"Why not, Shawn?"

Starting first with a halting, strained voice that gradually softened, Shawn explained everything about the bridge. He described his encounter with Justin, Justin's recent visit and the nature of their conversation. He told of Randy Wilcox and the possible cause of his death.

When he finished his narration, Shawn wiped his hand, limp and trembling, over his face and neck. Fred smiled benevolently, got up from the sofa and walked toward Shawn. He reached out for Shawn's shoulder, consoling him with a gentle squeeze of his hand.

Then Fred said, 'You've had it real tough the past few weeks. What you need is a break, a change of scenery."

Shawn looked up at Fred with a mixture of gratitude and surprise. A smile beamed across his face. "Yes, that's what I need. I knew you would understand. Get away from here. Go to some place where no one knows me. Then in a short time I could start again but in a new location." The words gushed from Shawn's mouth.

"Sure, Shawn, that sounds good," Fred replied. As he answered, Fred moved away from Shawn, turning his back to him completely.

Shawn remained seated. "I knew you'd understand," Shawn repeated with an innocent smile. "I told myself this afternoon that you'd understand. You're a reasonable man."

"Sure I am," Fred announced with dripping sarcasm. He then turned around, holding in his hand a gun pointed directly at Shawn's head.

Shawn gasped in horror, mesmerized by what was happening. Fred walked slowly toward Shawn, each step taken with meticulous care.

"You're no good, Kelly. You're a coward. Cowards cause problems. I don't need any problems."

As Shawn raised his hand in a pleading gesture, two quick spits from the gun tore off the top of his skull, spattering it on the wall behind him. As his body slammed back into the chair, a third spit ripped through his chest, crushing ribs and passing through his heart. Shawn lay slumped awkwardly in his chair, lifeless eyes gazing into nothingness, blood streaming through what remained of his hair and down around his ears.

Fred calmly replaced the gun in his inside breast pocket, made a rapid survey of where he might have left fingerprints, wiped them off, and, as deliberately as he entered, left Shawn's apartment, closing the door tightly behind him.

CHAPTER 73

Justin awoke early on Saturday morning. His system had yet not adjusted to sleeping later in the morning which summer vacation afforded him. He felt rested, though, and resolved to contact Shawn Kelly once more. He expected to schedule another committee meeting when he could talk further with Shawn. Since he heard nothing from either the state mediation office or from the state union office, he deemed the meeting unnecessary, thus the need to get in touch with Shawn.

A second visit to the Beaver Creek Bridge area revealed nothing new. Nor had Justin heard anything more from Officer Shier. Though Shier's implied accusations regarding Randy's death still disturbed Justin, they served as additional motivation for an energetic pursuit of the truth. Shawn Kelly had something to do with the truth.

Justin shaved and made himself a light breakfast of toast, juice, and coffee. Minor cleaning chores around the house occupied his time until nine o'clock when he considered appropriate calling Shawn. He allowed the phone to ring ten times before hanging up, disappointed in no answer. Some anxiety over what he envisioned as a contentious meeting with Shawn made him restless. Presently, he felt thwarted by having to wait to schedule the meeting.

Until almost noon, Justin called Shawn's apartment repeatedly without success. Fearing that Shawn might have left town only intensified his frustration. He would drive to Shawn's apartment without first talking with him.

As he drove the short distance to the apartment complex where Shawn lived, he rehearsed just how he would try to extract from Shawn information that would answer some of the questions which haunted him. The time for tact and diplomacy had passed. Justin decided he would candidly inform Shawn of the basis for his suspicion: his search of the bridge area, his discoveries there, his misgivings about Shawn's recent behavior, his unexpected appearance at the cabin, Officer Shier, everything. Determined to arrive at the truth, Justin concluded that like it or not Shawn had to listen. Justin was prepared to see that he did. However, he lacked preparation for a refusal by Shawn to confront the issue in a frank and honest discussion. He'd have to deal with that when the time came.

Making his way slowly up the familiar stairs to Shawn's apartment, this time oblivious to the worn, rundown condition of the building, he had a single purpose, to confront Shawn with what he found out. His firm knock on the door produced no response from inside. He knocked again, listening against the door for any sound of movement from inside. Nothing. He tried the door knob. It turned. The door was unlocked. Justin gingerly eased the door open a mere crack, not sure if he should enter. Shawn couldn't be far away, he assumed, if he'd left the door unlocked.

Despite his concern about entering the apartment in Shawn's absence, Justin refused to turn back. He had come this far. He opened the door farther and cautiously asked, "Anybody home?" He paused, waiting for some reply. Again nothing. Pushing the door open wider, he stuck his head into the apartment. His eyes searched the room until they came to rest on Shawn's outstretched body, slumped oddly in the chair behind the open door.

For an instant Justin assumed Shawn slept until his eyes reached his head. Justin froze, aghast at what he saw. The urge to scream gathered in his throat. He couldn't move, transfixed by the morbid sight before him. Shawn's eyes remained wide in a vacant stare, blood and tissue now encrusted in his hair and down the sides of his face, the wall spattered with dried blood and tissue, the odor nauseating.

Justin forced himself to enter the apartment. Attempts to avoid glances at the mutilated head of Shawn Kelly failed. An almost macabre fascination drew his attention. He fought the temptation to look at Shawn and made his way to the phone on the table not six feet away from where his body sprawled, cold and grayish, on the chair. He fumbled with the phone then dialed 911.

Justin waited in the hall outside the door to Shawn's apartment. Limp, he rested against the wall, his mind in a daze. The initial shock of the gruesome sight began to wear off. Still he fought to control the trembling that invaded his body.

In the distance he could hear sirens. Moments later he recognized the face of Officer Shier at the top of the stairs at the end of the hallway. Suddenly, the hall overflowed with people all talking at once, asking questions and speculating about what had happened and when. Aware of the commotion within the apartment, Justin refused to enter again. He watched as the ambulance attendants wheeled the lifeless body, covered with a sheet, out the apartment door and down the stairs. When Officer Shier approached, Justin still stood in the hall.

"Can we talk?" Shier asked glumly.

Justin explained to Shier how he called Shawn's apartment several times. Not wishing at this time to discuss with Shier what he discovered at Beaver Creek bridge, Justin told him that he intended to speak with Shawn about the impending mediation sessions. When he failed to answer, Justin drove to the apartment to discover Shawn's body and dial 911.

A look of dissatisfaction crossed on Shier's face at the scarcity of Justin's knowledge of what happened. Justin had the impression that Shier believed him to know more than he revealed. But Shier didn't pursue the conversation. He cautioned Justin about leaving town and said he would get

265

back to him later. With assurance he was going nowhere but home, Justin turned and walked slowly out of the apartment building to his car, knowing Shier would contact him soon, this time expecting specific answers.

CHAPTER 74

Sitting in his den, Vince shuffled through a small stack of papers on his desk. Stress and depression compelled him to leave the bank to try to work at home. For the two days since Connie told him about her resolution and planned special school board meeting, Vince debated if he should intervene.

Deep inside, he believed that somehow the turmoil that recently disrupted his life soon had to end. It simply couldn't continue. He was convinced of the inevitability of the discovery of his embezzlement at the bank. It was just a matter of time. What that would do to Connie and her grand plans for an elevated, political career he shuddered even to speculate.

What she did with Randy and what she planned to do to Shawn and Justin, he had no doubt, were wrong. If they were guilty or not supplied no justification in Vince's mind for the ruthless methods Connie used to establish a case against them. Vince understood Connie's motives for wanting the credit for exposing them. These motives failed to make her plan right. Enough wrong had been done already. Maybe he could salvage something from the shambles of his life.

Vince reached for the phone before him on the desk. If he was to take action, now was the time. Connie attended another of her country club engagements, leaving him alone in the house. Picking up the receiver, he dialed. He hesitated, replacing the receiver. He fell back in the chair, running his

267

hands over his face in frustration and doubt. With sudden resolve he straightened up, grabbed the phone, and dialed.

"Hello," answered the unfamiliar voice.

"Mr, Starling?" Vince asked weakly.

"Speaking."

"Mr. Starling, this is Vince Shetland."

Justin's hand tightened on the phone. He waited for Vince to continue.

"I don't believe we've ever met," Vince went on haltingly, "but I'm Connie's husband."

"Yes, I know," Justin acknowledged.

Generating more confidence as he spoke, Vince hastened right to the point. "Mr. Starling, I'm aware that you and Connie have had some kind of conflict over the past few months. I don't intend to know nor do I really want to know the details of your differences." Vince paused to clear his throat. "This time I think she's gone too far. I want to alert you to her plans."

Vince waited for some response from Justin. None offered, Vince continued with firmness and conviction. "She maintains that she has evidence that Shawn Kelly is involved in drugs and that you have taken advantage of some of the young girls in your classes."

The information did not shock Justin as Vince suspected it would. Calmly, Justin replied, "I'm not surprised, Mr. Shetland. She's threatened as much to me personally. Why are you telling me this?"

"Never mind about that. There's more. She has scheduled a special board meeting for next Wednesday. At that time she will formally present a resolution to the board charging you both and demanding your immediate resignations."

"So she's finally going to do it," Justin muttered to himself. Then more directly to Vince he asked, "Do you happen to know where she got her so called evidence?"

"She used Randy Wilcox," Vince answered with finality.

"That doesn't surprise me either, Mr. Shetland. I suspected as much. It also clears up a few things that have bothered me for some time."

"Mr. Starling, I don't have to remind you of the confidentiality of this conversation. I have done what I thought was right. Please leave my name out of anything you might do about what I've told you."

The whole situation was strange, husband betraying wife. Justin had nothing to gain by implicating Vince in anything. His battle was and would be with Connie. "I will not deliberately involve you in any way, Mr. Shetland. I don't know why you have told me these things, but I thank you and admire you for doing it."

"Good bye, Mr. Starling."

Vince replaced the phone gently. Finding a tissue in his pocket, he wiped the perspiration from his face and forehead. Relief washed through his body as did the assurance that what he did was the right thing to do. If Connie ever found out about the call, she would explode in fury. Right now Vince didn't really care. He didn't really care about very much at all.

CHAPTER 75

News travels fast in small towns. By late afternoon Justin received numerous calls besides the one from Vince Shetland. Norma, Rita, and other committee members called in virtual shock over the violent death of Shawn Kelly. Other staff as well as administrators phoned their dismay, astonished by the nature of Shawn's death. By seven o'clock in the evening, Justin sat by his phone, physically and mentally exhausted. When Norma Metcalf called back with an invitation to dinner at her house, he gladly accepted.

Norma lived about as far from Justin as one could and still live in the city limits of Twin Pines. Nonetheless, in no more than a few minutes, Justin drove the distance between his house and hers, a two story colonial where she, her husband, and family lived for nearly eighteen years. As one would expect, the house was immaculate both inside and out. Driving into the driveway, Justin noted, particularly, the exactness and precision with which the shrubs and small hedge were trimmed. The lush, green lawn, too, cut and edged neatly, sloped gently away from the house on three sides.

Norma greeted Justin at the door with, "Been a terrible day, I'll bet."

Slowly shaking his head from side to side, Justin concurred, "God, I guess so."

Norma led Justin into the family room where her husband sat engrossed in the evening paper's cross word puzzle. Justin knew Bill Metcalf from occasional meetings but not well. They exchanged greetings. Naturally, they plunged into a discussion of Shawn Kelly's death. Restricting his conversation only to what happened that day, Justin was not ready to reveal anything of his investigative activities of the past several days. He, of course, had absolutely no idea who killed Shawn nor did he wish to discuss the possible motive. However, in his own mind he knew that the motive had some connection with the shadowy world of drugs.

Recognizing Justin's reluctance to discuss the tragedy any further, Norma offered him a drink which he gratefully accepted. They talked of summer vacation, the mediation sessions yet to come, school in the fall, a conversation that generated very little interest. Shawn's death occupied their minds. All other topics just faded into insignificance.

The dinner was superb as Justin expected. A home economics teacher, Norma obviously practiced what she taught. She prepared the most delicious rolled roast Justin had ever eaten. That combined with over browned potatoes, scalloped corn, tossed salad, and rolls lured Justin into eating far more than he should have.

After dinner, the three of them gathered in the small screened porch off the dining room, the evening warm, clear, and bright. A gentle breeze filtered through the porch. The conversation unavoidably reverted to Shawn Kelly. Justin had yet to discuss with any one his discoveries at the Beaver Creek bridge. That plus the horrendous impact of seeing Shawn's body stretched out on the chair turned endlessly in Justin's mind. He decided he needed someone to talk to. Keeping it all to himself created more of a burden than he could handle.

To Norma and Bill, Justin told all, everything that happened to him that spring and summer: his suspicions, his investigations, and his confrontations with Connie Shetland. Norma, of course, knew of some of what happened to Justin. With astonishment she heard the full story as Justin pieced it together.

"My Lord," she uttered in disbelief, "if Shawn were really involved in drugs, how could he possible justify his job as a teacher?"

"What could possibly entice a man to deal in drugs at all?" Bill wondered aloud.

For well over two hours, they discussed the situation and what Justin intended to do about what he knew. For sure, he would eventually go to the police. First he needed to clarify a few things with Connie Shetland. This, Justin affirmed to the Metcalfs, was what he planned to do next. He now had weapons, thanks to Vince, to combat her threats and her resolution.

A little after midnight, Justin thanked the Metcalfs for their hospitality, including their attentive listening, got into his car and drove the short distance back to his house. He felt completely exhausted after one of the more traumatic days in his life. To his gratification, the chance to talk with the Metcalfs released some of the weight of all he carried around inside. The thought of his soft, cool bed was the most attractive thought he'd had in days.

Justin parked his car in the garage and casually strolled out onto the driveway to absorb the freshness of the midnight air. The nearly full moon, halfway up the western sky, shined through the large pine tree in front of his house, casting gently moving shadows across the driveway and adjacent lawn. He breathed deeply, exhaling in an audible sigh that reflected modest contentment.

Returning to the garage, he closed the overhead door and unlocked the one which opened into the kitchen dining areas. He closed the door behind him and turned. At that instant, a flash appeared from the other side of the room. Almost simultaneously Justin was hurled backward against the door by a driving, burning sensation in this left shoulder. Another flash appeared. The sound of splintering wood and shattered glass filled the dark room. Dazed, Justin fell to the floor, a searing pain in his shoulder.

He squirmed on his stomach to the dining room table, each movement of his left arm sending excruciating pain through the entire left side of his body. He lay beneath the table, trying to control his breathing, bewildered by what was happening.

He listened, hearing movement then complete silence. Another flash, a whiz and inches from his face a table leg splintered. He rolled again onto his stomach, frantically crawling toward the living room. A spitting sound broke the silence. Instantly, the side of his head burned. He struggled to clear his head. As he slipped toward unconsciousness, two thunderous bangs resounded in his ears. Then an overwhelming stillness, then nothing.

CHAPTER 76

Spinning, spinning, caught in some monstrous whirl of light and dark, Justin groped with his hands for something to hang on to. Pain shot through his shoulder; his head throbbed. Slowly, he began to gain an awareness of a bed and of more pain whenever he moved. He opened his eyes to disorientation. Nothing looked familiar. Visions of the kitchen, the flashes of light, the splintered wood raced through his mind. He remembered the shock of pain ripping through his shoulder, then his head. He blinked his eyes, surveying where he was. A young woman entered the room and approached his bed.

Softly, she asked, "How are you feeling?"

Justin studied her, reaching for recognition. Then in a halting, tiny voice answered, "I'm not sure. What happened?"

The nurse checked his vital statistics as displayed on the bed side monitor. While doing so, she explained, "Someone took a few shots at you last night." With a smile she explained, "Luckily whoever it was couldn't shoot very well. The emergency room staff was able to treat your wounds quickly. Fortunately, they were superficial. Later this morning a doctor will come in to explain the details of what happened here at the hospital."

Justin's eyes followed the nurse while she performed her duties of making sure he rested comfortably. "Do you know who it was?" he asked.

"I don't know, but an Officer Shier asked to talk with you as soon as you feel up to it. You will be here a few days to make sure your shoulder and head are healing properly. Right now you need rest." The nurse inspected the bandages covering Justin's head and shoulder before gently repositioning his pillow and adjusting his blanket. She turned to leave then paused to ask, "Anything I can get you?"

"Maybe something for this throb in my head."

"I'll see what I can do." She departed with a pleasant smile.

Justin closed his eyes. The throbbing in his head subsided a little. In this struggle to recall what happened, he could go only to his vague recollection of two loud explosions, probably gun shots. Beyond that he could remember nothing. The nurse returned holding a tiny cup containing two tablets. She poured a glass of water before assisting Justin in taking the pain pills.

"These should help," she smiled. "Now try to relax. I'll be back later. If you need anything, press the red button next to the bed." She pointed. She left with another friendly smile.

Alone, Justin stared blankly into the corner of the hospital room, a private room with just one bed, a small table, a closet, a bath room, and one chair. Who could possibly have wanted to shoot him? Considering the extraordinary events of the passed few weeks made almost anything possible. But getting shot? That approached the unbelievable.

So much of what happened during the recent weeks involved in one way or another Connie Shetland. Certainly, he didn't suspect her of running around town shooting her adversaries. However, Justin sighed, could she have some connection to this latest incident? He no longer would wait for her to come to him. This time he would seek her out. Waiting for the scheduled special, board meeting would waste valuable time. If he had no other option, he would have to persuade the hospital staff to release him before the Wednesday night meeting.

The pills he took did help. Gradually, he closed his eyes and drifted off in a deep sleep. When he awoke two hours later, the nurse stood beside his bed.

"You feel better?" she asked.

He muttered a nearly distinguishable, "Don't know."

Checking his vital signs, the nurse said, "Mr. Shier returned to inquire about your condition. The doctor said if you wished to talk to him, he had no objections."

Groggy from both the short sleep as well as the pain pills, Justin looked at the nurse. He gently nodded his head. "If that's what he wants, okay, I guess."

"I'll tell him."

In only minutes, John Shier walked through the hospital room door. He moved deliberately to stand by Justin's bed. "You able to talk now?" he asked without a hint of sympathy, all business.

His voice barely above a whisper, Justin answered, "You don't waste time, do you."

Justin didn't know how long he slept, but he felt better. A dull sensation lingered in his head. His shoulder hurt only when he moved the wrong way.

"We're not playing games here, Mr. Starling." Shier pushed on seemingly oblivious to Justin's condition. "We have one murder on our hands, possibly another, and now we have an attempted murder. I want to know where you fit into all this." He stepped back from the bed, placing his hands on his hips in a commanding gesture.

Justin looked up at Shier, pain distorting his face. "I wish I knew."

Shier now moved to the end of the bed placing his hands flat upon the bed's edge. He leaned closer. "Do you know a Fred Wyman?"

Justin thought for a moment, the effects of the medication slowing his response. He looked at Shier standing at the end of the bed. "No, I don't think so. Why?"

"He's the one who tried to kill you last night." Shier was abrupt and firm.

Justin wrinkled his brow in perplexity. "I've never heard of any Fred Wyman. How do you know he's the guy?"

"Because I shot him last night in your kitchen. He died this morning on the operating table.

In consternation, Justin uttered, "You shot him!" with as much force as his weakened condition allowed.

Shier relaxed, dropping his arms to his sides, "Yes, I shot him. After what happened to this Kelly fellow, I thought maybe you might bear some watching."

"You mean you tailed me yesterday?" Justin tried to raise himself, but the pain in his shoulder prevented it.

"Yes, I did. A good thing too, or you might not be talking to me now."

"I guess I should thank you for that." Justin swallowed then grimaced trying to shift his position in bed. "Who the hell is Fred Wyman?"

"From what I can gather," Shier moved to the only chair in the room and sat down. "he's some big wheel in the drug market out of the Twin Cities. Unusual that he would be doing the dirty work, but the bullets found in your house matched those we found in Kelly's apartment. In other word, they came from the same gun, the one I took from Wyman last night in your kitchen."

"I was right; I was right," Justin repeated, gingerly moving his head up and down.

Shier stood up. "Right about what?"

Justin locked eyes with Shier. "Right about your involving me in the drug game. Is that what you have in mind?"

Shier stiffened but said nothing. His hands returned to his hips.

In a voice with renewed strength, Justin explained, "I've done a little investigating myself into that game."

"What did you find out?" Shier moved to the side of the bed.

Justin slowly, with frequent pauses, outlined for Shier all the events which led him to suspect Shawn of some type of illicit drug activity. He explained that Shawn probably realized that he was on to him. He also explained the probable connection between Shawn and Randy's death. Unprepared to discuss with Shier what he suspected was her role in the whole affair, he avoided any mention of Connie Shetland as the force behind Randy.

"Why didn't you come forward with this information before?" Impatience echoed in Shier's voice.

"Because I just wasn't sure. I didn't want to start throwing wild accusations around. I would have informed the officials eventually."

A much more relaxed atmosphere pervaded the hospital room. Shier leaned against the bed, careful not to disturb Justin. "Taking the law into your own hands is dangerous business. It almost got you killed."

"I know. Thank you for saving my life."

"You're welcome. It's part of the job." Shier smiled for the first time, shoving his hands, self-consciously, into the pockets of his trousers. "Just a reminder. When you get out of here, we will need a full statement from you, including all of what you've told me today."

Shier turned toward the door. Before leaving, he looked over his shoulder, "You know, Mr. Starling, before our conversation I would have bet that both you and Kelly were involved with Wyman."

"And now?" Justin asked.

"Now I'd bet you weren't"

"That's very generous of you, officer. What changed your mind?"

"Nobody could make up a story like that and tell it with such conviction. I'll be in touch." With that he disappeared through the open door.

CHAPTER 77

By Tuesday, that the hospital would not release him by Wednesday became apparent to Justin. Therefore, he would be unable to meet with Connie prior to her special board meeting unless she came to the hospital. After what happened over the weekend, Connie's case would certainly collapse. What more could she do to Shawn Kelly?

Determined to settle the score with her, Justin intended to entangle her in her own intrigue. Though no lawyer, he believed common sense exposed the treachery of Connie's behavior which included collusion, bribery, invasion of privacy, manipulation and distortion of the facts. Her position in the community did not entitle her to use people and destroy them with impunity. If she would not come to the hospital, Justin would devise some other means of meeting with her. He did assume, however, that under the circumstances, she would agree to meeting him in his hospital room.

After several futile attempts to reach her at home, Justin finally succeeded at about three in the afternoon. Connie spoke cordially and solicitously about the unfortunate incident, as she described it, at his house. Justin avoided any mention of Shawn Kelly or of the special board meeting. He simply suggested they meet soon. Vague about a specific purpose, he indicated they should discuss problems of mutual concern. Connie agreed to meet him in his room at ten thirty Wednesday morning.

Justin's wounds healed rapidly. He experienced periodic throbbing in his head, but even that had improved. A soreness remained in his shoulder which didn't significantly restrict the use of his left arm. He just exercised care in the movement of that arm. Apparently, the hospital would release him on Friday, assuming no complications. The prospect of going home grew increasingly attractive to Justin with each day he spent in the hospital.

Despite the sensitive care and attention he received, Justin suffered from the hospital routine along with the boredom. The absence of freedom to walk around, to get up, to lie down, to eat when he wanted or not eat when he wanted became the major problem he faced.

At one time, half dozing in his bed, he lapsed into a semi dream in which he found himself in prison. He awoke abruptly, amazed at the many parallels between life in a prison and life in a hospital even though he'd never spent time in prison and hardly any in a hospital. In fairness, he also noted some of the differences, particularly the one of greatest importance; he was not sentenced to the hospital.

As he lay waiting for Connie Shetland's arrival, Justin puzzled over why he compared hospitals and prisons. He attempted no further analysis of his psychological behavior, content with the simple explanation that the mind does strange things.

As usual the hospital staff awakened him at six o'clock for breakfast. They assisted him in bathing after which for nearly half an hour he strolled slowly and by himself through the corridor outside his room. Since then he tried to read the morning paper. He grew weary of reading about himself and the wild shoot out, as the paper described his nightmare. A book obtained from the hospital library also offered little appeal.

At precisely ten thirty-five, the door to his room opened slowly. A soft, gentle voice requested, "May I come in?"

"Sure," Justin responded firmly.

CHAPTER 78

Connie was dressed tastefully. Justin couldn't remember ever seeing her dressed any other way. She wore a lightweight, summer suit, light blue in color which contrasted beautifully with her flowing black hair and distinctive tan. Looking delightfully fresh and animated, she displayed no signs of worry.

"How are you feeling?" You look great," she announced as she entered the room and seated herself in the one chair.

"Oh, I'm fine, I guess. A little sore here and there but fine," Justin assured her.

"I just can't believe this could happen in Twin Pines."

"Believe me. It does."

"I don't believe I've seen you since the brutal killing of Shawn Kelly. I do wish to tell you how sorry I am over what happened."

Justin suddenly became very serious and looked directly at Connie, "Are you really sorry about anything that has happened?"

Connie sat rigid; her face tightened, and her eyes narrowed. She clasped her hands in her lap. She answered, "I don't know what you're talking about."

Justin raised himself up with a grimace. "Mrs. Shetland, let's not try to fool anybody. I didn't ask you here for a social visit. Some horrible things have happened in the past few weeks. Only recently have I begun to understand some of them. I think you can confirm my understanding.

"What do you mean?" Connie asked in a tone of disdain.

"For what purpose have you scheduled a special, board meeting for tonight?"

"The agenda is posted in the district office."

"That hardly does me any good. You tell me what the agenda includes."

Connie shifted uncomfortably in her chair. "Routine district business," Connie uttered.

"Come, Mrs. Shetland, be honest! You don't call special, school board meetings to consider routine district business. Don't you think it's about time you leveled with me and with yourself?"

Irritated, Connie stood up and faced Justin. "You asked me here to discuss mutual problems or some such thing. Now, I'm a busy woman. Get to the point, or I'm afraid I'll have to leave."

Justin took a deep breath and released it slowly. "What's in the resolution that you intend to present to the board tonight?"

Connie flushed with anger. She spit back the words, "What do you know about any resolution?"

Calm and determined, Justin replied, "I know that you have prepared one that recommends termination for Shawn Kelly and me."

Connie's face turned white. Her eyes burned with contempt, with hatred. "Who told you about any resolution? She asked almost breathless.

"It doesn't matter now who told me or if anybody told me. Nor does it matter what the hell is in the resolution. There is not much you can tell the police about Shawn Kelly that they don't already know. You can't do much more harm to a dead man.

"As for me, your allegations that I have been involved in unprofessional and intimate relationships with my students is a blatant lie, and you know it. So what you intended to accomplish with your resolution has been reduced to absolutely nothing, except making you the laughing stock of the community."

Connie stood, rigid, pale, and filled with suppressed rage. "Mr. Starling, that's your opinion. I have witnesses."

"All the witnesses in the world wouldn't make it less a lie." Justin raised himself up so he sat nearly upright in the bed, on about the same level as Connie. "Besides," he continued, "I don't think you want too many people to know that you paid Randy Wilcox to do your dirty work for you."

Connie leaned closer to the bed and screamed in Justin's face, "What are you talking about!"

Into her face Justin replied, "You know what I'm talking about. Do you want me to make a list: the beating in the parking lot, nearly running me off the road, Lion's Park? Do you want more?"

"You can prove nothing!" Connie stepped back from the bed.

"I don't think I have to. You push this and the State Labor Relations Board will be here in Twin Pines within hours. Yes, I may have to answer to your fabricated charges. You, Madame Chairperson, will have to answer to much, much more.

"You're crazy!" Connie shouted.

"Am I? Look at the facts. You attempted to tamper not once but twice with the negotiating process. You attempted to bribe me, to coerce me into supporting a settlement that I did not and do not believe is in the best interests of the patrons, the children, or the teachers of this district."

Justin stopped. He leaned back, resting his left arm on his stomach. Not taking his eyes off Connie, he continued, "The State Labor Relations Board would, I'm sure, be interested to hear that a board chairperson would submit to such unscrupulous and illegal tactics." He paused again, then with finality added, "Do you really want to drag all this before the public?"

Connie stood expressionless. Her shoulders slumped.

"One more thing, Mrs. Shetland," Justin could sense his victory as he spoke, "if Randy hadn't been after Shawn Kelly, he would not have been shot. The accident probably would not have happened either. You are as much responsible for his death as anyone."

He stopped and looked at Connie, who remained rigid. She aged remarkably since first arriving in his room. Her face was colorless, her suit almost ill fitting, the sparkle gone from her eyes. She turned to make her way slowly to the door.

"Do we have a bargain?" Justin smiled benignly.

Connie glanced over her shoulder without interrupting her progress toward the door. Without a sound, she hurried out.

CHAPTER 79

Wednesday was turning out not much better than other days. Vince sat in his office at the bank depressed and distracted by what would likely happen at the evening board meeting. The fleeting elation he experienced after discussing with Justin Starling Connie's resolution turned to guilt over a betrayal of his wife. With fists clenched tightly, he pounded softly on his desk, his face contorted in anguish. He felt he didn't know what was right any more.

Recently, he devoted much of his time to trying to identify when and how his life started to crumble. So suddenly his life changed from one of happiness and promise to one of misery and destitution. It just couldn't go on this way. Something had to change. Each day became worse than the previous one. Placing his hands over his face, he sobbed.

The sound of his phone stunned him. Whenever it rang, he felt threatened by one more shock in the nightmare that his life had become. He wiped his eyes with the backs of his hands then his hands on his trousers. The phone continued its incessant ringing.

"Yes?" Vince answered meekly.

"Your father wishes to see you in his office," announced the his secretary.

"Be right there."

Vince studied the silent phone for an instant before slowly replacing it. He got up from his chair, reached for a tissue, and wiped his brow. He straightened his tie and adjusted his suit coat. Looking briefly around his office as if for the last time, he opened the door to walk briskly in the direction of his father's office.

His father's familiar voice requested him to enter. Vince opened the door and hesitated. Beside his father's desk stood his father and another man he only vaguely recognized.

"Good morning, Vince," his father spoke without the gentleness to which Vince was accustomed. "I believe you know Mr. Evans. He is with the State Bank Examiners Bureau."

Leonard Evans stepped forward, extending his hand to Vince. "Good to see you again, Mr. Shetland."

Vince clasped his hand limply and only nodded.

"Please sit down," Vince's father directed while he moved around his desk and seated himself. "Vince, I'll get right to the point," his father began. "Mr. Evans has examined the bank's records and has found some irregularities in your accounts. Is there some explanation for this?"

Vince sat humbly in his chair, his head bowed, his hands clinched in front of him. A complete silence consumed the office.

"Vince," his father asked again, "is there some explanation for the irregularities? The records indicate a shortage of over five thousand dollars. There are withdrawal records without corresponding deposit records."

Vince rose from his chair and stood before his father's desk. Without emotion, he confessed, "Yes, Dad, there is a simple explanation. I needed money." He then turned and walked quickly out of the office, leaving the door open behind him.

Vince rested his head on the steering wheel of his car. He closed his eyes and breathed deeply. Somehow he felt relieved that at last someone knew about his embezzlement. It didn't really matter any more.

He started his car, slowly backed out of his parking space, and drove onto the street. For the first time in weeks his mind was clear. He knew precisely what he wanted to do. He relaxed behind the wheel of the car, enjoying the fresh summer air that flowed through the open window.

For just a moment he thought of how it used to be and how maybe it could be that way again. He then laughed to himself in full realization that what used to be could never be again. Too much had changed; things happened; people were different.

Connie would not be home. She would be at the hospital meeting with Starling. As he turned into the driveway, the garage door stood open. Connie's car was gone. He parked on his usual side then reached to the sun visor, pressing the button to close the garage door. He did not turn off the engine. He opened his window fully and slouched low in the driver's seat.

The thought of leaving Connie filled him with remorse, but Connie could get along by herself. She proved that already. However, the disgrace he brought upon himself and his family had destroyed his dignity and self respect. At this moment he felt no despair. He was not frantic. He sat is his car, calm and resolved.

The pungent, deadly fumes filled the car. Vince began to feel a mild head ache. Soon he only felt tired, his eyes refusing to stay open. He submitted, closing his eyes and quietly uttering, "Forgive me, Connie. I love you."

CHAPTER 80

Connie tried to assure herself that she could still salvage something from her encounter with Justin Starling. So little existed for her to grasp onto.

How in the hell did he find out about the resolution? she asked herself, and about Randy? Only Vince knew for sure. She could not accept that Vince so blatantly betrayed her.

As she drove toward home, Connie was distraught. Tired and frustrated, she worked against Justin Starling for weeks only now to face defeat. He was right about one thing. The resolution meant little now. Virtually nothing remained that would give her an advantage. God, she thought, I'm not a loser.

They did, though, have a bargain, she and Justin. They would go to mediation; a settlement still would be reached. She remained the chairperson of the school board. Who could predict the rest of it? After all, they did have a bargain.

Connie regained some of her strength and composure by the time she reached home and turned into her driveway. She pressed the automatic opener control then slowed as the door eased its way upward. With surprise Connie noticed Vince's sitting in his car. Driving into the garage, she realized that his car was still running.

Seconds later she screamed, "Oh, my God, my God!" Stopping her car, she jumped out and raced around the driver's side of Vince's car. Frantically, she reached in and switched off the ignition. Already his skin had turned a sickening, bluish gray. She gasped in fear and indecision. She pulled him out of the car, his body limp and extraordinarily heavy. Somehow, she managed to drag him out of the garage and onto the driveway.

Searching for his pulse, she found none. She ran to her car for her cell phone to call 911. She rushed back to her husband lying completely motionless on the driveway. Not knowing what else to do, she kneeled next to him, staring at the man who had for so many years shared her home and her life. Slowly she reached down, wrapping her arms around Vince's head. She held him tightly, sobbing uncontrollably.

CHAPTER 81

Justin sat on the edge of the stage, his legs hanging freely. Next to him sat Norma Metcalf and Rita Williams. All three watched casually as members of the Twin Pines Teachers' Union filed into the high school lecture hall and auditorium. The auditorium, like the rest of the building, was clean and polished in preparation for Monday, the first day of school.

Teachers gathered in small groups of two, three or four, sharing summer experiences and renewing friendships allowed to lapse over the summer. An atmosphere of reunion filled the room as teachers appeared happy to be back, prepared to engage in another nine months of teaching.

Justin slid off the edge of the stage, wincing at the slight pain in his left shoulder. Besides that, he felt exhilarated. A summer that began in turmoil, in mystery, was ending with promise and with hope for better teaching conditions and for a better educational program. He surveyed the assembling crowd, remembering all the times he imagined this occasion when he could bring to the membership a contract for ratification, a bargain between the teachers and the school board.

After Vince Shetland's suicide, progress toward agreement was swift. Connie Shetland resigned from the school board, and Charles Langley assumed temporarily the duties of chairman of the board's negotiating team. One mediation session saw the board's acceptance of contract language ensuring class sizes of no more than twenty-five students in academic classes and limiting teaching assignments in the middle and high schools to no more than five academic classes per day.

With this acceptance, Justin and his committee agreed that these provisions were subject to review and possible revision at the conclusion of the two year contract. The board also renewed its final salary offer which the teachers accepted. After that, two concluding meetings dealing with extra curricular compensation and fringe benefits completed the contract package.

The teachers finally settled into their places and the conversation gradually diminished. As Justin approached the podium, the group fell silent, all eyes focused on him. He cleared his throat, smiled and began, "Welcome back. I trust you've had a refreshing summer." He looked into the space above the heads of his audience and swallowed almost audibly. "Needless to say, for some of us, this summer has been something less than typical."

A slight stir floated through the auditorium. "I don't think I have to go into any detail about the tragic events of the past months. I think we've all suffered shock over what happened." Justin paused to look over the crowd that sat before him. Selecting his next words carefully, he continued, "Let us learn from our mistakes and the mistakes of others. Let us get on with what we have dedicated ourselves to do: to teach young people of this community. To me no commitment of any kind has more importance in society than that."

Justin paused, this time to look down at the papers placed before him on the podium. He shifted his weight from one foot to the other. In a strong, confident voice he addressed the group, "You have in your possession a rough copy of the contract that has been tentatively agreed to by your negotiating committee and the committee of the board. I wish to review it with you before we vote on ratification to determine if, indeed, we have a bargain. If you have questions as I highlight its provisions, please feel free to interrupt me. Now, if you would turn to the third page of your booklet, we'll get started."